NORTH in the SPRING

The Apprenticeship Series
PART II

NORTH in the SPRING

Frank Kelso

Beachfront Press

A Beachfront Press Book

ISBN: 978-1-7335433-3-0

Cover photograph by Ed Haefliger taken on supply run
in the Olympic National Forest in Washington State.

First edition: 2019
V2

North in the Spring is a work of historical fiction. The names, characters,
places, and incidents are either the product of the author's imagination,
or, if real, used fictitiously.

Visit the website: TheApprenticeBook.com
Join Frank's Blog, Traveling the West http://frankkelsoauthor.com

Beachfront Press, LLC
25778 John M Snook Dr, Suite 2402
Orange Beach, AL 36561

Dedication

Thanks to those fans who follow my Facebook, Twitter, Instagram, Pinterest, and LinkedIn pages. Special thanks go to my mentor, and writing partner who kicks me in the butt to keep me focused on better writing, my friend, John O. Woods.

A special thanks to Ed Haefliger for the wonderful pictures of pack mules at work, just as they did in 1853.

No dedication, or even my books, would be complete without the support and encouragement of my lovely island bride. Thank you for all you do for me, but mostly for tolerating my grumpy behavior. I have the T-shirt to prove it.

Frank Kelso

Other Books by Frank Kelso

The Posse – an anthology of 8 western stories

The Apprenticeship of Nigel Blackthorn

California Bound (Co-Author – John O'Melveney Woods)

Zach's Gold

Juan's Revenge (Co-Author – John O'Melveney Woods)

Short Stories

Flop-eared Mule
The Windmill
True to the Union

Links to Frank Kelso on Social Media

Please visit Frank Kelso's web page:
frankkelsoauthor.com
visit Facebook: facebook.com/AuthorFrankKelso
visit on Twitter: @authorfrankelso
linkedin.com/in/frank-kelso-89b077100
facebook.com/AuthorFrankKelso
authorfrankkelso.blogspot.com
frankkelsoauthor.com
TheApprenticeBook.com
facebook.com/thepossebook.1
facebook.com/CABoundBook/
facebook.com/TheApprenticeBook

Chapter One

October 1855

Black Wolf lost his family again. Sadness and grief weighed upon him, although not the same wrenching horror of witnessing the brutal death of his father or finding his mother's smoldering body two years earlier. The ache from his mother's death burrowed deep within him, festering like a splinter oozing to the surface, but he tamped it down, as his time for revenge as a man had yet to come. One day, he vowed, the Comanche would pay for killing his mother. Only fifteen years old, the Cheyenne believed he'd become a man during a test in combat against their mortal enemy but the elders advised patience until his body grew and gained strength while he learned a warrior's skills.

Six months ago, concerned for his safety, his godfather, Pascal LeBrun and his mute partner, LaFleur de A'lune, ordered him to remain in a Cheyenne village while Pascal and the mule-borne trading company rode across the western mountains for a "trade season." He left in the early spring, and as promised, returning to the Cheyenne village late on this October morning.

"You bring an extra saddle and blanket?" Black Wolf asked in Spanish as his godfather rode close to greet him. He waited beside his horse after racing three miles from the Cheyenne camp, leaving after a display of his riding skills and bow and arrow accuracy at a full gallop.

"*Oui*," Pascal LeBrun replied in his favored French, dismounting to stride close before grabbing Black Wolf in a bear hug. "*Noir*, I've missed you, my son. It's been too quiet in the camp without someone asking damn fool questions." Pascal brayed his booming hee-haw laugh.

Surprised by Pascal's hug, Black Wolf hugged his godfather in return. In French fashion, Pascal kissed him on each cheek, twice, before he danced with Black Wolf in his arms and laughed. "*Bon retour!* Welcome back!"

I used to think of Pascal's six-two as quite tall, but now I reach past his shoulders, he thought as Pascal's bear hug engulfed him. After Yellow Blossom hugged him goodbye in the Cheyenne village, he failed to imagine another family hug riding with Pascal and the men on the mule train. *Pascal is full of surprises.* Approaching forty, the former Jesuit priest radiated vitality as he stood tall and broad shouldered, with thick arms from repeated lifting of 250-pound packsaddles four times a day. His once dark brown hair and chin-strap beard grew streaked with grey.

"I've spoken The People's language so much, I must stop and think what I want to say," Black

Wolf said in Spanish, without glancing at Pascal. "I relied on Spanish at first with the woman who makes peace and the one who became my mother."

"Your Spanish sounds like a squeaky gate," Phillippe, the mule train's Arapaho scout, said in Cheyenne. He'd proclaimed himself the bastard son of Jean Baptiste "Little Pomp" Charbonneau and grandson of Sacajawea, the Far Walking Woman. "None of these tongues translate well into The People's language. You'll forget it soon enough."

Black Wolf ignored Phillippe's remark, and continued to wipe his sweaty horse with a handful of dried grass. A wave of sorrow washed over him, causing a slight shiver to ripple when he remembered riding away from his adopted Cheyenne mother and brother, knowing Yellow Blossom cared for him as much as she did for her own son, Running Elk. She offered him the same unconditional love his birth mother provided. *Two years have passed, and I still listen for my mother to call me to eat.* It seemed his birth mother loved him, to the exclusion of her husband and daughters and sacrificed herself to save him from the Comanche. She had loved him past the point of reason, spoiling him into an overweight, lazy, brat.

Breaking Black Wolf's reverie, Pascal said, "I feared LaFleur would peel my hide because we returned late. He sighed with relief after young Bent reported none of Black Kettle's band came for trade this fall. Antonio and the Ortega cousins chattered like magpies after we crossed La Veta Pass and descended to the plains. They want to compare adventures with you. I won't spoil it and tell you what. They plan to brag about what they've done this trade season. I suspect you may have a story or two to tell." Pascal tugged on Black Wolf's single Cheyenne braid.

Two years earlier, Pascal and LaFleur found *Noir*, as Pascal called him, alone and starving after the Comanche killed his missionary family near old Fort Adobe. Memories of his life in Wales and England faded as he learned French and Spanish apprenticing on the mule train.

"I met a warrior called Old Wrinkled Wolf. He said he knew you." Black Wolf nodded at Pascal. "Old Wolf let me ask questions in French about things I didn't understand, but he said I must show the village I'm not an *ignorant savage* and learn The People's language. He taught me to craft my own bow and arrows. You often shared your brandy and cigars with him. Mayhap, I lost Phillippe's brandy flask and his tin of cigars beside Old Wolf's tipi." With a glance at Phillippe, he said, "I'll replace them when we reach El Paso."

Pascal grunted, shaking his head. "I met him when I first ventured onto this grand prairie. They called him High-back Wolf in his younger days. He served as the war-chief under Red Hawk. This happened long before they elected Black Kettle to the ruling council. I think, at first, he tolerated me because he liked to show he spoke French. He liked to play jokes."

"He still does," Black Wolf said. "I'll save his story until we join the others. Are they near?"

"*Non,* we're on the west side of Bent's." Pascal waved an arm toward the Arkansas River and Bent's Trading Post at Big Timbers. "We crossed from Fort Massachusetts empty, and you know how I *hate* dragging empty mules. Lucky for us, Bent contracted for cartage to haul five English tons by mule to El Paso. I've decided not to return through Santa Fe with such a load. We'll ride south beside the Pecos River toward Pope's Crossing at the Texas border."

Riding with Pascal and LaFleur turned his life on its head. He worked, *and walked*, from a dark dawn to a dark supper time, falling into his bedroll while mumbling prayers for his family. At the first *Anglo* settlement, Pascal gave him a choice of an orphanage or joining the mule train as an apprentice. Then came the lessons. He liked the former Jesuit's lessons only because he rode during lessons, where he learned French and Spanish, using English only if in a book.

"You returned in time to work on a heavy load." Phillippe slapped his arm. He stood an inch under six feet with a slim muscular build matching his slim, somber facial features.

Black Wolf stood next to his horse, gazing across the open prairie. "Did you bring any clothes for me? How about a bar of soap? I need to wash clean before I wear fresh clothes."

"*Oui.*" Pascal held his nose. "Phillippe advised

it'd be best if you didn't ride into Bent's Post dressed as you are. Separate clans of Kiowa and Comanche are camped north of the Post." He handed Black Wolf a bundle tied with the long sleeves of a grown man's shirt.

"A dozen Utes followed us from Fort Massachusetts," Pascal said in French. "I suspect they intend to raid us on our return, if we cross through La Veta Pass with loaded mule strings. It's why I'm turning south, attempting to cross the badlands to reach the Santa Fe Trail Cimarron River cut-off.

"I think we can elude the Utes and Kiowas by going straight south before they're ready to leave Bent's Trading Post." He pointed south. "I'll keep your breechcloth and leggings with your furs on the supply pack mule. Change your clothes before we ride."

"*Non*," Black Wolf said. "Wait until we stop for the night, where I can wash before we eat."

"I know what it means to you," Phillippe said in The People's language, "but you cannot carry your lance with a scalp. The others will recognize a Cheyenne lance, and consider it an insult. It'll be a fight starter because you are not a warrior to them. They will attack without mercy if you carry a scalp as a prize. It alerts them you're a lone Cheyenne taking prizes."

After running two steps, he heaved his lance into the prairie. "I can make another if I rejoin The People," Black Wolf said, glancing away and ignoring Phillippe.

"Let us ride as soon as you're ready," Pascal said. "We are getting a late start and won't reach Bent's Post tonight. Bent sold us smoked ham to eat tonight and side meat for breakfast."

Once underway, Pascal drew alongside Black Wolf's horse. "I didn't intend this season to become such a rigorous rite of passage for you. In earlier times, titled men sent their sons away as wards of another leader. It allowed a lad space to grow and learn. If you hope to become a full partner in our business, use your Cheyenne time as a foundation to build upon, and grow from."

"Another lesson?" Black Wolf smirked.

"Of course." Pascal barked a laugh. "When have you known a Jesuit who didn't teach?"

The evening camp grew quiet as Black Wolf adjusted to leaving his Cheyenne family.

"Tall Bear met us before we reached their camp," Pascal said. "He wanted to trade two ponies for you. I guess he has no sons of his own. He thinks you'll be a fine warrior, if you live."

"The tall one told me he wanted me to live in his tipi. He'd teach me to become a warrior," Black Wolf said. In the way of The People, he avoided saying the name of a person not present to avoid sending evil spirits after the person named.

"Digging Badger came to me later, when I waited on the rise above the village," Pascal said. "He reported you stood alone against five Pawnees to prevent them from stealing Cheyenne women. He has younger sons, but he wanted you for a son."

"That one told me if I stayed, he'd ask the Bow

Strings to accept me as one of The People," Black Wolf replied in French.

In Cheyenne, Phillippe said, "You cannot be two people. If you're one of The People, you must return to them now. If you stay here longer, it means you're a white man inside."

"If I were part of them, as you are," Black Wolf said, "with a respected father and grandmother, I'd stay. I'd fight and die beside them, but I'm a white man. I think they understood and wanted me to make my choice, to understand where I belong."

He missed Yellow Blossom, his adopted mother and her son, his adopted brother, Running Elk. He discussed subjects with Yellow Blossom he never considered speaking about with his birth mother. She spoke with candor about her grief in losing her husband, Running Elk's father, and of being required, by Cheyenne tradition, to become the second wife of his brother, Tall Bear. She spoke of Tall Bear's anger, saying it voiced his fear the Cheyenne people couldn't survive in a white man's world, and The People would fade away like the buffalo.

When Black Wolf spoke of his anger over his family's death, she listened, letting him voice his angst at failing to protect his mother. He told how fear had paralyzed him during the attack and how he worried if cowardice kept him from fighting to stop the Comanche killing his family.

Her words came to his mind unbidden as he sat in Pascal's camp. "How would it have helped your mother for you to die beside her? She sacrificed herself to give you a chance to live and grow into a man. Don't deny her last wish for you. Remember her message for you, 'Don't look back.' She wanted you to live and go forward."

Her counsel, mixed with her grief about losing her own husband, eased his guilt about his family's death when he alone survived.

The men in the small camp remained silent for a quarter of an hour.

Without breaking the silence, Black Wolf rose to stride from the camp, pretending to check on the animals, before he washed in a small creek feeding the Arkansas River.

Yellow Blossom's words stayed with him. "Our men worried your name might be too strong for a young boy, but I saw the man blossoming inside. You are Black Wolf, my son. Bring honor to your name so we become proud to call you one of The People." She hugged him before he rode away.

By custom, The People didn't demonstrate affection in public because they considered it rude, and it might embarrass onlookers, but she hugged him anyway. He remembered her and Running Elk as family while he yanked a handful of dried grass to wipe his horse and smiled at the thought of his display of his riding skills, his arrows striking the grass-filled rawhide targets Running Elk tossed into the air when he raced through the Cheyenne village to the creek and returned in a gallop standing on the horse's rump, waving his lance as he rode away. The moment dissolved when the Mule Man and the Arapaho spoke in the camp behind him.

"Huh," Black Wolf grunted. *I think of my godfather and friends in Cheyenne terms*, he thought. *Are they my family and friends now or only my travelling companions?*

~~~~~~

Sitting by the fire, Pascal decided he shouldn't inquire about what transpired with the Cheyenne.

"The Little Wolf is becoming a man and it frightens him," Phillippe said. "He understands how unprepared he's been to live on the prairie. I believe he's learned how valuable your protection has been. His ... *summer adventure* has ended. It's time for him to become a man."

"I understand," Pascal said. "I lived a life of ease in distant and strange lands without recognizing the danger. My biggest threats came from cuckold husbands, and to my eternal shame, they punished LaFleur for my transgressions. It wasn't until I came to this grand prairie before I realized how a man walks with death every day. I don't think I could return to such a life, even if they would accept me again. Life would have no meaning in a monastery."

~~~~~~

The next morning, Black Wolf spoke in French to the two men as they gathered their gear from the camp. "I'm not the Nigel you found on the prairie two years ago and I cannot live with The People. I want to remember who I am today and what is expected of me. I will keep the name of Black Wolf, but in an English fashion as Blackthorn Wolfe with an 'e' on the end. I think I understand why Pascal calls me *Noir,* for the dark time in which he found me. Those who speak French may continue to call me *Noir,* but to everyone else, I'll be Blackie after the Black Wolf. No longer will I be that whiny Welsh brat, Nigel."

"Amen," the two men said in unison as they prepared to ride to Bent's Post at Big Timbers.

Chapter 2

October 1855

The mule team's reunion grew raucous in the evening when they gathered for supper in the common hall at Bent's Post. Pascal's partner at the Rancho in Zaragoza, Mexico, Victorio Ortega, had encouraged his sons and nephews to work on the mule train's seasonal jaunts. The young Mexican men, cousins, formed a strong bond as a working team. The cousins laughed and joked as they recounted their adventures on the Western trails. The common language on the mule train became Spanish, while Pascal, LaFleur, and Blackie used French among themselves.

"We traveled west from Fort Massachusetts," Antonio Ortega, Victorio's second oldest son, said, "following the Rio Grande into the San Juan Mountains. The Utes traded with us at first, but later, tried to steal our horses. In the excitement, Reynaldo let the hammer slip when cocking his rifle. He shot a shiny bangle hanging from their leader's headband. The leader grew angry and asked, 'Why are you shooting at me? We're only trying to steal the horses.'

"Phillippe laughed aloud before saying to the Utes, 'You only *tried* to steal them, so we only *tried* to shoot you. If you steal our horses, then we *will* shoot you.'

"The Utes laughed like they enjoyed it as a big joke," Antonio said. "They let us ride away as if nothing happened. After the close encounter, the Utes grew more serious about trading."

"I still don't think it's funny." Reynaldo scowled, causing more laughter.

Antonio, twenty years old, rode on his second season with Pascal, and had tanned a deep brown like old leather. He topped out at five-nine and had developed the broad shoulders and thick arms of daily heavy lifting. The Ortega cousins, ranging in age from seventeen to twenty-one, had been slim when they joined the team, but after a year or two of working on the mule train, they too grew the broad shoulders and thick arms a man developed with daily heavy lifting and eating three filling meals a day. Working on a mule train made for demanding daily labor, which made their seventh day, a rest day for man and mule, a welcome relief.

"We caught some luck." Phillippe interrupted Antonio. "We found them in a good mood. The Utes hadn't suffered recent problems with the white man. Such will change as more and more whites move in their direction and settle on their lands. The northern tribes held a treaty ceremony in 1851, and the people of the north plains believe the treaty will protect their land from the white man. You know my feelings about treaties with the white man."

With repeated urging from Pascal and LaFleur, Blackie recounted his first meeting with Old Wrinkled Wolf. He reported the story the way he remembered it, admitting his fear when the old Cheyenne man surprised him by tapping his shoulder from behind, but relaxing after the old man beckoned him to his fire where meat cooked.

"He said his name in Cheyenne and tapped his chest. I pointed to my chest, saying my name in Cheyenne, the only Cheyenne words I knew. The old man sat in front of a small fire, pointing for me to sit, and saying words in Cheyenne I couldn't understand. He roasted an animal larger than a rabbit on a green willow limb over glowing coals.

"The old man pointed to himself, saying his name again in Cheyenne. He signaled for me to repeat the words he said. The old man nodded, saying his name again. I repeated it, trying to make the exact sounds with guttural stops. The old man nodded his approval.

"Old Wolf pointed at my knife and mumbled words I didn't understand. He repeated the sounds and pointed at his mouth. I needed to repeat the word four times before Old Wolf nodded. The old man said a Cheyenne word and pointed to the knife on my belt, repeating the word. After I repeated the Cheyenne word a couple of times, the wizened man nodded once in approval. He reached his open hand to me, grasping with his fingers. I handed my knife to him, wondering if I should have.

"Old Wolf tested the blade with his thumb,

smiled his approval, and sliced several pieces of meat from the roasting animal. He speared a slice of meat, offered me a hot piece, and said, '*me-se-estse*,' *eat*, and put a piece in his mouth. I repeated the Cheyenne word before I ate the meat. The meat tasted greasy with a strong gamy flavor I didn't recognize.

"The old man smiled, pointing at the roasted animal. He uttered a guttural Cheyenne word and motioned for me to repeat it. I repeated it five times before Old Wolf approved.

"While we sat across the fire from one another, Old Wolf pointed at different items, said a Cheyenne word, then motioned for me to repeat the words, over and over again. After a dozen items and words, he pointed to the first item again, testing if I remembered all the new words. Old Wolf signaled me to repeat words, while he sliced meat from the roasting animal.

"After I said the new words to his satisfaction, I pointed at the roasting animal, saying its name. Old Wolf nodded, but the twinkle in his eyes reminded me of Pascal when he'd played a trick. I didn't get his joke at the time, but he laughed aloud, tilting his head to each side. He sliced another piece, handed it across the fire, and grinned.

"Old Wolf and I cleaned the meat from the roasting animal. The wrinkled old man broke off a hind leg, gnawing on the remaining meat around the joint with gapped teeth before he threw the bone to a dog waiting nearby. He wiped his greasy hands through his hair, then wiped the greasy blade on his hide shirt and handed my knife to me.

"He rose, patting me on the shoulder before he turned toward his tipi and said, '*Merci. Je va a'dormir,*' in spoken French.

"'*Ce que? Vous parlez Français?*'

"Old Wolf replied in French, '*Voila!* Do you think I'm an *ignorant savage?*'

"'Why did we spend this time learning those words, if you speak French?'

"He replied, 'I couldn't find my knife in the dark. I saw you carried one, so I invited you to my fire with your knife. Once here, I tried to discover if you're an *ignorant savage* who can't speak Cheyenne.' Old Wolf laughed before he flipped open the flap to enter his tipi."

Old Wolf had made him feel every bit the fool, but Blackie barked a laugh in the retelling.

While the men laughed and slapped one another's shoulders, Blackie said, "The worst part came the next day when he showed me the skinned hide of the animal we ate—a black-and-white hide. I'd eaten skunk. I didn't know what the word meant when Old Wolf said it. When I found out, I gagged to throw up before realizing it'd been a day since I'd eaten it. I hadn't been sick or died from eating it. I'd not hunt one, but it's better than no meat at all, if you're hungry."

The Ortega cousins found eating skunk even funnier than Old Wolf speaking French.

While the men laughed, Pascal said, "He's a

trickster. Pay attention if you trade with him."

"Oh yes," Black Wolf said.

As he glanced at them, Black Wolf said, "I've changed my name. Please call me Blackie."

The Spanish-speaking cousins liked the name change because they found it difficult to say the French *Noir* without rolling the "r" as in Spanish. They said they found Blackie easier to say.

"When are you going to tell us about Black Kettle refusing to allow you on a buffalo hunt?" Phillippe asked. "The Comanche and Kiowa camped near Bent's Post tell the story for a laugh."

Blackie covered his face with both hands, flushing hot with embarrassment.

"I heard one version of the story," Phillippe said, "Wolf Dragger."

To stop Phillippe's comments, Blackie said, "We crawled on hands and knees learning to stalk animals or an enemy. I carried my possibles-bag, but the Cheyenne don't use one. As I crawled, my possibles-bag caused a deep gouge in the dirt where it dragged between my legs. The boys behind me assumed only my pizzle would drag between my legs. They nicknamed me Dragger."

"What about Black Kettle and the buffalo hunt?" Phillippe asked with a raised eyebrow.

"He worried about letting me hunt buffalo. He said if I dragged my wolf's pizzle on the hunt, I'd scare the buffalo away. Black Kettle joked and laughed about it with his hunters."

The men laughed and teased about 'Wolf Dragger,' much to Blackie's embarrassment.

After returning to camp, LaFleur led Blackie aside for a private conversation, as if one held a conversation with a man unable to speak in words. Blackie had yet to learn what led to cutting off LaFleur's tongue. Whatever happened, Pascal and LaFleur found it too shameful to discuss.

LaFleur grabbed him, hugging him tight, and Blackie returned it, holding the mute man tight. After three minutes, LaFleur kissed each cheek as Pascal had done, but in doing so, Blackie tasted the tears running along LaFleur's cheeks.

LaFleur used his lit cigar to ignite a small candle, and with its light, he searched Blackie's face and arms for signs of injury or abuse. He wrote on his slate, *You all right? They hurt you?*

"They kept me safe. It happened as the woman who makes peace predicted. The Cheyenne leader's honor rested upon treating me well. I became one of their children, allowed to roam, explore, and get into mischief. The entire village watched the children, even one as large as me."

In the moment, Blackie realized, after years of trading and visiting a Redman's village, Pascal and LaFleur had little understanding of a Redman's daily life.

"Until I lived, ate, and slept with them," Blackie said. "I thought *them* savages, incapable of salvation in the teachings of Christ. How ... prideful of me, and my father, to come to their land, thinking to teach them to live a better life. I've learned they aren't savages. The People believe in a creator, Maheo, or The Wise One Above, and a god inside the Earth sending green plants as food for all. Maheo created buffalo, elk, and deer to feed The People. They understand evil, and bad spirits cause ill fortune and death. The People don't need the white man to *teach* them. I trembled with fear and loathing, but they responded with care and concern for me as one who'd lost his family to their enemy, the Comanche. They understood my grief, they sheltered me, and gave me another loving family while they taught me to live in the way of The People."

Blackie answered LaFleur's written questions until the candle guttered and expired.

~~~~~~

The next morning, while the team worked to sort and arrange the cartage for loading on the mules, Blackie hiked to William Bent's Trading Post. The Big Timbers Post replaced his older brother's well-known Bent's Fort, ruined by the U.S. Army in 1849. The new Post sat on a bluff beside the river, twenty feet higher than the surrounding plain, which kept the Post above the seasonal floods. It sat beside a grove of old cottonwoods, earning the name, Big Timbers.

Blackie carried an armful of skins he'd collected during the summer. He dressed in a white homespun cotton shirt with a yoke neck and thong lacing, coarse wool trousers with a three-button front held by a three-inch-wide leather strap belt and wore his Cheyenne moccasins and fringed leggings. He gathered his long black hair in a leather cuff, like Pascal and LaFleur wore. Bent sold white, Mexican-made, broad-brimmed straw plantation hats with a tall crown. Such a hat topped his list of items to purchase from the Post. It's what the men on the train wore in the blazing sun.

William Bent glanced at him, and then gazed below to his moccasins. Bent spoke in Cheyenne, "What band are ya? I recognize the pattern on yer moccasins. What's yer name?"

"I am Black Wolf, son of Yellow Blossom, in Black Kettle's band. The People camped by the blue river toward the rising sun. Comanches roamed too near the sandy creek for our liking."

Bent chuckled aloud before he spoke again. "Young'un, I didn't glimpse yer eyes when ya strode in. Ya've grown into a strapping lad, a hand's spread taller than when I last seen ya. Yer Cheyenne is right good. The only way I can tell ya ain't one of 'em is yer eyes. Ol' Pascal named ya right when he called ya a 'wolf cub.' No true Cheyenne would wear 'em yellow-green wolf eyes."

Bent laid a hand on Blackie's shoulder to whisper, "Ya walked inside tall and proud, like a man of The People. I'll tell them such when they come to trade, but ya must be right careful while the Kiowa and Comanche are trading here. If they think yer alone, they'll try to kill ya, even if there is a truce on my trading grounds. If ya have boots, or plain moccasins, wear them until ya leave. I don't want none of ya to make trouble here and break the trade truce."

"Do you have boots to fit me?" Blackie asked.

"Ya could be kin to ol' Bigfoot Wallace such feet," Bent said. "I believe I have an old pair I can give ya. Toss 'em away after ya leave. They're third-hand and ain't much good."

"What about my skins? How much will you pay for them?"

"Well, I might could give ya a dollar a piece for 'em, only cause yer with Pascal," Bent said, shaking his head and taking a trading stance of leaning away to signal lack of interest.

"No, thank you." Blackie waved a hand to push away. "They pay five Yankee dollars for such skins in El Paso. They don't find mule deer this large or elk along the Rio tanned and treated in the Cheyenne way. I'll take them south rather than give them away at a dollar a piece."

Bent guffawed. "Young'un, ya sure got ol' Pascal's training. No mealy-mouthed puffery with ya. Goin' right after top dollar. Pascal must have ya saying 'rithmetic tables at night instead of yer prayers." Bent continued to laugh. "If'n ya can get five dollars in El Paso for 'em skins, I better send my skins south right soon."

"Such sounds like his kind of a deal. Pascal will make you a decent price to carry your trade. I'd expect he'd not charge you more than two dollars for each skin, being how you're such good friends." Blackie rotated on a heel, moving away from Bent as he strolled toward the door.

Four men standing around the iron stove

erupted in laughter and Bent joined them.

Blackie turned, laughing with them as well. He nodded at Bent. "I'll take four dollars for the skins if you've finished joking."

"Pshaw. I'll not pay ya more than two dollars tops." Bent said, slamming his open hand on the counter, but still grinning.

"I'm not in the mood for haggling. We'll split the difference, and settle for three dollars per skin," Blackie shined a toothy "trade smile," as LaFleur taught him to smile when trading.

"Why in tarnation would I do such a fool thing?" Bent asked, leaning forward.

"Simple profit," Blackie replied by spreading his hands wide. "If you buy my skins, I'll buy trade goods from you with the money. If you don't buy my skins, a tradesman in Las Vegas or El Paso will get my business and you gain nothing." He heaved a version of Pascal's classic French shrug, bunching his shoulders, lifting his palms, tilting his head, and wrinkling his lip.

Bent stepped away, shaking his head. "Yer worse than ol' Pascal. Ya're plain ornery mean," he said before he laughed and slapped a hand on his thigh.

One of the men standing beside the stove, straightened, and said, "I'll bet there ain't no wolf hides in his plew. The young'un is still wearing it and he's sharpened its teeth, too."

The men erupted into laughter, slapping one another's arms, and pointing at Blackie.

When Bent agreed to three dollars per hide,

Blackie smiled and enjoyed their good time.

After leaving Bent's, he strode to Pascal's camp. Trading with men in the Post brought home Pascal's statement from their first night together. "If you plan to become a full partner in my trade business ..." Blackie had never considered what he would do for a living when grown and yet he became aware other men treated him as if already a grown man. *Could I operate Pascal's business alone, or will I always be a scout or a mule wrangler?* If he planned to be a partner in Pascal's business in a few years, he must heed Pascal's lessons and learn the business.

Chapter 3

October 1855

At first light the next day, Pascal ordered LaFleur and Phillippe to ride west across La Veta Pass to reach Fort Massachusetts. They planned to travel without a pack mule, intending to ride a fast pace across La Veta pass and into the San Luis Valley. Pascal believed two riders might not attract the attention of the Utes, or the Comanche, who hunted bigger prizes.

"If the Utes haven't crossed La Veta for their winter buffalo hunt on the plains, do you want us to wait before crossing the Pass?" Phillippe asked.

"Bah. What kind of scout are you if you can't face a few Utes?" Pascal grumbled.

"The kind who wants to keep his scalp," Phillippe replied, drawing a bark from LaFleur who touched his nose, meaning "me, too."

"Don't take unnecessary risks but reach the San Luis in time to find grain for sale," Pascal said. "I want you to purchase three surplus wagons and teams outside the fort. Contractors often abandon used wagons there to avoid paying the drovers return and sell the stock. Find sturdy wagons and teams before buying grain to carry to south. Feed grain always sells for a profit in Santa Fe."

After selling the grain in Santa Fe, LaFleur planned to purchase any items on sale at "end of season" low prices and use the wagons to carry the trade goods to El Paso. Pascal relied upon St. Vrain to find local men to drive the wagons to El Paso and pay for their return to Santa Fe.

With LaFleur and Phillippe away, Pascal needed to hire two or three men at Bent's Post. He sought Bent to inquire about the best men available.

"Ya done waited too long," Bent said. "The better workers returned to Westport Landing in late September before the last wagons headed east. The men returned to their families along the Missouri for the winter where living is cheaper. Most of 'em will hire on to work a wagon train coming west next spring. The men remaining here represent the dregs, lazy and unreliable. I've run off a few and I'll send the rest packing once ya leave with the last of my cartage goods."

With no choice, Pascal hired two men who loafed around Bent's Post, men who'd worn out their welcome by eating for free at Bent's table once too often. Pascal hired them because they'd become the only men available and willing to ride south with the mule train.

Afterwards, Pascal introduced Luke and Alfredo, who went by "Fredo." Luke stood over six-foot tall and weighed 250 pounds, running to fat. He wore a slouch hat and his clothes appeared worn thin and dirty. Fredo barely reached five-seven and lean as a fence post. He had dirty black hair and a stringy beard. They made a scruffy-looking misfit pair.

After speaking to each mule team member, Pascal warned the team to keep a close watch on Luke and Fredo. The team needed the two men as workers to lift the packsaddles, but the team shouldn't trust the new men or turn their back on Luke and Fredo. He assigned the two new men to different work groups to assure those two never stood night watch together.

While Pascal grumbled about new assignments, Blackie confronted him. "I stood nighthawk duties in the Cheyenne camp. I expect to stand a shift each night to guard the mule train. I can pull my weight on the team. I don't need protection. Assign me work."

His mouth open to argue, Pascal placed a fist on his hip, and leaned into Blackie's face, as they locked eyes with one another.

"Before you begin, answer the question," Blackie said. "Am I a member of this team, or a passenger? If I'm part of the team, give me an assignment. I refuse to let you coddle me any longer."

As Pascal's shoulders slumped as he sighed aloud. "We'll find out."

Blackie leaned forward, staring at Pascal. "While we're discussing this, with Phillippe gone, Antonio will need relief as the scout. You ought to have a man watching our back trail when Antonio's in front scouting for the next waterhole."

"Next thing I know," Pascal grumbled, "You'll be

asking to carry a Sharps."

"What?" Blackie's eyebrows lifted. "You want me to fight with my target pea-shooter?"

"You're getting too big for your britches. I make the decisions on this train."

"Fine," Blackie said. "I'll rummage through the camp supplies to find LaFleur's horse liniment. Your old bones will be aching from pounding in the saddle all afternoon."

"Old bones!" Pascal threw a tin cup at Blackie before chasing him around the mules loaded with the camp supplies. He chased Blackie as Tomas, one of the Ortega cousins, loaded the mules. Benito, another Ortega cousin, followed Antonio, guiding one ten-mule string into rolling grassland south of the Arkansas River. The other Ortega cousins were Reynaldo, Javier who they called "Javy," Fernando, called "Nando," and Dominic, called "Dom."

After Pascal and Antonio became accustomed to Blackie's presence, Pascal assigned him to alternate riding scout and watching their backtrail to relieve Antonio of the extra tasks. Blackie carried one of the spare Sharps rifles Pascal kept with the supply mules. While the mule train moved south, Blackie settled into his old routine of running each evening before eating.

The two men from Bent's Fort lacked basic trail and survival skills, which worried Pascal. "Be extra vigilant when either of them is on a nighthawk shift with you," he told the team. "I'm sure *Noir* could sneak up on either of them in the dark. If *Noir* could, you know a full-grown warrior would slit their throat and be gone with our horses before their bodies hit the ground."

Blackie grunted his agreement and nodded.

"I don't mean those words to slight your skills," Pascal said. "You're better than any man in the camp."

"I know. My Cheyenne brother teased me, saying I might as well wear a bell, I made so much noise. I never told him about using a bell mare, but the Cheyenne knew we did."

"You don't speak of them. Was it so bad living there?"

"*Non.* I grew up with older sisters and had no boys as close friends in Wales. It became a challenge to have a male companion. We weren't rivals. Other than shooting a rifle, my brother beat me at everything else. I struggled to learn new things related to becoming a Cheyenne. The one who was my mother was patient. She taught me things she didn't teach her true son. The men and boys grew intolerant of my mistakes, particularly if I struggled to learn a new thing."

"I notice you gained several new scars with them. Did those come from punishment?"

"Oh, no. The tall one struck me only once in anger. He struck me because I spoke to him with disrespect. I challenged him after I'd been warned, and he taught me to follow the way of The People. The tall one treated me rough when he thought I lacked a fighting spirit. Later, he said I carried the wolf spirit."

"And the scars?" Pascal asked in French.

"Young and foolish, like a bear cub sticking my nose where it didn't belong. When I got stung, the camp guard came to my rescue. I lacked good tracking skills and blundered into a raiding party from the Wolf People, the whites call Pawnee. It's true God protects idiots and fools. They could have killed me three or four different times that day. The Pawnee gave me these scars as a reminder I'm not yet a warrior of The People. I fought to save my horse and my rifle, and I counted myself lucky to survive."

"I thought it best to keep you somewhere safe this season. LaFleur and I didn't think you'd be in danger in such a well-established camp, and never expected you to fight for your life."

Blackie laughed. "I'm in more danger here than at any time with The People. They have forty warriors and twice such number of young men like me, young braves in training to become warriors. The Pawnee might try to sneak close, grab something, and run away. But none would attack the camp itself." Blackie grew silent, glancing around the rolling prairie as they rode.

"Did it upset you to kill the Pawnee and take your *prize*?" Pascal asked with hesitation.

"They gave me no choice. It became kill or be killed. I wouldn't let them take my horse."

"And after the heat of battle?"

"They came to steal our women. I failed to protect my mother and my family in their time of need. It has made me determined to never again fail those who depend upon me for protection."

"You didn't fail your mother. You have become the man she wanted through her sacrifice," Pascal said. "I hoped by living with the Cheyenne, you'd understand your revenge on Comanche is a fool's errand. The Redmen have few rules in their society, but they'll kill to protect their hunting grounds because it's for *their* family's survival. We are always in danger on the prairie. It's what I've been trying to teach you the past two years."

"Our biggest danger along here," Blackie said, "is from young Redmen, from any people, who seek to prove themselves by stealing horses—our horses. We must kill whoever attacks on the first raid. If we let them strike and ride away unhurt, every Redman in the area will come after us and pick the train to pieces. It is unbelievable how fast news travels with The People, even between those who don't often take one another's counsel."

"You sound hard and unforgiving," Pascal said, his voice soft.

Blackie gazed across the rolling grassland south of the Arkansas River. Green grass, tall as a horse's belly, as far as the eye could see without any trees. Few young trees survived pruning by a buffalo or used as a back-scratch. The area formed a huge natural pasture for roaming buffalo herds.

"Yes. You taught me the prairie is hard and unforgiving, and survival comes first. If we are to survive, we must strike hard at those who attack first. Others won't risk attacking us later."

"I hope I haven't made you too hard. You said you didn't notice any on our backtrail."

"It doesn't mean there aren't other Redmen around us. It's hard for forty-six mules and ten riders to pass through without a Redman glimpsing us or our tracks. We must remain alert."

"Yes. I'll join the night watch, too. We'll have three people on guard all night."

"Tell the team *don't scalp them.* Leave the raiders where they fall. Make sure Luke and Fredo understand this. If the warrior falls in battle, they believe it's an honorable death, and their friends won't be driven by the need to avenge them. But if you mutilate the bodies, it will make them angry at us. It isn't necessary to provoke them."

"I'm glad to have you with us again, *Noir*, even if you wear the hair of the Wolf."

He thought Pascal and LaFleur odd. They had lived on the prairie for twelve years, and yet acted as if visitors, passing through. The best example came from Pascal referring to the original people as Redmen while the "white men" called them "Indians." Pascal insisted Columbus had become lost and believed he had reached India, a half a world away. Columbus called the American native people "Indians" when he presented them to Spanish royalty.

"Great explorer," Pascal ranted, "He missed India by 8,000 miles!"

However, Pascal reserved his greatest scorn for the English, whose East India Tea Company financed much of their Navy. The English, with an attitude of superiority, failed to notice the natives of India are small brown men while the natives of this continent are sturdy Redmen, but they persist in calling both "Indians" when the two native people don't resemble one another.

~~~~~~

Blackie rode away to secure their back trail, as Pascal gazed after him. *He's lost the baby fat in his face. His plump double chin disappeared last year. I hope he's outgrown the whiny, "Do I have to?" crap of last year. He's developing the oblong face, narrow nose, and lantern jaw of the English upper crust. God knows I hate those pompous asses, but I shall do my best to drive such an attitude from him.* He barked a laugh. *How long will he keep his innocence after the cousins spread the word about the "Wolf who drags his pizzle"? If he weren't such a Methodist, we could laugh and joke about it.* Pascal glanced at the mule string as he rode. *Ah, mayhap LaFleur will offer him guidance and understanding while teaching him to laugh.*

~~~~~~

Later in the day, Blackie rode past Pascal to change horses. "I wonder how long before the buffalo herd north of the Arkansas moves south to graze here. The Cheyenne will love it."

"When the snow comes," Pascal said, before he waved an arm. "The Vigil land grant holds this land, spreading across five million acres from the Arkansas's south bank. It begins at Pueblo and south along the Purgatoire River and runs east past Big Timbers and extending south into the badlands.

"St. Vrain is a full partner on the Vigil grant. The Union of States refused to recognize most of the Spanish and Mexican land grants. St. Vrain pays lawyers to fight for his rights since old Don Vigil died. The legal costs keep St. Vrain working hard and leaves him strapped for cash."

"This is the Redman's land. How can one man own it? What will happen to the buffalo?"

"It is why I sent you to watch the great herd the first year you joined me," Pascal said. "The rising tide of pilgrims from the east is changing the prairie. I fear the buffalo and the Redman will be swept away with their tide." Pointing at Blackie, and then the mules with a sweep of a hand, "We must change what we do, or we will be swept aside with them."

"What?" Blackie asked. "Are you reading tea leaves? Where do you get these ideas?"

"You're a scout. Read the signs. First, the Santa Fe Trail, then the Oregon Trail, then the Mormon handcarts. The real change came after finding gold in California. The great Mississippi kept the weak away, but the railroads are building iron trestles. They'll soon span the Mississippi and connect with the west coast. We must change or go the way of the Redman and the buffalo."

Blackie rode to the horse remuda, shaking his

head in puzzlement at Pascal's ideas.

~~~~~~

Pascal tried to gain an extra ten miles each day to reach the Cimarron. The "badlands" evolved from ancient lava beds produced by volcanic cones visible around the area. He'd ridden the route once without mules, and thought if they pressed hard, they'd reach the river. Dragging the train south drained the team. The extra two hours in the saddle left them weary and tired at night.

The Kiowa raided late one night after watching the men droop in their saddles. The raiders must have intended to feint a strike at the camp before withdrawing to steal the animals when the white men gathered to save the camp. Antonio disrupted their timing when he plodded among the remuda to relieve himself before he stumbled across a warrior lying on the ground, untying a horse's hobbles. He fired the opening shot of the skirmish.

A shot from the grazing area alerted Blackie, who stood camp guard. He carried a 10-gauge cap-n-ball double-barreled shotgun—each barrel loaded with eighteen lead pellets he'd cast for his .25-caliber target rifle. Without hesitation, he shouldered the shotgun and fired, killing the first Kiowa who rushed into the scant firelight and wounded those behind with the other barrel.

Luke's old cap-n-ball rifle misfired, but he attacked the last warrior using his rifle as a club to knock the Kiowa from his feet before killing the

Redman with his broad-bladed knife. Luke and Fredo used their knives to kill the wounded warriors while Blackie reloaded the shotgun.

The three men plodded through the camp, thinking they'd driven the Kiowa away, but a fifth warrior lay quiet in the grass, wounded. He rose, screaming, to strike the first man to walk past— Bent's man, Fredo. The warrior gutted Fredo before Luke fired his cap-n-ball pistol, killing the wounded Kiowa. Luke pulled the Kiowa's body from Fredo to check him but shook his head.

After removing his hat, Luke gazed at Fredo on the ground. "Damn, *hombre*, why'd ya let that there injun kilt ya?" Luke donned his hat again and twisted his head about to glance at the assembled men in the scant firelight. "He was my pard-na, an' I claims his kit an' horse."

"Damn it to hell," Pascal barked, "have the decency to wait until he's buried before you claim his gear."

Chapter 4

Early November 1855

Pascal had miscalculated. The mule train suffered a hard, dry, five days of trailing south before using the last of their water for the stock. Antonio informed Pascal the next waterhole lay twenty miles south. Loaded with packsaddles, the mules couldn't walk ten miles without needing water.

Before making the final decision to unload packsaddles and ride for water, Pascal led Blackie aside for a question. They spoke in French to assure Luke couldn't listen to their words.

"I can't leave him here alone," Pascal said, avoiding using Luke's name. "Will you stay here with him, or should I leave one of the Ortega cousins with you to guard the cargo and him?"

"The mules will be tired and thirsty tonight," Blackie said. "They'll be hard to control when you get close to water. You'll need every man to control them." He waved an arm at the horses. "Take every horse with you. I don't trust him, but he's too lazy to *walk* away from here, carrying whatever he believes is valuable. I'll stay with the cargo and keep him and the coyotes at bay."

"You're sure?" Pascal asked.

"If nothing else, we can sit here making ugly faces at one another until you return." Blackie shrugged, mimicking Pascal's French version.

"I'll leave drinking water for three days. The animals will need a rest tomorrow after working hard overnight without water. We'll return by evening of the second day. It'll be an easy trip without loaded packsaddles. While waiting at the water, we'll call it our rest day." Pascal winked before he smiled. "You and Luke can have two days of rest while we're away."

"*Monsieur* is too kind. May I assure the hired man you will not dock his pay for the extra day's rest?"

Pascal laughed. "*Non*, but it is a good idea. Thanks for the suggestion." He reached across to tug the front brim of Blackie's plantation hat. With a smile, Pascal said, "I'm glad you're finding your sense of humor. Life becomes much easier when you can laugh about it."

"Black Kettle told me I should ask you to teach me how to laugh aloud like you do."

"I don't believe I ever met the man. How does he know I laugh aloud?"

"The People are watchful, even if you don't notice them, they watch how the 'white man' acts. They like that you don't kill buffalo and waste their meat or hides. They think you respect the land as they do, and they tolerate you."

Pascal boomed his laugh. "They *tolerate* me? How kind."

"It is. Otherwise, they'd kill you and eat your

mules. They like the taste of mule meat."

Pascal chuckled as he shook his head in amazement.

The team unloaded the packsaddles from the mules before the siesta break. After the break, Pascal, Antonio, and the six Ortega cousins rode beside the mules to keep them moving and to help refill the water barrels when they reached water after a long night's dry march.

Pascal stood in his stirrups and waved his hat, signaling the team to ride south, four hours before sunset.

~~~~~~

In twilight's gloom, Luke and Blackie sat across their pot of reheated bean stew on the fire. Blackie had completed his usual run and returned to camp hot and sweaty. When he first joined Pascal, two years ago, he could not run the length of the train without stopping to rest. After that, Pascal ordered him to run ahead until the train dropped out of sight, and then run to return with the admonishment not to get out of sight from the train. Only after living with the Cheyenne did he understand how running had trimmed his fat while strengthening his body. He removed his shirt to get cooler and grumbled his frustration at being unable to wash the sweat away.

"Was ya scart when ya was fighting the Injun what gave ya them scars?" Luke asked.

"Yes." Blackie nodded.

"Good. Ya need to realize ya can die from another man's knife that-a-way."

"The People, the ones you call Cheyenne, have a chant they repeat before going into battle—'Die facing your enemy.' They chant it so they do not fear dying in the fight. They believe it helps them survive by fighting and killing their enemy.'"

"Don't know nuthin' 'bout injuns, but it sounds right. Ya must be willing to give it all up to win a knife fight. Ya must accept ya're gonna get cut, an' it'll hurt, an' be ready for it. Were ya ready to die in yer fight?"

"I didn't expect to live. I refused to let them treat me with disrespect because they were bigger and stronger."

"T'at so?" Luke snorted. "Young'un, keep such a thought in mind when ya work w'th other folks. Ya give a heap of disrespect to others for one who says he don't like it none."

Luke's comment stayed with Blackie. He didn't like Luke and it showed. Tall Bear taught him to extend honor and respect until a person gives a reason to withhold such courtesies. He didn't like it when others treated him with little or no respect. Now, in reflection, he realized he had acted no better than those who he resented for not showing him respect.

"Ya get any sleep last night?" Luke asked the next morning while Blackie coaxed buffalo chips into flames to heat water for a pot of coffee.

"I slept enough. You notice the coyote prowling

around the food pack last night?"

"Nah. The boss's brat forgot to assign a night watch. I enjoyed a full night of sleep."

"I'm frying side meat while the fire's hot. You want a few pieces?"

"Sure, if yer doin' the cookin'," Luke said.

In five minutes, Blackie set the coffee pot aside before pouring in a cup of cool water along the side to settle the grounds. "Buffalo chips," he muttered about fast burning chips. The side meat sizzled in the iron skillet as he shifted around the fire to prevent turning his back on Luke.

"No call to act so edgy, young'un. If'n I wanted ya dead, I'd have a shovel ready to cover the smell and keep the flies away. Ya surviving with t'em injuns don't matter to me none." Luke tossed a fist sized rock from hand to hand. "Whipping a runt like ya ain't a thing to brag on."

"Good. It's easier to defeat an over-confident enemy."

"See, there's the disrespect in ya. I don't think ya're no enemy. Yer a dumb and annoying brat, too big for yer britches, but ya ain't no *enemy* to lose sleep thinkin' or worryin' on."

"Let's settle this right now. Toss the rock you're playing with six-foot up into the air."

"What? Ya think ya can hit it from twenty feet away w'th yer little Colt pistol? I gotta see such a thing." Luke tossed the fist-sized rock seven feet above his head.

Blackie's shot boomed across the camp as rock shards splattered Luke, who fussed and cussed about the rock-chips stinging his neck after he ducked.

"Young'un, I never had no mind to challenge ya to a shooting match, but I'm hankering to learn if ya have it in ya to face another with only a knife in yer hand." Luke slapped his hat on his leg, dumping the rock shards from the crown and brim.

Blackie stared at the burly man. "You outweigh me by 150 pounds and have a five-inch longer reach than I do. I'm not going to let you get close enough to beat me senseless." He dumped the coffee grounds from the fire-blackened pot and readied to bank the fire. Blackie shook his head and waved his hand back and forth. "Not today, for sure."

Luke said, "I came from Kin-tuck working on river rafts hauling freight on the Tennessee River b'fore I worked on the ol' Wabash itself, not much different than Frenchie and ya." He flopped on the ground beside his saddle and leaned against it. "T'em river rats would knife fight for the pure meanness of it, takin' pleasure in hurtin' a man, or watchin' another get hurt. I wager I'd learn ya new knife tricks t'em injuns never knowed."

"If you come at me with a knife, I'll shoot your knees from under you. As you lay moaning, I'll shoot the hanging down parts in your crotch. I'm *not* knife fighting with you."

"Aww, little preacher's kid cain't say naughty words," Luke teased. "Come on, ya can say it. *Balls.* A lad like ya must have little green peas, but a man like me has *balls* as big as peaches."

"You and Pascal should compare. It might be you could bowl ten-pins with them."

"There ya go. A good joke, but ya ain't said the word, *sissie.*" When Blackie didn't respond to his taunts, Luke said, "B'fore ya douse the fire, place two packsaddle struts in the fire and burn one end. Give t'em a good char, an' I'll learn ya how t'em river rats showed lubbers like me to face a blade." He waved a hand, "Ya see, knife fighting ain't about a strike to the heart. It's about cuttin' yer man until he bleeds to death before ya do." Shaking his head, he said, "Don't attack like ya plan to drive a knife deep, stay loose an' shift to slice as ya pass. Only plunge yer knife when yer foe is weak an' tired. Weaken 'em with muscle cuts." He slid a thumb across his shoulder, chest, and forearm. "Bleed 'em with a slice across the belly, or in the back, slice deep into their kidneys. The best bleeder is the inner thigh from groin to knee, anywhere along there. A man my size'll be dead in two minutes with his thigh slit open."

"Good times with your pals along the river?"

"It ain't for the weak-kneed, like preacher's kids, or *girls.*" Luke winked at him.

Blackie ought to have known better than to listen to Luke, but his *game* sounded like an interesting way to pass two days without any harm.

The two stripped to their waists and carried no edged weapons but each held an ash-tree shaft an inch around and eighteen inches long. Blackie had charred three inches on one end of each. A man *won* by leaving a charcoal mark on his opponent without receiving one in return.

Luke often appeared clumsy, but he used it as a ploy to do less work. He surprised Blackie with his speed in his char-knife strokes and deft footwork. It appeared he favored using his size to bully Blackie, often knocking him to the ground with an elbow or hip in passing.

Blackie learned Luke used roughhousing as a tactic, particularly when fighting a man as light as Blackie's 120-pounds. Luke won a dozen mock battles before Blackie learned Luke's strike patterns and how he shifted his weight and his feet before an attack. As the morning progressed, Blackie avoided body contact with Luke and the mock battles often ended in a draw with each man scoring a char mark on the other. The mock battles lasted longer, as Blackie's youth and conditioning from running and working each day let him strike a char more often as Luke tired. The big man gasped for breath as sweat streamed from his body, soaking his pants.

Blackie said, "Let's take a siesta break, eat a bite of bean stew, and sleep for a while."

Luke nodded in agreement, too winded to speak with ease.

The bean stew had heated atop the smoldering buffalo chips while the two battled.

The two men shared their meal in silence, again sitting across the fire from one another.

"You say I don't respect you," Blackie said. "I'll

trust you to stand watch while I sleep during siesta." He turned his back to gather a blanket from his bedroll next to his saddle.

"An' yer threat if'n I don't?" Luke tilted his head and squinted an eye at Blackie.

"If I trust you, I don't need to threaten you. We'll treat one another as equals. We may not like the other, but we can learn to respect the man."

"Ya act as if ya bested me in the char fights an' ya don't need to fear me," Luke said, wrinkling his brow. "Ya don't think I tried my best, do ya?"

"You won most of them with fatal char strikes. I don't think I *bested* you at anything. You faulted me for not respecting you. I'm offering a sign of my respect – trust."

"I'm an asshole if I attack while ya sleep an' I'm a fool if I let ya get away with it. T'at it?"

"There's no trick. You said I failed to respect you. I'm offering trust and respect, if you want it," Blackie said. "If you don't want my respect, don't complain about not getting it." He snapped his blanket flat on the ground and laid upon it.

After Luke rose from his siesta nap, he grew restless in the afternoon. "Ya wanna try 'char' knifes again?"

"I need to scout the area, making sure we haven't been spotted by a passing Redman. We don't want them sneaking close while we play." Blackie gathered his rifle and possibles-bag, which held the 'possibles' a hunter needed to survive on the prairie, like food and powder. "Get some sleep. You have first watch from dark until midnight. I'll call when it's my shift."

"Shoot some fresh game. This here bean stew is done two days old," Luke said.

"I don't want to fire a shot unless I have to. I don't want to alert a passerby we're here."

Same old stew, reheated, and stirred. The two reached an agreement—the three-day-old stew rated a smidge above starving but made it a tough choice.

"As soon as I catch sight of Antonio tomorrow," Blackie said, "I'll hunt for fresh meat for supper." When he returned from his trot around the camp, he carried a gunny sack of buffalo chips needed to heat the coffee and stew the next day.

After setting the coffee pot on the smoldering chips the next morning, Blackie said, "I'll hunt for sign of Redmen in the area. Fry the side meat while I'm gone. Leave me a few pieces."

When he returned, Luke left him two pieces of crispy, damn-near burned pork side meat.

"A party of seven ponies rode past after dark last night 250 yards east of us. They're heading southeast, so I expect they're Comanche. We caught some luck. In the dark, they missed the mule tracks, and with no fire and no horses in our camp, they failed to catch our scent."

"Ya saying I fell asleep on my watch?" Luke growled.

"No. They'd have been hard to notice in the dark. I'm telling you to stay alert even if we don't see them. This is their territory. Seven on the hunt would come at us for the sport of it."

Luke napped for an hour but rose to stretch and loosen up. "We ain't got nothing better to do, wanna *char* fight again?"

"No, but I'll give you one last chance. First one to score a fatal *char* mark is the champion, with full bragging rights. You up for winner take all?" Blackie asked.

Luke's grin spread across his face as he rolled and stretched his heavy shoulders. He acted like he decided Blackie might try to beat him in a long fight and rushed close to batter and bully Blackie with his larger, heavier body. Blackie's agility let him avoid most of Luke's bullying tactics. In a short time, rivers of sweat covered their bodies.

A heavy arm smacked Blackie's shoulder as he slipped past, sending him rolling on the ground. Dry dirt coated his sweaty body as he rolled away. He dared not wipe his face for fear of smudging dirt in his eyes. Aware of the danger of being on the ground, Blackie relied on the Cheyenne wrestling skills he learned alongside the other young Cheyenne men. With one arm pushing off, he rolled across the ground to scissor-kick Luke's left leg, placing the ankle of his left foot in front of Luke's ankle, while the right foot kicked Luke's left leg behind the knee.

The surprise move caused Luke's knee to fold, dropping the big man to the ground. He, too, understood the risk of being on the ground in a knife fight. Luke grabbed a handful of dry dirt and aimed for Blackie's face, trying to blind him by throwing grit into his eyes.

While dust clouded the fighting area, Luke scrambled to his feet before spreading his legs. He wobbled as he stood, but Blackie dived through the dust cloud, sliding across the ground between Luke's legs as the big man spread his legs apart to gain his balance.

In a roll to his feet, he smiled as Luke spun to face him. Blackie nodded, "You lost."

"What? Ya think tossing dirt in yer face is cheating? Hell's fire boy, there ain't no rules in a knife fight. If'n I got a mark on ya it's hidden under the dirt on ya."

Blackie pointed his char-knife at Luke's left pantleg where a black char mark ran from crotch to knee. His char-knife had marked Luke's left thigh when he slid between Luke's legs.

Luke glanced at his marked thigh and then at Blackie. His angry grimace grew into a howl of rage as he loosened and removed his wide leather belt. From the belt's inner-side, he slid out a razor-sharp thin blade, six inches long, ending with a brass finger ring. "Gonna cut ya, boy. Learn ya some manners an' respect. We'll learn if'n Frenchie can sew the pieces together again."

In his anger and rage, Luke charged Blackie like a bull with his knife thrust forward.

Cheyenne wrestling techniques didn't have the fancy names of Roman-Greco wrestling, but The People understood body mechanics and how to apply them. In the Cheyenne camp, young boys and men practiced daily. The purpose of regular practice is to respond in an instant when threatened. Blackie responded as would any man of The People.

Luke's angry rush provided the momentum Blackie needed to apply a hip-toss. With his left hand, he smacked Luke's blade aside, grabbed Luke's right arm and spun to place his butt in Luke's stomach. He used both hands to pull Luke's arm across his shoulder as he bent forward, letting Luke's momentum carry him over and land with a heavy thud. Still gripping Luke's knife hand in both of his, he slipped his thumb into Luke's fist gripping the thin blade. Blackie's thumb gave him leverage against Luke's thumb as he spun, twisting Luke's arm, forcing the man to roll on his stomach and release the knife in order to ease the pain in his shoulder.

Blackie grabbed Luke's knife from the ground but resisted his Cheyenne training to slit his enemy's throat. He expected treachery from Luke and had wrapped a one-pound iron spike for picketing the horses within the lacing of his fringed leggings. He gripped the heavy spike in his fist, its butt-end, mushroomed from regular pounding, extended beyond the heel of his fist to serve as a hammer's head to strike a blow behind Luke's right ear.

Luke had pushed to rise when Blackie struck him the first time. Stunned, Luke lay a moment before he shook his head, trying to rise again. On his second strike, Blackie slammed the iron spike's butt-end above the jaw hinge on Luke's left side. Luke collapsed in the dirt, face first.

In three minutes, Luke's body shook, and he moaned. After another two minutes, he groaned and rolled on his back. He laid a hand on his left jaw. "Damn. What mule kicked me?"

Blackie tossed a water skin on Luke's chest. "Don't waste it. It's all the water you have until Pascal arrives near dark tonight."

Luke sat up in another ten minutes, resting his head on his forearms between his knees. He glanced at Blackie. "Who's here?"

Blackie slid his Colt Navy .32-caliber pistol from his belly holster, cocking it as he drew and aimed at Luke. "We're alone. You lost … twice. If you as much as raise your voice or give me or the team a bit of trouble, I'll leave your body where it falls. We hired you to work. I expect you to work, and work hard, until we reach La Junta del Rios. Don't push your luck until then."

The team returned an hour before sunset with the camp mules carrying eight full water barrels. Antonio rode into camp with a field-dressed doe on his horse's rump. He'd gutted it and removed the rear legs at the knee-joint to keep their scent glands from tainting the meat—fresh meat for supper.

If Pascal wondered about Luke's swollen left eye, he never asked Blackie about it.

Chapter 5

November 1855

By first light the next morning, the mules stood saddled and ready. Another day of watching mule butts. The trip to water had changed the order of the mules in the strings. They brayed and snapped at new neighbors throughout the day until they accepted their new order.

The nights grew cold and they carried no wood for fires, nothing but buffalo chips, which grew scarce in badland areas with little grass. Buffalo chips got hot enough to boil water but burned fast, failing to produce the warmth of a dry woodfire. After Pascal shifted east to avoid the worst of the lava beds and badlands, the team hoped to find water at the Cimarron River, but found it dry in this season. Upstream three miles, they followed Cold Spring Creek to its headwaters at the spring. They camped on the plateau above the spring, which served the Santa Fe Trail's Cimarron Cut-off, or Dry Route, to relax and enjoy a rest day at Cold Spring. The men moved the horses beside Cold Spring Creek where the grass stayed green and then switched with mules at midday, so each group had a turn at green grazing.

During the rest day, Blackie pulled Benito aside. "How is Luke's work? Is he helping?"

Benito curled his lip. "He helps lift the packsaddles but does nothing without being told."

"If he makes trouble, I want to know," Blackie said.

"You going to tell us about his black eye?" Benito raised an eyebrow.

"He didn't want to follow my orders. I convinced him not to make trouble."

Luke remained sullen but caused no problems.

The team enjoyed the easy pace of the smooth Santa Fe Trail as they plodded west. In five days, they reached Canadian Crossing, with a stone bottom. Upstream, the Canadian's sandy bottom bogged wagons. Downstream, it dropped into an impassable steep-walled canyon. They created the Trail to form the easiest wagon path, and the mule team enjoyed its level, easy route.

The winter flow failed to reach the men's boots in crossing. Once across, Pascal led the bell mare southwest and the mules plodded along, following the clanging bell. He sought La Junta del Rios where the "Dry Route" rejoined the Santa Fe Trail's "Mountain Route." The Mountain Route led southwest from the Arkansas River at Bent's old fort to the eastern edge of the Sangre de Cristo mountains, crossing at Raton Pass. It led the wagons south to Fort Union, New Mexico, which lay in a quiet valley of the Mora River, twenty miles into the mountains northwest of La Junta del Rios. The lush Mora Valley offered clear water and good grazing for the wagon teams, whether mule or oxen.

Early Spanish settlers called the grassy meadows surrounding the junction of Sapello Creek and the Mora River, La Junta del Rios, the junction of rivers. The area served as a campground for Spanish travelers and Redmen alike, where they often traded goods. The entire area lay within the Mora Land Grant. In 1825, Samuel Watrous, an early Santa Fe Trail trader, bought several sections of Mora land. He established a large ranchero along the Sapello's south bank, where the rancho prospered in a few years, and when it did, he added a store.

The mule drive from Bent's Fort to La Junta del Rios had taken eighteen days. As agreed, Pascal paid Luke his wages, nine dollars.

"Ya owe me four dollars due to Fredo 'cause we was pard-nas," Luke said.

Pascal replied, "It's worth four dollars to have you gone."

The next morning, the team loaded the mules in the dark and readied the string's alignment to move at first light, when Luke stomped from the cantina, cussing, and hollering.

Luke had spent the night drinking in an adobe cantina behind the Watrous store. He worked up his courage to challenge Pascal before he led the mule team away.

"Frenchy," Luke called, waving his arms as he stormed to the mule train, "I've come to find if ya're half as good as ya want them pups to think ya are. Climb off'n yer horse and let's get to knife fighting whilst we find who's best."

"If you insist," Pascal said, shifting to dismount away from the challenger by turning his horse's rear in Luke's direction.

Luke rushed toward Pascal as soon as he shifted to step down, trying to catch Pascal with his back turned, but once on the ground, Pascal jabbed his thumb low in the horse's belly where its ribs ended. The gelding kicked hard with its rear legs, catching Luke in the chest as he came past to attack Pascal.

The horse's kick straightened Luke to a standstill, dazing him.

Reaching Luke in two long strides, Pascal lifted his elbows as he rotated his shoulders, drawing his right fist behind his ear. He uncoiled his shoulder's twist faster than a snake's strike and pushed off his rear foot to shift his weight into an overhand punch, striking Luke's temple.

The punch staggered Luke, who teetered to fall.

Pascal grabbed him around the waist to lift Luke. As he rose, Luke's body jack-knifed across Pascal's shoulders as he stood tall, lifting Luke's 250 pounds high before he shifted forward, slamming Luke on the ground.

Luke exhaled a loud gush of air when he landed hard on his back. He lay with his mouth open, gasping like a fish out of water.

Blackie and the Ortega cousins gazed at the action from their mounts in slack-jawed silence.

"Didn't this flap-yap tell you there are no rules in a knife fight?" Pascal said as he mounted. "He fell for an old trick and set himself up by rushing close when he thought I turned my back."

Luke laid on the ground, long past fighting, when the mule train trod from sight.

The next evening, the mule team reached the village of Las Vegas, New Mexico. They camped east of the small village alongside a small stream called Gallinas Creek. Locals called it a river, but it only flowed deep during the spring snowmelt. The well-used camp area lay on the east side of the Santa Fe Trail, which meant by the season's end, local firewood and graze had been stripped bare by the Trail's travelers. It also meant they'd find no wood for fires and no fodder for the stock. Pascal had to buy both, and he complained to everyone when he had to *buy*.

The team enjoyed a rest day in Las Vegas, which let Blackie visit the Methodist church before riding south along the Pecos. While in town, Pascal hired two local Mexican lads to help with the daily loading and unloading of packsaddles.

"1 found two strong, willing workers at the Fonda to add to our work crew," Pascal said. "They are young Mexican men happy to find work and a chance to travel. Their names are Ignacio Valdes and Luis Ortiz. Ignacio said to call him 'Nachi.' They'll join us tomorrow."

The trip south along the Pecos passed without any remarkable events. The weather turned cool and rainy, but not stormy. The rainy season in this area came in the late fall. It helped green the gramma grass, the so-called *buffalo grass*, and the new growth lifted it off the ground before it froze in winter, allowing it to retain its forage quality during the dry winter.

After four days, the team took an unexpected rest day across from the Bosque Redondo, a cottonwood grove on the east bank of the Pecos River. Pascal said, "We've entered Mescalero Apache territory. We must remain vigilant at night." He scheduled extra men on nighthawk duty.

Pascal and Blackie rode for a half day to reach the Llano Estacado, the high mesa above the Pecos's eastern bank. "This is a huge flat-topped mesa. It's 250 miles long, north to south, and 150 miles wide, east to west," Pascal said. "It's renowned for its flat, featureless expanse. The only water here comes from rain, which collects in buffalo wallows, if you can find one. Few white men are known to have crossed it, although Gregg claimed he did in 1831 or '32."

"Why come here if it's so remote?" Blackie asked.

"It's the domain of the Kwahadi, the Antelope band of the Comanche, although a few Utes and the Lipan Apache have been known to ride here. There is sparse game there because water is so scarce. The *cibolero*, buffalo hunters, killed the buffalo roaming here in earlier times. The Redman claimed exclusive use of the area since the days of Coronado, the Spanish explorer, who crossed it

300 years ago. Coronado's expedition named it the 'staked plain,' or Llano Estacado."

The pair sat on their mounts, awed by the stark beauty of the flat, grassy plateau stretching to the horizon in every direction. It appeared God had slapped a huge frying pan to flatten it.

"We don't come here," Pascal said. "I'm told Comancheros drive their carts up this edge to trade with Kwahadi. The Comanche steal cattle, horses, and children to trade the Comancheros for weapons and liquor. The Comancheros are evil people without a shred of moral conscience. They traffic in slaves and in selling young girls into prostitution. Young white girls bring the highest prices. Avoid the Comancheros at all costs."

"If people know they do these evil things, why don't they stop them?" Blackie asked.

"You must catch them first, and even with their carts laden with hides and plunder, they are elusive. I brought you to the Llano to show you how desolate this area is, and why we avoid it. It's akin to a death sentence to attempt to cross it in summer, if you don't have strong healthy horses and extra water." Pascal gazed across the flat plain, marked, on occasion, with the *agave lechuguilla's* tall flowered stalks, and from a distance appeared like wooden stakes, which lead to the name *staked plain.*

"I intended to warn you about Comancheros. Be alert for two-wheeled cart tracks. Those tracks are different than a wagon's, more wide-set and broader rims. If you come across their tracks, warn us without delay. They'll ambush us, in a savage attack, killing everyone before they steal our mules, horses, and cargo."

"I understand about cart tracks, but what do Comancheros look like? Are they Redmen?"

"*Non.* They're dirty, filthy animals who may have been human once. Most are of Mexican descent, but there are few whites among them and mixed-breed Redmen. Often, you'll smell the hides before seeing them, but don't rely on it. They are silent killers at night like the Redmen."

"Where do they live? How do we avoid them?"

"They hide their camps well. The Army never finds them. I'm told they hide in the barren mountains, west across from the Bosque Redondo. When they have slaves, cattle, and hides to sell, they travel south along the Pecos, like we're doing, and continue straight south into Mexico following the old *Camino Real* to Ojinaga, Mexico, across the Rio. They don't follow a pattern or season, so we must be alert. I'm expecting a lot from you as a new scout. Antonio and you need to search around the train in a regular schedule. I want you on opposite sides of the train from one another so we can get the earliest warning of their presence."

"And you are worried about the Mescaleros, too?" Blackie stroked his horse's neck.

"Yes, we must be alert for both. The risk of Comancheros is smaller, but they are more deadly because they'll ambush and kill without hesitation. The Mescalero often consider us traders and let us pass, as do many of the

Redmen. Enough gossip." Pascal waved a hand to point west. "Let's return to the train and find if Tomas has supper ready."

~~~~~~

To amuse themselves in the evening, Blackie showed the cousins how to practice knife fighting with fire-blackened sticks as Luke had shown him. The Las Vegas pair, Nachi and Luis, reported they'd seen one such fight and found it bloody.

"I wondered how a man learned to fight in such a way with a knife," Nachi said. "I would have to be angry with a man to choose to fight in such a way."

"Sometimes," Antonio said, "the other man gives you no choice. Fight or live as a coward."

After the first night, char-knives became a regular event among the young men. During the noon siesta a week later, Blackie demonstrated the knife and tomahawk throwing skills he developed with the Cheyenne. After learning, the young men often spent a bit of siesta time practicing accuracy and distance with both weapons in daylight.

"If you have extra energy, I can give you more work," Pascal grumbled after they got noisy rooting for one or the other during a char fight. "I can make the rest period shorter, too."

The trip south along the Pecos in early winter became almost boring. They saw no one, not even Redmen scouting in the distance. Neither Antonio nor Blackie found fresh tracks of carts or horses. The mule train continued south alongside the Pecos but when it grew bitter from nearby salt deposits, Pascal ordered them to swing west, closer to the Guadalupe mountains.

"Don't grow careless. The Mescalero will give you a close shave," Pascal said. He led the train southwest into mountains with an alert. "After Pine Spring, we'll find no water for four days. We will keep a fast pace across the dry stretch. Be thankful it's early winter while we cross this area and not the scorching hot summer season."

"It's hot enough now," Dom said, causing the cousins nearby to laugh.

A week later, Pascal led the mule team across the Rio into El Paso, in time for siesta. The team unloaded the cargo during siesta time because they wanted to party into the night. Pascal received gold in payment for the cartage delivery, which always put him in a good mood. He paid the men half their wages and announced he'd treat the team to *cena*, the traditional after siesta evening meal, once they cleaned up. The young men visited a barber Antonio liked with outdoor bath stalls and hot water. With their gold, the young men bought ready-made clothes to wear that night, dressing like fancy *caballeros* before they rode to the Rancho in a few days. After their *cena*, Pascal awarded each young man a gold Eagle, advising them to stay out of trouble.

Blackie, as he often did, wandered through the open shops, where he observed people's behavior and listened to how they spoke to improve his spoken Spanish. He caught a glimpse of Nachi, one of the Las Vegas pair, as he headed into an alley behind a young girl.

Blackie shifted to follow Nachi when two women carrying packages strolled past. One woman called the girl a whore. "Why do they let *them* strut about town?" she ranted. "And in daylight."

He straightened as if he'd been slapped. *How could I have been so dumb? Those aren't sporting houses—they're whore houses. The men fornicated with whores.* His strict Methodist family life abhorred the thought and practice. *This is the vile sin my mother warned me about.*

Blackie grabbed a post at the alley's edge. His preacher's kid family life warred with the stark reality of his last month in Black Kettle's camp. Two young girls grew bold enough to touch him as he explored them. Despite his promise to his true mother not to commit adultery, he'd been invited to *sleep* with the wives of two different men in Black Kettle's camp in honor of his saving Cheyenne women from the Pawnee. *It would've been an insult to refuse their offer, wouldn't it?* The experience both excited and terrified him.

What's the difference? To fornicate with a paid one, or to fornicate with another man's wife? Sin is sin. Those painted whores don't appeal to me, but the Cheyenne women were neither pretty nor young. Not even the white girls in town compared to Morning Star. I'd have fought an entire Pawnee clan to lay beside Morning Star one time. Let Nachi lay with whom he chooses.

He wandered to the corral where they kept the mules. Without a camp and animals to guard, he visited the gun shops and found four small-caliber target rifles. *I'll suggest Pascal buy these rifles to train new workers to shoot without the Sharps' ear-pounding boom.*

~~~~~~

LaFleur arrived in El Paso two weeks after Pascal and the team. Phillippe didn't accompany him south from Santa Fe, which aggravated both Pascal and LaFleur. Fortunately, St. Vrain found three men to drive the wagons south, carrying the trade goods LaFleur had purchased in Santa Fe. The wagons added rolling stock to the freight line and Santa Fe goods produced a profit.

Pascal, Blackie, and several from the team rode to El Paso to greet LaFleur. His safe return became a cause for celebration, and a good excuse for the men to visit the sporting houses.

~~~~~~

Pascal and LaFleur wintered at the Rancho at Zaragoza and helped the Ortega family improve the Rancho like they had the previous seasons. LaFleur worked in the vineyards on the high, dry plateau above the Rancho, where springs watered his vines.

Pascal resumed the task of improving the

community's *acequia*, a shared irrigation canal, allowing the Rancho to grow corn for its families and workers and maize for its animals.

The wagons LaFleur bought in Santa Fe bolstered Ortega's freight venture to Chihuahua. The young men refurbished or repaired the wagons and trained new mules to work in harness or carry packsaddles. At the Rancho, Pascal kept people busy with his plans for the next season.

Once again, Blackie wondered why they called it the "winter rest," when no one rested.

Chapter 6

November 1855 – March 1856

Pascal and LaFleur planned another trade season to the north—their primary source of income. This season, Pascal decided to try new areas and wanted to reach Santa Fe by late March. St. Vrain sent a letter asking Pascal to deliver 2,500 pounds of goods to Fort Massachusetts, which solidified his plan. Rather than drive and feed extra mules he wouldn't need after he delivered St. Vrain's goods, Pascal figured to load the relief mules from Taos across the San Luis to the Fort.

After trading in southern Utah at Mountain Meadows, St. George, and Pipe Springs last season, Pascal discussed by mail with St. Vrain what trails to follow. The letters suggested Pascal follow an old fur-trader route northwest from the original old Spanish Trail, which saw little use after Mexico lost California in the Mexican-American War.

Pascal planned to lead a forty-eight-mule train, with a twenty-four horse remuda and a bell-mare, twelve relief mules, and eight mules with camp supplies. He wanted a team of himself, LaFleur, Blackie, Phillippe, and the Ortega cousins, consisting of Antonio, Benito, Javy, Dom,

Reynaldo, and Tomas, plus the Las Vegas pair, Nachi and Luis.

On March 2, 1856, the team arrived in El Paso. Phillippe had agreed to arrive by March 1, but no one had seen him. Pascal arranged to deliver cargo to Santa Fe for Señor Valencia. The season shaped up as the pieces came together. It appeared reasonable on paper, but their test would come when they entered the mountain trails north of Santa Fe.

"If Phillippe doesn't arrive by first light tomorrow, we'll leave without him," Pascal said.

~~~~~~

While Pascal organized the mule train's departure from El Paso, the San Antonio-San Diego stage arrived, nicknamed the San-San. Travel by coach along the *express* mail routes became so unreliable, one never knew if they maintained a schedule at all. On an errand, Blackie noticed the coach driver, a big man, taller than Pascal's six-two, step from the box to wheel to boardwalk as a crowd gathered to greet the coach's arrival. Later, Blackie glimpsed the big man enter the hotel's dining room while Pascal, LaFleur, and he ate dinner. The big man called to Pascal and LaFleur as he passed. He spoke with a heavy drawl, and spoke around a wad of tobacco, forcing Blackie to struggle to understand him.

Pascal introduced the man as "Bigfoot" Wallace. After Pascal said, "Bigfoot," Wallace lifted one to show his huge foot to Blackie.

Bigfoot said, "I'll jabber with y'all after I fill my gullet."

When the men gathered after dinner, Blackie left, saying he'd scout around town to "see the sights." After an hour, he strolled to the corrals where the team kept the mules before loading them, searching for the cousins or the Las Vegas pair. He failed to find his friends, and instead, he glimpsed Mr. Wallace speaking to the hostler who switched the stagecoach's mule team.

Blackie wandered close to gawk and listen. After he stepped closer, Wallace glanced at him and asked, "Ya the young'un ol' Pascal found on the prairie?"

"Yes, sir. The Comanche killed my family and stole my sisters. I'll take my revenge on them one day."

"I done such myself once't, young'un. My brother gallivanted to the Alamo with ol' Davy Crockett. He got killed with 'em other heroes. I come to Texas from Tennessee in 18 an' 38 and I swore I'd kill as many of 'em Mexicans as I could to settle for what they done to my brother. In the Mexican war in 18 an' 48, I kilt a passel of 'em. While riding scout to find stragglers from the Mexican Army, I kilt a bunch who gathered to fight." He wiped a hand across his mouth.

"I met Kit Carson doing the same, scouting and killing stragglers with his Cavalry company. Ol' Kit waved at me, 'Hey Bigfoot, has ya kilt 'nough Mexicans yet?'"

Bigfoot laid his large hand on Blackie's shoulder. "A strange thing happened, and the more I thought about it, the more I understood it. I nodded, replying, 'Yep, I think I has.' I found I didn't need to avenge my brother no more. It was done. I let it pass behind me."

The big man shifted, spitting a big gob, and glanced at Blackie, "Ya take revenge on yer Comanches an' kill as many as ya can when ya grow some bigger. One day ask yerself, 'Have I kilt enough?' and once't ya ask the question, ya can stop. Ya have avenged yer family. It's enough. Let it pass behind ya. Ya'll be a better man for it." With such words, Bigfoot shifted, ambling toward the corral, giving Blackie a wave over his shoulder, "See ya around, young'un."

~~~~~~

Pascal found Phillippe waiting for them in Mesilla, two days' north of El Paso.

"This town has better saloons and cleaner sporting houses than El Paso," Phillippe said. "The Texas side of the Rio gets too wild-eyed loco. Besides, Texans don't want my *kind* in a saloon."

Pascal found no humor in Phillippe's remarks.

The Ortega cousins wanted the opportunity to try Phillippe's recommendations. After their evening meal, he led the cousins and the Las Vegas pair for a tour of Mesilla's night life.

With a grin, LaFleur used his slate to ask Pascal, *Have you never done such?*

Pascal jabbed an obscene gesture at him.

When Blackie laughed at their antics, Pascal nudged him with an elbow, "What are you laughing at? You promised your dear mother you would abstain from such carnal knowledge."

"I'm still waiting for you to explain what *sport* they play in the *sporting houses*."

"Bah," Pascal barked. "You're getting too big for your britches. You need a belt to the seat of your knowledge." Pascal pulled his wide leather strap belt loose to shake at Blackie.

Using LaFleur as a shield, Blackie blat a raspberry at Pascal as LaFleur howled laughing.

"Try being useful," Pascal barked. "Go stand night watch. I'll relieve you at midnight."

The next morning, Pascal rousted the team from their bedrolls. "I hope you enjoyed last night. Today, we enter the *Camino Real's* version of *Jornada del Muerto*. It has lava beds like the Cimarron crossing on the New Mexico border last season. Expect a six-day ride without water. You'll sweat out the beer and whiskey you enjoyed last night."

"I don't see volcano cones like in the northern badlands," Blackie asked. "Where did the lava come from?"

"It may come as a surprise, *Noir*," Pascal said with a wink. "There are things I don't know." After a moment of gazing about, he continued, "The trail across here is well marked, but the lava beds are jumbled and broken, forcing us to take care. It gives the impression the mountains split apart letting lava ooze and bubble from a tear in the rock. It's rough ground, and iron shoes don't protect a mule's hooves. It's another reason to go slow."

To Blackie's surprise, a thick carpet of black-gramma grass covered its surface. He expected the absence of water to reduce all plant life in the *Jornada* desert. The eighteen-inch tall grass rippled in the hot winds from the Chihuahuan Desert. No trees or bushes grew on the valley floor, but higher on the surrounding mountains juniper, piñon, and mesquite bushes took root.

"I thought you warned this desert would be without water for six days." He glanced at Pascal in wide-eyed wonder. "There must be water nearby to support this grass."

"The old-timers in Mesilla told me buffalo grazed along the *Jornada* until Yankee soldiers killed them in 1847," Pascal responded. "This area receives seasonal rain in the fall, and I guess it provides enough moisture for the grasses to survive year-round. The old men said if the seasonal rains are absent, the grass turns brown and withers, but returns after a rainy season."

"Why would you talk to the old men about rain and grass?"

"Fodder. If there's no grass, the animals get no nourishment and can't work. I'd have to bring twice as many mules to carry their food." Pascal sighed. "More lessons. You must learn not only to seek a rest area with water, but also one with enough graze for our animals." Pascal batted

Blackie's hat brim. "Such will become one of your jobs as a scout and hunter."

"More lessons," Blackie mumbled as he stomped away. When he returned from his run, he asked, "Does anyone want rabbit for dinner tomorrow? There are dozens of rabbits in the grass."

"I don't want jackrabbits," Dom said. "They're tough as leather."

"There are jackrabbits around but most of what I glimpsed are cottontails," Blackie answered. "I bet I can trap a dozen overnight."

"You'll need three dozen if you're going to feed this group," Pascal said.

Blackie produced forty skinned rabbits for roasting the next evening but used his small-caliber target rifle.

"Did you notice the sparrowhawks after the mice and the larger hawks and eagles after rabbits?" Blackie's voice pitched higher in excitement. "It looks like they are using us to spook the critters from hiding before grabbing one. It's fun watching them swoop to attack."

"The *Camino Real* trail is well marked," Pascal said. "Be careful wandering away from it. There are open pits where lava once flowed. Don't be gawking at the sky and fall into one."

At the halfway camp, Pascal decided to send Blackie and Phillippe ahead to the Rio crossing with four mules carrying the water barrels they'd emptied. They'd leave after siesta the next day on the Jornada trail and ride to the Rio at Val Verde crossing, the Jornada's north end, during the night, rest the mules a day, and return to the team by siesta on the fifth day.

When the two returned with extra water at midday, the hard glare Blackie gave Phillippe alerted Pascal the two had argued. Pascal asked, "What happened?"

After loosening his cinch, Blackie pointed at Phillippe, "You tell him."

"I knew where you'd stop tonight," Phillippe said after an indifferent shrug and spreading his hands apart. "I wanted to rest at tonight's camp site until you arrived, saving another four hours of riding. You won't need the water until this evening. I didn't see a need to hurry."

"Either we grew careless watering the animals or we're losing water from the barrels," Pascal said. "We had enough water to give each animal a drink before we ran out. They'll need another drink before we push north after siesta."

Phillippe nodded and shrugged.

"Next time I send you out, returning promptly is part of the assignment," Pascal barked.

As if trying to change the subject, Phillippe asked, "Did Little Wolf report the bats?"

"What?" Pascal straightened and turned to his scout with brows raised.

"A swarm of bats came from the ground east of the trail a day's ride north of here. We'll probably pass the area about midday tomorrow and not notice any activity. Hawks attacked them, but the bats flew through them. I recognized the large Mexican bats. Smaller bats flew north for the river, choosing not to fly across the San Cristobal. You asked me to remain alert for them."

"Thanks for reporting. You have narrowed the search area to find their roost."

"I hate to squawk like Little Wolf, but why do we care where bats roost?"

"We are too far from the source of quality black powder. DuPont's mills are on the Atlantic coast. It is a four-month wagon journey to deliver powder to Bent's. The cheaper, and poorly made, Mexican black powder degrades when jiggled in a wagon for months, and its ingredients separate."

"Bent's always has a supply of DuPont powder. Why worry?"

"He didn't have powder in the last three months before the Mexican war ended. The U.S. Army confiscated two of his shipments, and DuPont couldn't produce enough to meet demand before the war ended." Pascal said. "Mexico is about to collapse into civil war, and the Union are at one another's throat over slavery. If the Union prohibits the sale of black powder to prevent civil unrest or buys the available supplies in the East, what will happen in the West?"

"The white man must learn to use a bow and a lance in a hurry." Phillippe smirked.

"The best natural source of saltpeter is bird or bat guano," Pascal said. "Napoleon scoured bird nesting areas on islands across the Mediterranean to make powder for his cannons."

"What is bat guano?" Phillippe's usually placid features wrinkled as he raised his brows.

Pascal laughed. "Bat shit. It's been collecting in those caves for thousands of years. I believe they awarded a land grant for this area. I must find whose grant claims this land."

"You intend to manufacture your own black powder?" Phillippe stepped away from Pascal.

"Not until we must, but saltpeter is essential to the process. Collecting, drying, and powdering guano should be quite profitable if war comes, as I expect," Pascal winked. "Mining here will be easier, and more profitable, than dragging mules from one end of the mountains to the other, and this area is accessible by wagon from El Paso."

Phillippe cocked his head, gazing at Pascal. "White men are crazy. Bat shit?" he strode away shaking his head while muttering, "Bat shit."

Along the *Camino Real,* a week later, they rested for a siesta break at Albuquerque where they met southbound freight wagons led by "Uncle Dick" Wooten.

"Dick, I thought you worked at Bent's new Post at Big Timbers?" Pascal called.

"I do. This year, Bent contracted to deliver freight to the new Army post they're building west of Albuquerque. He uses my wagons on usual shipments and hires others, like your mules, when a shipment comes out of order."

Wooten waved an arm at the road. "I'll tell you one thing for sure, the Army ain't got this road measured right. They claim it's sixty miles from Santa Fe. It's taking far too long to get here.

They're cheating me on delivery costs. I'm going to the camp commander about it. Fair is fair. They've shorted me on mileage."

While the men talked, Pascal said, "I'm going to follow the old Spanish Trail north to the Green River to find what trade I can sell in Utah, and then go northeast to Fort Bridger. I need to find new trade areas along the mountain routes. The wagon freighters like Majors & Waddell make it too hard for me to compete with their large wagon loads. I'm not making any money hauling cargo for hire along the front range. I must carry trade items to sell to make any profit these days. Have you traveled across the old Spanish Trail to Utah?"

"Kit Carson's the man to ask," Wooten said. "He done it once, all the way to California. I don't think it worked for him, 'cause he don't like to talk about it."

After they parted, Pascal said, "Wooten is a first-class frontiersman and trader. He worked along the eastern edge of the mountains and the front range before the Mexican-American War when Bent's original Fort William represented the prairie's only civilization. Wooten served as the messenger between the trading posts, north to St. Vrain's Fort on the Cache la Poudre River, and then to Fort Laramie on the North Platte River. Wooten rode that circuit alone every two months for many years, except in winter."

"He sounds like he's bragging," Blackie said, "when he talks so loud."

"I think he's losing his hearing, but he does like

to talk about himself," Pascal said.

Late the next afternoon, the mule team reached Santa Fe. They unloaded Valenzuela's cargo with merchants in Santa Fe before resting a day. This town became the men's favorite stop because of its saloons and sporting houses.

At first light the day after the rest day, the team rode north and reached Taos late the third day. During their evening meal, Nachi asked, "Why do we stop in Taos? It's smaller than Santa Fe. In season, Santa Fe has more goods coming in from the Trail or Mexico. Taos has little compared to Santa Fe."

"Taos grew popular with the early trappers because the Santa Fe Trail didn't exist," Pascal said. "In its day, Taos became the nearest place to the northern mountains for supplies."

"They didn't have other stores back then, like we have now, so why keep stopping here?"

"After the Mexicans declared independence from Spain in 1821, the Santa Fe Trail began with Mexico's blessings. In 1826, the fur-trappers carried supplies by boat upstream on the Missouri, and then upstream on the Yellowstone River to their private forts in the mountains. Once they established the Missouri River route, trappers working in the northern mountains no longer used Taos." After a moment's reflection, Pascal said, "The Santa Fe Trail ended the French influence in the area. Few speak French now."

"You mean only the old-timers speak French now." Phillippe laughed.

Pascal and St. Vrain like to compare the size of their purse, LaFleur wrote, leading the men to laugh about comparing the size of a certain piece of their anatomy between the old bulls.

Blackie guessed the answer lay in the friendship between the Frenchmen.

~~~~~~

Phillippe had little experience in the Colorado mountains, forcing Pascal to rely on directions provided by Kit Carson. After the Mexican-American War, gold seekers flooded to California. Carson borrowed money from St. Vrain to herd a flock of sheep along the Old Spanish Trail into southern Utah. From there, he had once scouted the mountain passes of Utah for the Fremont expedition, and followed his nose across a high pass to Sacramento and into the goldfields.

The miners welcomed the fresh meat, and Kit found prices high. While Carson didn't like to speak of it, after selling the sheep, he re-crossed the high pass from California, where bandits attacked, robbing him of his hard-gained profit. It left Carson in St. Vrain's debt for many years.

Pascal and Phillippe met with Carson at St. Vrain's trading post in Taos where Carson had his home. Although he never learned to read, Kit sketched a map while giving hand signals for "a jog" here and "a scooch" across the ridge there. The sketch contained important landmarks to check for location and turns. Names often meant little, for the locals called a creek one name, while folks across the next ridge called it another. Its location, and direction, became the most crucial elements. Did the creek flow west? Did the ridge run north? Such directions became the extent of Pascal's guidance from Carson along the Old Spanish Trail to Utah.

~~~~~~

After delivering St. Vrain's cargo to Fort Massachusetts, they adjusted the packsaddles to distribute the load evenly before climbing the mountains. The team rode west to find the Old Spanish Trail upstream on the Rio Grande in the San Juan Mountains. After they climbed higher, Phillippe followed the South Fork to cross Wolf Creek Pass. The pass held deep drifts in early March, forcing Phillippe, Antonio, and Blackie to break trails through the snowbanks.

Once across the Wolf Creek Pass, Phillippe followed the San Juan River downstream to the Sulphur-tainted hot springs the Ute's called *Pagosa*. The Ute word meant "water smells bad." The Utes considered the hot springs as healing waters and visited the area often.

From Pagosa, Pascal led the train over a ridge to follow a fast-running creek flowing west and through a broad tree-lined canyon until it turned south. He followed Carson's "a jog north" before riding west past the south side of a rounded mountain resembling a haystack. Without a trail, the mule train meandered back and forth across the creek to avoid boulders and deadfalls. They often sawed a deadfall to leave a gap for the train to pass between fallen trees.

To avoid slipping and falling on a creekbank, Pascal preferred to cross perpendicular to the water's flow. It made the shortest time in the water and reduced the chance of falling by going straight up or down the bank, not crossing at an angle.

He ordered them to avoid bunching the mules together at the water's edge and crowding one another. "Keep the string away from the creek bank until the path is clear, then move them across without stopping in the water."

It seemed to Blackie, if he got settled into a daily routine, Pascal sought ways to keep him alert under the guise of improving his survival skills, or with the dreaded "lessons."

Small game had grown scarce, and Blackie suggested, "Let me use the Sharps rifle. I can shoot an elk or deer. You know I'm a good shot from our practice sessions at the Rancho."

"Yes, you're a good shot." Pascal nodded. "Victorio Ortega's vaqueros improved from your instructions, as did the Las Vegas pair." Pascal glanced at Phillippe. "If we need more meat, I'll send him. He is the hunter and scout for the team. You must sharpen the skills learned last season with the Cheyenne. I want you to learn to fool those animals with your stealth, as Yellow Blossom advised. One day, an unexpected event or accident will happen, causing your horse to stumble and fall, or a Redman shoots it. In the fall, your rifle is damaged. What will you do?"

"I'll run away as fast as I can," Blackie said, "Like you taught me."

"Don't be smug. Yes, you could run, but how will you eat, or replace your moccasins without a rifle? This is your next lesson in survival. I want you to practice the stealthy approach you learned with the Cheyenne. Don't let the animal know you are there until you kill it with your knives. In your escape from the hostiles, you may not have the time or materials to craft a strong bow and find bird feathers to guide straight-shooting arrows.

"You must learn to use cunning and skill by lying in wait or killing your prey by pouncing on it as if a silent panther, leaping to sink your knives into it to bring it down. Find a game trail, locate an ambush spot without leaving your scent in the area. Wait for game to come along the trail and take it unaware. When you succeed, trot to us with the animal across your shoulders, as you'd have done to escape the Redman hunting you. Show me you can kill one in such a way without a bow or rifle."

Phillippe, who liked to raze Blackie, said, "Be careful of their hooves. They can kick almost as hard as a mule, but a deer's small split hooves will cut you to pieces if you fall beneath one."

The mule team moved west, stopping to trade with Utes south of Haystack Mountain. Pascal said, "We will come in the spring each year to trade with the Utes," offering tobacco, foofaraw trinkets, and sweets for trade. As usual, he refused to sell liquor or weapons to the Redman. The Utes had little use for flour or dry food, but traded in finished skins, or hand-worked leather.

Blackie watched as they offered handmade silver and turquoise jewelry, but the Utes wanted weapons, or liquor, or both for their best work.

Pascal refused to trade in such items.

The spring heat added to their long hours and hard work. The mountains made it harder for everyone, including the animals. Blackie became aware it didn't get dark gradually in the mountains like it did on the prairie with a lingering sunset. It grew dark in a rush, as though someone blew out the lantern, and then it grew cooler.

The next day, the team crossed a stream where the water didn't reach his feet as they crossed—his measure of an easy crossing. As he rode up the far side, he noticed the water dripping from their hooves had made the trail climbing up the far bank slick. At the top, he reined his horse aside and called to Benito, leading the next string.

"Hold the string on your side." Blackie dismounted. "Send Geraldo to the camp mules and bring two shovels here."

When Geraldo arrived, Blackie stood at the bottom of the west-bound bank. "The trail is muddy and slick. Let's use the shovels to knock down the grass overhang on each side of the trail, making it wider, and throw the dry dirt on the slick area."

In five minutes, the crossing's path grew wider, less steep, giving the mules a wide path and avoiding the slick mud. Busy working with Geraldo, Blackie failed to notice Pascal had dismounted to watch from atop the streambank.

"Those are the tasks a scout does to protect our animals. *Merci.*" Pascal said.

~~~~~~

Pascal ordered Phillippe, as the primary scout and hunter, to take Blackie on hunts, but they grew edgy around one another with petty bickering and sniping. Because of this hostility, Blackie didn't trust Phillippe. It became a *respect* issue for him like Luke's complaint from last season.

After listening to Blackie's complaints, LaFleur wrote on his slate. *What did Tall Bear teach you? You must give respect and honor before you can receive it.* LaFleur wrote a second message. *You two alike. Proud. Unforgiving. No Trust. No respect. Give one to get other.*

Chapter 7

April-May 1856

At some point after leaving Pagosa, Phillippe asked Blackie to hunt with him in the Haystack Mountain where the forest grew steep and isolated. Phillippe suggested they tie their horses in a meadow by a creek and hunt on foot to prevent the horses' noise or scent from spooking the game. The two stalked forty yards apart across the valley, hunting for elk. They reached a house-sized boulder in the stream, forcing the creek to carve a channel around it, when a grizzly came from behind the boulder, growling for her cubs to come to her.

Phillippe shouted, "Climb a tree as quick as you can."

Blackie glimpsed Phillippe climbing a fir tree.

Phillippe called, "I can't be sure of a killing shot from here. I don't want to shoot the bear because we don't eat her meat and the cubs will die."

Mama Grizzly acted undecided for a moment as to which man to chase before she came after Blackie who ran for a tree. She chased him to the side of the tree away from Phillippe.

A tall blue spruce became the closest tree for

Blackie. It had dead branches at its shaded bottom allowing Blackie to climb with ease, but it also made it easy for the grizzly. He grew surprised at how tall she stood once on her rear legs and reaching with her paws stretched high. He climbed twelve feet up the tree before climbing higher. Fortune favored him when the bear's weight snapped several of the dead lower limbs, daunting her desire to climb. The she-bear shifted between standing and walking on all fours, anxious about leaving her cubs, and wanting to prevent Blackie from getting them. She prowled around the tree's base, growling at Blackie and swatted the tree twice, shaking it, but she often glanced to the creek to watch her cubs.

Blackie sat on a high limb, listening because he could no longer see the grizzly through the limbs below. He couldn't tell if she had settled on the ground to wait for him or had moved on. In the quiet waiting, the footfalls of a large animal descending the mountain grew more distinct as it descended from the slope on the far side, moving with care. After twisting his head to gaze around the tree, Blackie glimpsed an elk cow nose her way between the trees into the valley, checking to find if the bear still prowled the stream. Blackie caught the shuffling noise of another elk behind her, probably a bull, but didn't spot it before Phillippe shot the lead cow.

Blackie descended the tree in a rush. Once on the ground, he searched for the grizzly but failed to catch sight of her. He strode toward the creek to cross to where the cow had fallen.

"Bring our horses," Phillippe called. "We need to get this elk butchered and leave."

Blackie trotted away, returning with the horses in fifteen minutes to where the elk lay.

Phillippe had crudely skinned the elk before using his trade-tomahawk to quarter the elk cow. "We must move quickly before the smell of blood arouses the female grizzly to hunt."

No sooner had he said the words than she growled followed by two wolfing snorts to catch a scent of what animal bled nearby.

Each of the elk cow's hindquarters weighed close to 200 pounds.

"Mount up. I'll lift the hindquarters to you." Phillippe said.

"No, we'll both lift before tying one onto each saddle. We'll walk the horses to camp."

"Do it fast. We mustn't be nearby if the she-bear wants to fight us for what remains."

Each grabbed the reins to lead their horses across the hill when the she-bear rushed from the stream to stand on her hind legs, roaring a challenge. She charged them as far as the remains of the elk, where she stood to roar again, letting them know she'd claimed the carcass and the front quarters. The cubs waited at the edge of the nearby streambank excited by the blood scent.

The two men strode into camp after dark leading horses with the raw meat. Each man on the team carved a piece from the elk's hindquarters, and soon each man roasted fresh meat over the fire.

The Vegas pair started another fire and Blackie joined them with the hindquarter he carried.

Pascal grumbled, as usual. "Fresh elk is wonderful, but in this weather, it won't keep." He instructed them to slice it thin like jerky, roasting it to keep it from spoiling and going to waste.

Phillippe and Blackie resumed bickering once roasting the elk meat settled into a routine.

Phillippe called to Pascal, "I'm surprised Little Wolf didn't panic, wounding the bear with a rushed shot, and making the situation worse after the grizzly treed him."

"I'm surprised at how such a *great hunter* missed a large grizzly with cubs," Blackie said.

"We are a team, act like it," Pascal barked but added nothing else aloud.

Blackie wondered if Pascal caught the meaning of his message about "missing" a *grizzly*.

~~~~~~

Phillippe took pleasure in lording his tracking and hunting skills over Blackie, but it presented Blackie with the opportunity to learn more about surviving in the mountains, which needed different skills than hunting on the prairies. The majestic elk remained elusive, and skills Blackie learned tracking on the flat land often didn't apply in the steep and rocky mountainsides.

Blackie stood in amazement the first time he thought he'd cornered an elk with dense woods behind, believing the animal had no way to escape without hooking his antlers in the trees. The bull elk raised his nose, laying his antler's tines on his shoulders to trot between the packed trees. The antlers, wider than the bull's shoulders, pushed the small trees aside while the tines didn't hook. Distracted by the elk's swift escape, Blackie failed to fire a shot from fifty feet away.

~~~~~~

Fish rarely became a dependable food source on the prairie, but Phillippe taught Blackie the Shoshone way to hand-fish for trout in the mountains. Picking a fishing stream here never was a problem. Water splashed from the mountainside streams, each loaded with plump fish.

Phillippe stood in a pooled stream without moving, luring them close to catch them by hand. In the same time as Blackie caught four trout, Phillippe caught over a dozen. When they caught two for each man, they gutted the fish and inserted a wild onion inside. Phillippe coated each with mud from the bank. In camp, he roasted them in the glowing coals of the firepit, hot enough to cook the meat but not so hot as to burn it. The men enjoyed a supper of fresh mountain trout.

"I've tasted none cooked finer when I lived in Europe," Pascal said.

A real compliment, for he found few things better than those in France.

~~~~~~

The team continued west beside a high plateau before locating the Dolores River, flowing west at this point. The team followed natural avenues between the snowcapped mountains to their north. A day became a week before they shifted west toward the La Sal mountains, and north after passing on the La Sal's western base, and another week to reach the Colorado River with a ferry crossing at Moab, where the river ran high with spring snowmelt.

Pascal ordered them to remove the packsaddles before loading on the ferry.

The ferry operator said, "With the river high, you've too much weight for one crossing. You'll have to make two crossings with them packsaddles."

"Ah, an honest man caring for his neighbors," Pascal said with a smile as he shifted to one side. "But under your skin you're a sinner like the rest of us, and *a lying cheat*," Pascal barked. "This load is equal to a wagon load without the wagon's weight. This ferry can carry two loaded wagons, *and* their animals. You know it and I know it." He nodded to Phillippe, who had shifted the opposite direction, to prod the ferry operator's kidneys with his Sharps.

"You can't do this," the ferry operator cried. "This is my ferry."

"It may be your ferry," Pascal said. "but if you continue to make trouble and cheat people, you'll cross the ferry on the River Styx. I'll pay ten dollars for each crossing—your standard fee—not a penny more. If you don't like it, I'll drop you in the middle on our last crossing."

The mules brayed and squealed during their crossing, but the team followed Pascal's orders to crosstie their alternate legs to keep them from kicking one another or bolting overboard. The ferry crossing consumed a full day.

On the north bank, the team reloaded the packsaddles on the mules. They climbed a ravine leading to the plateau and north for the upper Green River allowing them to avoid the deep goose-necked canyons to the west formed where the Green emptied into the Colorado.

Pascal, LaFleur, and Phillippe discussed the information learned from other men at Moab. They decided to leave the Green when they reached the next higher plateau and ride northwest to Mormon Utah instead of following the Green's west bank north to Idaho. The Mormons created many farms in the upper Salt Basin, and Pascal wanted to try trading with them. He needed to find new trade areas in the towns and villages hidden in the fertile valleys between snow-covered peaks and to establish a reliable route into trade areas in the mountains' interior.

~~~~~~

Pascal allowed a rest day on the plateau above the ferry for the team to explore the sculpted canyons and rock formations north of the Colorado River at Moab. The upper reaches grew semi-arid grasses, but to the west, it fell into vast canyons. Even Phillippe who'd not seen them before stood in awed silence at the beauty and wonder. The team remained silent as they gaped, open-mouthed, at the radiant colors in the rock formation of the deep canyons. Soaring rock towers stood on multicolored layers of rock foundations. The river, when visible, appeared like a bright green ribbon looped below the towering rock formations, reaching thousands of feet from the canyon floor. Each riverbend unique, each a treasure of nature. Along a ridge above the canyons, they found a natural stone arch more than 200 feet long at its eastern edge. The graceful, natural stone arch, lit by the setting sun, glowed burnt orange reflecting from the canyon's hues. Blackie's mouth gaped open as the scene mesmerized him.

"The size of these puts to shame any man-made arches I've visited in Europe," Pascal said.

"The Shoshone say if one continued downstream on the Colorado, the canyons grow deeper, wider, and more colorful," Phillippe said. "I haven't traveled south, so it is only a story."

~~~~~~

After riding two days north, the mule team waded across the Green River with the water short of reaching Blackie's feet. The plateau above them continued to follow the Old Spanish Trail north toward the San Rafael River, flowing with snowmelt. Two days later, Pascal halted at siesta time to explore the wonders of the upper San Rafael canyons.

In one canyon alongside the San Rafael, they found a vertical rock wall 125 feet high, marked with primitive etchings and paintings from early Redmen. The men discussed if they thought one type of markings represented deer or elk. Other symbols formed elongated, tall people with short arms and legs. Several etchings showed what appeared to be a snake. Others appeared as figures of people and baskets with food. If the etchings told a story, none of the team understood what it meant. The original people created the etchings in several different sizes and their work covered a 100-yard-long section of the canyon's vertical wall.

"These etchings demonstrate Redmen have lived in this area long before the white man ever came to this country," Pascal said. "The patterns changed with time. This may have been a place to rest or visit as they changed locations with the seasons or needed water."

On a rock shelf upstream around the next bend in the San Rafael, the Las Vegas pair found what they called a huge paw track, three-foot across. They called for the others to come.

After studying the imprint, Pascal said, "It must be something other than a paw print. No animal we know has a paw of such size or weighs enough to push its paw into solid rock."

He paused to light a cigar while sitting in the shade beside the mystery. "Before I left France and England to come to this continent," Pascal said, "I read a newspaper report from a British museum claimed a piece of a buried skeleton came from a giant lizard with a long neck. It claimed giant lizards lived in an age before man. I don't know how an animal, if it existed, could leave its track in a rock. It's puzzling and amazing. Only God knows the answer."

As he gazed along the bend of the little San Rafael, studying the large stand of cottonwood trees beside the flowing water, Pascal said, "This area must have been known for water and a place for the Redman to escape the barren high plateau for more years than we can measure. Who knows what types of animals roamed this area in the beginning of time?" He heaved his classic French shrug.

"How is such a thing possible?" Blackie asked, his lips curled. "My father believed the Holy Bible is the history of life on earth, and taught God created man and animals at the same time. How can animals have existed in a time before man? It defies God's holy words in the Bible."

"I'll not argue with the Holy Bible." Pascal shrugged. "However, there are many things in life not explained in the Bible. We must acknowledge evidence we see with our own eyes, even if it contradicts the Bible. Nature cannot be denied. Water always runs downhill. The Bible doesn't tell us why such occurs, but it does, whether the Bible allows it or not."

Pascal snorted. "The Italian Pope in Rome still believes the sun rotates around the earth." He waved a hand of dismissal. "Religion and science are often at odds." His comment reflected his bitterness at the Church who had excommunicated him as a priest twelve years before.

"I understand," Blackie grumbled. "Learn to accept nature as it is, not as you want it to be. Work in harmony with nature. Don't resist nature." *If I just understood what such means.* While the team gathered to remount, Blackie tightened the cinch on his horse.

The mule team climbed from the San Rafael canyon and reoriented to their westerly course beyond the canyon. Miles in the distance, they caught sight of rock cliffs layered in various shades of green rock in one high bluff, while to the north of it, a bluff colored in layers like spilled Burgundy wine. In the far distance, in the same direction they rode, a black cliff rose 100 feet or more above the plateau. The colors attracted the eye in the barren upland desert.

"Those colors are so varied," Pascal said, "it's as if this plateau is a giant artist's palette, with mounds of paint colors arranged about the edge, awaiting the master's brush."

Distracted by the spectacular visual scenery, the men of the mule team realized, to their surprise, they had ridden upon three Redmen waiting on the plateau.

"They are Unitah. I don't know their language," Phillippe said in a soft voice.

One of the Unitah signaled in trade sign, *"Why here? Beaver gone. Elk gone. Buffalo gone. Nothing here for whites. Go. Leave this place."*

Pascal signaled in trade signs, offering each of them two cigars. *"Not hunt beaver. Not hunt elk. Ride to the setting sun for trade. Cross high mountain."* He pointed at the snow-covered mountains to the west and trade-signed, *"Where place to cross mountain?"*

The Unitah leader pointed northwest before he signed, *"Ride three days. Wak-see River."* He spoke the river's name, then signed. *"Follow up hill. Go across mountain. Leave this place."*

Pascal glanced at Phillippe, "You know this place? How do you translate the river's name?"

"I don't understand the name either," Phillippe said. "The Duchenne River crosses farther north before joining the Green River in five or six days of riding, if he's talking about its headwater. They're angry with us being here." He glanced to the area nearby "The reason they haven't attacked is we outnumber them. Let's ride on. Tell them we'll leave as they asked."

The mule train continued northwest. The next day they passed near the black cliffs they'd glimpsed before the team met the Unitah warriors.

"The black rock reminds me of coal mined in Wales. You think it is coal?" Blackie asked.

"I suspect so. It may not be the quality they mined in Wales, but I believe it'll burn."

"Even if you could burn it, who would need it, or use it out here?" Blackie asked.

"I'd wager the winter gets mighty cold in these mountains. After a day outside, you'd sing hallelujah for a coal fire to warm you. Notice there aren't many trees here. What else burns?"

They rode north, three days of dry trail and cold camps, while searching for the stream the Unitah mentioned. After the mule train crossed a meadow at the base of the western mountains, they moved north onto a higher plateau, as they searched for the "Wak-see" River.

Six Arapaho rode from an arroyo, signaling with hand-signs they wanted to trade. In the past years, Blackie had experienced anxiety and fear when strange Redmen greeted them, but after living with Black Kettle's Cheyenne, he gazed into their faces without being hostile.

Phillippe proved his worth as their lead scout when he recognized one of the warriors. He called the warrior's name and rode close to speak in their language, offering them trade cigars.

After speaking with them, Phillippe returned. "After our trade parley, this small group had planned to report to a larger hunting party a day away about our mules and what arms we carried. If two warriors hadn't known me, the larger group would've attacked the mule train later."

"Do they want to trade?" Pascal asked. "Are they going to let us pass?"

"The larger Arapaho party consists of twenty-seven warriors. We would be hard pressed to fight them. These Arapaho came from the Northern or Mountain Band, who roam west and south to hunt the high meadows in the warmer months," Phillippe said.

"I thought you're an Arapaho?" Blackie asked.

"My mother is from the Southern Band. These are the Northern Band. We're related but compete for hunting grounds across the prairie. I think they grew pissed at me when they thought I led you here to hunt on their grounds. They understand trade and will allow us to pass."

More good news came when Runs-After-Antelope, the hunting party leader spoke French. He led a dozen warriors to talk. Pascal shared cigars with Runs-After-Antelope. They sat on a blanket and drank brandy from the same small silver cup as a sign of friendship.

After a period of smoking, drinking, and sharing elk jerky, Antelope pointed at Blackie and asked, "Who is little man? He speaks our language like a Cheyenne."

"Yes. He lived with Black Kettle last season to learn their way and become a man."

Antelope grimaced. "The Cheyenne are our friends, but they are not the best warriors. If you want little man to be a warrior and learn the way, send with me. I will make him a true warrior."

Pascal gave the simplest answer that came to mind. "He is a slave who must work for me five more years. He must stay with me and work."

"Work him hard, beat him often, then sell him to me. I need a strong slave to work for me."

Runs-After-Antelope expressed his approval upon learning Pascal didn't trade in whiskey. "It makes the warriors act stupid. When you come to trade again, bring coffee, corn meal, and foofaraw for the women. We can sit, smoke cigars, and enjoy a brandy." His statement told them Pascal would be welcome to travel this way again and not be attacked by the Northern Arapaho.

The team followed the landmarks given by the Arapaho and rested for a day at the Wak-see River, little more than a step-across stream. If the white settlers in the area had a name for the stream, none ever mentioned it, but then again, they had yet to encounter settlers.

While the team camped, Pascal ordered Phillippe and Antonio to ride upstream and determine if it led to a pass or saddle to cross the mountain chain blocking their way west.

In their absence, Pascal assigned Blackie a useless task more unfathomable than usual. "What will this prove?" Blackie asked. "Is this another of your dumb ideas about survival?"

"Of course." Pascal smiled. "Why would you expect anything else?"

Blackie exploded in youthful angst.

"Survival! Survival! Is it all there is to life? Work from before the sun rises, wrestle with those stupid mules all day, before collapsing in my bedroll well after sunset's dark. Day in, day out, day after day, work without end. Is this all there is to life? To work all your life only to survive? Is that *it*? Is work all there is to life?"

"*What is the meaning of life?* Such a philosopher's question. I think I'm making you into a Jesuit. I'll add those questions to your lessons. Be prepared to discuss them tomorrow."

"Arrrrr!" Blackie screamed as he stomped from the camp to do as bidden.

Phillippe and Antonio returned the next day during the siesta rest and reported the mountain saddle passable. The next morning, mules began the slow climb, zigzagging to ascend into the saddle. Phillippe and Antonio rode ahead, returning to the pass to search for the easiest route to descend through the rugged rock formations on the western side. Uncertain as to where the saddle across the Wasatch Mountains would bring the mule train into the Great Salt Basin, they rode forward watching for landmarks and the easiest path to descend into the Great Salt Basin.

Chapter 8

June 1856

After two days of a hard climb followed by a day of easy descent, they reached the floor of the Great Salt Basin. Travelers told Pascal he'd find Mormon settlements north along the Basin's eastern edge. As the mule train trod north, the first settlement after leaving the mountains was Spanish Fork. The mule train reached the Great Basin forty-seven days after leaving Taos.

Spanish Fork laid along the eastern shore of Lake Utah, a freshwater lake fifty miles south of the Salt Lake. Provo laid ten miles farther north. The settlement of Provo spread alongside the Provo River before it emptied into Lake Utah. Etienne Provost, a fur-trapper with the Hudson Bay Company, worked this area. Provost used the French pronunciation, and his name became spelled phonetically as "Provo." The Provo River flowed south from the Heber Canyon area before it turned west to the lake. John Heber, an early fur-trapper with the Ashley-Henry Fur company, put his name on the river. The use of a name identified a trapper's claim. The fur companies fought over the best trapping areas in their time.

The locals in Provo expressed their surprise

when Pascal's mule train appeared in their settlement and grew more surprised upon learning they crossed the mountains from the southeast on the Old Spanish Trail. As Pascal had planned, his trip from Santa Fe let him reach the Great Salt Basin on May 17, two months sooner than wagons coming overland from Westport or St. Joseph on the Missouri River. A loaded freight wagon leaving St. Joseph by April 15 wouldn't arrive at the Great Salt Lake until July or August. The huge wagons wouldn't leave the Missouri Valley departure areas before mid-April because the prairie grass wouldn't be green enough to provide forage for the teams, whether oxen or mule. Also, in March and April, the ground remained soft from winter snow, often causing the wagons to get stuck in the mud. Spring flooding from snowmelt always created problems fording major streams across the West.

Many people thought Pascal the luckiest man they knew. Others failed to recognize Pascal's "luck" came from planning. They also failed to notice how Pascal studied one man's misfortune or problem to find an opportunity for him to turn a profit. One example came in the team's visit to St. Vrain's trading post in Taos before venturing to Utah.

~~~~~~

St. Vrain griped and grumbled the moment Pascal and Blackie entered his trading post in March. The problem came from his flour mill on the Mora

River. The Army at Fort Union had canceled a contract for 7,500 pounds of flour the day before St. Vrain delivered it—in bulk. He had to pay to have the wagons turn around and return to Taos. St. Vrain realized he couldn't keep the flour around all spring or summer in Taos without it becoming infested with mealy bugs.

While the lost flour contract consumed St. Vrain's time and attention, a trader leaving on the return trip to Westport Missouri "forgot" to carry a load of empty whiskey kegs to the distillery. One reason the trader slipped away without the kegs happened because part of his outbound delivery to St. Vrain contained 1,000 bottle corks for him to rebottle the whiskey, but the corks didn't fit the bottles the trader delivered. He slipped away before St. Vrain could exact a settlement and let the supplier deal with St. Vrain on the next order.

This caused a new problem for St. Vrain who lost profitable warehouse space now used to store empty whiskey kegs. He stored the empties as he used them through the summer trade season, but before the last wagons headed East rolling empty, he'd pay them to carry the empty kegs to Westport Landing, where he'd be paid a dollar for each one returned to the distiller.

St. Vrain learned the hard way about buying whiskey. A fifty-three-gallon barrel of whiskey cost less, but at 560 pounds, the barrels couldn't be lifted, only rolled. Worse yet, it split open easily if dropped, losing all its contents. He minimized his losses by ordering whiskey in ten-gallon kegs, but now he'd been stuck with 100 ten-gallon wooden kegs, called a hogshead.

"I'm losing money from every pocket," he complained. "Why, on my last shipment a crate of candles, *candles* mind you, got crushed when the wagon slid from the trail. A tree kept the wagon from toppling, but it crushed the crate and broke the candles into pieces of wax held by a string. Imagine if the candle crate had been a barrel of whiskey? The drovers would have fallen on the ground to lap up every drop. A pox on all freight drovers. May their pizzle rot and fall off." He waved a hand, as if batting a fly. "Now I must find a fool to buy wax on a string?"

LaFleur whistled before he patted his chest and nodded.

"What will you do with broken candles?" St. Vrain asked, leaning away in disbelief.

LaFleur twirled the ends of his mustache, grinning.

"Mustache wax? Where will you keep it?" St. Vrain asked, expecting a joke.

LaFleur stepped into the storage area to return with an empty ten-gallon whiskey keg. He tapped his knuckles on the empty keg before pointing his finger inside.

Playing along with the mute man, St. Vrain asked, "How will you get it out?"

LaFleur mimed reaching a finger in the top hole to scrap out the wax before pulling on his mustache ends.

St. Vrain shook his head. "How will you get the

wax when it's deeper than your finger?"

LaFleur grabbed his crotch, shook it, and pointed to the bottom of the eighteen-inch-tall keg.

St. Vrain and the men gathered in the trading post burst into laughter.

Pascal nodded to LaFleur, wiping a finger across his nose to signal, *follow my lead.*

Frenchmen from birth, Pascal and St. Vrain always spoke in French when together or in arranging a deal. With the French-Canadian fur-trappers passing on, few in Taos understood it.

"*Mon ami,*" Pascal said, "I think LaFleur's heart is in the right place. He wants to help an old friend. I'll buy your broken crate for a half Eagle."

"Bah! You thief, you know I paid more than such a price for shipping it." St. Vrain squinted an eye, glaring at Pascal. "What scheme have you to sell candle wax?"

"I think LaFleur has an idea. We'll sell mustache wax to the wild-haired mountain men to make them resemble the prissy Austrians." Pascal roared in laughter as St. Vrain joined him.

"If truly my friend," St. Vrain said, "you'd carry away those troublesome whiskey kegs."

"Some friend," Pascal countered, "Next thing I know, you'll want me to buy your useless corks. The corks don't fit anything, and don't even make good fire starters."

Blackie observed Pascal's trade talk often enough to suspect this ploy led to a deal where Pascal bought items he didn't want at a low price, to gain a better price on the item he wanted. He listened to the banter, trying to guess what Pascal wanted before either side mentioned it.

"The corks aren't useless," St. Vrain countered, "You failed to find the proper hole to plug."

The men laughed, making rude remarks about what hole need to be plugged and by whom.

"The problem with your kegs is I have no way to refill them, and they're too small for a decent water barrel," Pascal said. "I wouldn't buy them, even at a copper penny each."

"Waugh! Those kegs are worth a dollar each at the distillery."

"*Oui*, but the distillery may as well be in Paris for all the good it does us. The kegs are here, and in your way, and cluttering your much-needed trading space. It's a fair price for a friend."

"What's this?" St. Vrain barked. "Do you want the corks or the barrels?"

LaFleur tugged on Pascal's arm.

"Neither," Pascal shook his head. "You distracted me from the wax. I'll pay six dollars for the broken crate of wax candles."

"You can't fool me, trickster. I'll sell you 100 kegs for fifty dollars and give you the wax and the corks to seal the price."

Pascal wiped a hand across his chin. "I'll make you a better offer." He took a sip of the brandy on the table between them before he relit his cigar. "The flour the Army returned will be infested with mealy bugs by May's end and you won't be able to give it away. I'll buy 6,000 pounds of flour at three cents per pound and pay you $15 for the kegs, wax, and corks."

"You traitor!" St. Vrain gasped as if struck. "You claim friendship and then take advantage of my misfortune. Flour sells for thirty cents a pound, and you well know it. And the price of the kegs, wax, and corks is still fifty dollars gold."

LaFleur raised his hands, fingers pointed at the ceiling, and heaved an exaggerated sigh.

"You're right," Pascal said as he returned LaFleur's shrug. "We have no way to fill the empty barrels with flour."

LaFleur hand-signed a message, *Don't ruin a friendship trying to make a bargain.*

After translating LaFleur's message, Pascal said, "I'm sorry to learn of your troubles, old friend. We must ride to the Rio and make ready to ride north for trade. *Bonne nuit. Good night!*"

"What?" St. Vrain shouted. "You scoundrel, leading me on as if you intended to make a deal. You're nothing but a tease, raising my hopes I'd not lose my shirt with this disaster."

"No. No," Pascal said, rubbing his hands together in worry. "I had a foolish thought with LaFleur's joke. Barrels are too hard to fasten on a packsaddle. They would be a constant problem loading and unloading all the way to Utah. I beg your pardon for raising false hopes."

Blackie shifted toward the door, mumbling, "Outhouse," as he trotted outside.

St. Vrain continued to harangue Pascal, positioning himself in the aisle to the door.

Blackie stuck his head in the door twenty

minutes later, and called, "Antonio reports the mules loaded. We must leave or we'll not make the trail to the San Luis Valley in the dark."

"What can I do?" Pascal shrugged. "We must leave while the weather is fair."

"*S'il vous plaît*, I'll take twenty-five dollars for the kegs, if you buy the flour at fifteen cents per pound," St. Vrain said, slapping his hand flat on a countertop. "It's my final offer."

"I … I … I have no way to refill the kegs, or to seal—"

Blackie interrupted again from the door, "Antonio warns if we don't leave, you'll need to buy forage now, and in the morning before we leave. The hostler wants a half Eagle."

"Why don't you send the flour to El Paso, while it is fresh?" Pascal offered in consolation.

"Bah. Corn meal certainly, but never wheat flour to El Paso. The locals there don't use it."

"I must go," Pascal said. "Your price is fair, but I have no time. *Adieu, mon ami.*"

"You're a scoundrel to take advantage of a friend," St. Vrain growled. "I'll take twenty dollars for the kegs if you buy the flour at twelve cents per pound. My final offer."

Outside the mules braying grew louder in a warning they'd grown agitated standing loaded.

"I must tend to my animals," Pascal said. "We'll be at risk taking the trail north to the Rio Grande tonight." He rose, stepping to go around St. Vrain. "It'll cost me more to stay longer."

"Damn you," St. Vrain groaned. "Sixteen for the

kegs, wax, and corks, but I hold firm at ten cents a pound for the flour." He held out his hand. After a moment, Pascal sealed the bargain.

When Pascal and LaFleur strode onto the porch a half-hour later, the team had unloaded the mules and nosed them into the corral's feeding troughs. The team waited by the corral rails.

Blackie strode close, "I asked the men to pretend being upset about the delay, and to assuage them, you'll take them to the Mexican cantina for supper and drinks." He grabbed LaFleur around the neck. "Did I make enough distraction?"

"I'm pleased to learn you've paid attention to closing the deal," Pascal said. "Your timely distractions disrupted his rhythm. He'd have gone on into the night dropping a penny at a time until I tired of dickering with him, which is his ploy."

Pascal laid a hand on LaFleur and Blackie's shoulders. "Tomorrow," he nodded at Blackie, "LaFleur will teach you how to remove the top metal ring from the keg and pry out the lid."

LaFleur, trained as a vintner, had experience with preparing, filling, and shipping both large barrels of wine and often filling small kegs for use by the winery family, staff, and locals. The house staff decanted the keg wine into glass carafes or other bottles prior to serving. He had a sketch of a barrel-head tightener ready for the blacksmith the next morning.

The local blacksmith studied LaFleur's sketch for five minutes before he nodded. "I have a forged chain that'll work on your gadget, and square-head bolts and nuts in one-half inch." His lips puckered in thought. "How far does the bolt need to travel in tightening?"

The mute man held his thumb and forefinger a half-inch apart and winked.

The blacksmith wrapped his large hand around his chin. "You're sure it won't crack a barrel stave, when you tighten it?"

Twirling his mustache, LaFleur nodded. Then held his fists together and twisted as if breaking a stick. He blatted a raspberry by fluttering his lips and turned his thumb down.

"What, you'll be mad if it breaks?" the blacksmith asked.

While the mute fetched his slate, Blackie said, "If a stave breaks, it's a bad stave." Touching his nose, LaFleur pointed to Blackie, who said, "The staves won't crack on a good barrel."

In two hours, the blacksmith fashioned two barrel-head tighteners and made six, small flat pry bars, each heated and hammered into a flat spade-tipped chisel.

LaFleur showed the young men how to slide the tighteners on the keg to below the top metal ring before tightening the bolt with a cast-iron wrench until the chain dug into the barrel staves.

After LaFleur divided the men into pairs, he gave each one an ash-wood packsaddle strut to use as a mallet. He mimed tapping the chisel to drive the top metal ring from opposite sides equally until it loosened enough to remove. Once they observed the process work on the first keg, they removed the top metal ring from 100 kegs in two hours.

While they worked, LaFleur wrote on his slate asking the blacksmith to make four drill bits smaller than the cork size. With a brace and bit, the men drilled a hole in the keg's flat top, into which they inserted a one-half-inch metal rod the blacksmith heated and bent to a right angle before quenching. With the top metal band removed, LaFleur showed them how to pop loose the wooden top with the correct technique. He warned them in advance to keep each top metal band and wooden top tied by a string to the barrel they came from. They didn't make these handmade parts interchangeable. He wanted the kegs opened to dry overnight before adding flour.

While LaFleur kept the young men busy, Pascal hunted around the shanty town close to the warehouse district. He soon found an old, rusty and pitted cauldron, three feet across and two feet deep. The man in the shanty accepted Pascal's offer with glee and sold the old cauldron for two silver dollars. Pascal loaded it on the pack mule he led on this part of the adventure.

Next, he visited a store where the local laborers bought cheap clothes, purchasing nine sets of rough-spun white cotton drawstring pants and split-neck shirts, typical of what the Mexican workers wore. He also bought nine plain cotton bandanas, and nine pairs of reed *huaraches* for the team. Even a man as frugal as Pascal recognized the labor in cleaning an item could exceed its cost. After transferring the flour, the men would toss these clothes away rather than waste time in multiple washings and rinsing to remove the flour imbedded in the cotton threads.

When St. Vrain's flour wagons arrived in Taos the next day, Pascal and LaFleur assigned work teams, each wearing the cotton outfits with bandanas covering their hair and *huaraches* on their feet. The Vegas pair, Nachi and Luis, lifted empty kegs into the flour wagon. Antonio and Benito filled each keg with flour with a wooden scoop. Blackie weighed each keg after Dom or Hector set one on the balance scale. Reynaldo and Tomas lifted the kegs from the scale and set them aside in rows, waiting to have the lid's refastened. Ortega cousins, Javy and Geraldo filled in when another grew tired or needed a rest. The last step required reseating the lid and fastening the iron strap ring around the top to retain the keg's seal or tightness.

By day's end, the team transferred the bulk flour into 100 ten-gallon kegs, each containing fifty pounds of flour. The team unloaded over 5,000 pounds of flour from St. Vrain's wagons, with 1,000 pounds remaining. Pascal purchased twenty-five cotton flour sacks, planning for each to hold twenty pounds. The team filled the cotton sacks with the remaining flour. Pascal figured they'd lost less than 200 pounds to waste, but by the end of the process, the team members, coated in flour, appeared like white "snowmen."

Pascal ordered them to the bath stalls with instructions to give the flour-coated clothes to the old couple who operated the stalls. Pascal and LaFleur strode away to have supper with St. Vrain, while the team tromped to a nearby cantina with good food, music, and a bawdy house.

LaFleur left them a note while they bathed and dressed. They had completed only one-half of their task of packaging the flour.

The next morning, a woodsman delivered several bundles of firewood by mule. Pascal directed the team to stoke a fire under the cauldron to melt the broken candles he'd purchased from St. Vrain.

"By removing the top band and the lid," Pascal said, "we may have weakened the keg's seal, allowing moisture inside to ruin the flour. To be sure we didn't waste our effort in hauling flour 800 miles, we'll dip the kegs in hot wax to coat the outside. Air-tight, the flour we sell in Utah will be as fresh as it is today. We'll do the same for the sugar and bicarbonate of soda we carry."

At day's end, they laid their cargo beside packsaddles ready to load the following morning.

St. Vrain visited before dark to grouse about Pascal getting the better end of the deal in a low price for the flour. "I should have known you had a trick up your sleeve when you and LaFleur concocted the story about mustache wax," he said. "Carson says you'll be two months on the trail to Utah. If they're hungry after a long, cold winter, you might yield a good profit."

"I offered you a chance to join and pay the

cargo's cost, while I provide the mules and the labor. In the end, we'd split the profit," Pascal said, lifting his hands and shrugging.

"I don't like the risk in the high country." St. Vrain shook once. "I'm surprised when you return each fall. I'll not join with your venture." He waved a hand, *"Au revoir, mon ami."*

~~~~~~

Once again, Pascal enjoyed exceptional timing. A drought, begun in 1855 continued into 1856, and caused flour and basic cooking supplies to become scarce, *and costly.* Pascal carried 5,000 pounds of flour, 2,500 pounds of red beans, 1,250 pounds of sugar, and 100-pounds of soda bicarbonate, as baking soda. Each mule carried 250 pounds, plus the packsaddle. Pascal needed forty mules to carry 10,000 pounds of trade. Eight more mules carried iron goods and notions.

During the wax-sealing process in Taos, they double-wrapped the beans into rough gunny-sack cotton packages weighing twenty-five pounds. They placed ten pounds of brown cane-sugar into a fine-weave cotton sack before wrapping it in old newsprint, tying it with a string, and dipping it in wax to prevent it from getting wet and melting away. Before the wax cooled and set, they placed the waxed, paper-wrapped bags into a coarse gunnysack and dipped it again to maintain the wax seal while preventing an easy rupture of the package.

Flour, beans, and sugar amounted to three-fourths of the total weight the mule train carried. Pascal's gamble paid a handsome profit. However, if not for a flour shortage, the profit wouldn't have paid the cost of hauling.

In a market fashion, he offered one-quarter of the flour, beans, and sugar on the first day. In part, to test the price limit during the shortage, and second, because the merchants in Provo and Spanish Fork lacked the gold to buy more.

Chapter 9

Pascal extended no credit nor accepted paper money or script. He traded only in coins, either Spanish or U.S. gold coins. He avoided silver. It took too many coins for the same value as gold.

A devout Mormon castigated Pascal. "Why are you shirking your Christian duty of charity to make a profit, and charging a dollar-a-pound, when the people need flour for survival?"

"I don't understand your complaint." Pascal's brows furrowed. "You prayed to God for relief, did you not?"

"Of course, we prayed." The man scowled at the insinuation that he lacked piety.

"God sent me with flour, which I have delivered. Who are we to deny God's wisdom?"

The man became so flummoxed by Pascal's response he became speechless, gasping like a fish. Others nearby hid their smiles behind their hands or turned away.

After the man left, Pascal muttered in French, "Next time, pray for God to send you free flour and see what you get." He spat on the ground and rubbed his boot on it, to seal the bargain.

Pascal noticed Blackie working his lips like a cow chewing its cud. The former black robe asked, "Do I detect disapproval from the son of a

Methodist minister?"

"The people are in need. Why are you exacting a profit?" Blackie asked.

"Did your father require you to read the Holy Bible?"

"Yes," Blackie said, resisting the impulse to add *constantly.*

"Do you remember Timothy 5:10?"

Blackie's eyebrows raised. "Do not muzzle the ox that grinds ...? What does—"

Pascal interrupted, "You are the 'ox.' Are you not worthy of being fed while you labor?"

"Yes." Blackie dipped his head. *When would he learn not to debate a Jesuit?*

"The scripture continued on to say, 'The laborer is worthy of his reward,'" Pascal said. "We labored to bring trade to these people. Are we not worthy of a reward?"

"But what of charity?"

"These gentle folks have gold but learned they could not eat gold. *Charity,* as you call it, is for those with nothing. We traded our food for their gold. If they believed we cheated them, they could've turned away. It's the basis of any trade, 'what *thing* am I willing to exchange for the *thing* I want.' Such ideas are what I hoped you'd learn in this business, if you intend to run it."

"But what if they had no gold?" Blackie asked. "What would you have done?"

"Let us ask the question another way. What say you if we arrived here after an abundant wheat harvest, and harvested wheat rotted un-milled into flour for lack of a market? Would these gentle folks have fed us and our mules in charity? What if the price of a meal for each of us cost a mule or a horse? How would we return to the Rancho?"

"They would feed us for free if they are Christian. Charity is an obligation of Christians."

"Charity is an obligation of all religions." Pascal laughed. "When we ride, we shall discuss other religions and the obligation of charity as opposed to fostering sloth."

Blackie shoulders sagged. *More lessons.*

A non-Mormon drover hauling freight called to Pascal as they passed by. "If you follow the Provo River up into the hills," he said, "you might find more trade at the farms in the hills away from the bigger settlements." The drover pointed, "Up higher, it's joined by the Weber River, and follow the Weber to its headwaters. Send your scout ahead to locate a saddle to the northeast and cross into the Bear River Valley. You should find small farms in need of trade goods. There's a passel of farmers up that-a-way, so you should be able to sell your goods. If you know how the mountains go yonder, you can head east to find the Black Fork to old Fort Bridger. Brigham Young done forced Bridger to surrender his Fort. It's fallen under Mormon control."

Pascal's eyes opened wide. "It's the first I've heard of such. What happened?"

"Don't rightly know for sure. All I know is ol' Brigham Young claims that corner as part of his Deseret Utah. If'n it belongs to Utah, he says,

Bridger's land claim ain't no good in Utah."

"I planned on Bridger being there and conducting trade. Is the trading post closed?"

"Not so I've heard. There's been talk of Brigham Young setting up a trading post of his own, but I ain't been that-a-way this season. So, I can't say nothing but rumors."

"*Merci*, thank you for the information. I don't know if we should visit Fort Bridger now."

Pascal found a local farmer, Petr Olsen, who, in exchange for a flour keg and a sack of sugar agreed to let the team stay at his farm, feed the men two meals a day, and included a whole smoked ham. Olsen agreed to let the animals graze his green pastures. "His price is high." Pascal barked a laugh. "I got my price from the merchants in town. Let him have his price."

They found no grain available to feed their animals at any price. Olsen had a spacious and dry barn and it became comfortable sleeping quarters for the team. Olsen told them he'd sold his animals because he had no forage and his pasture wouldn't last the summer without rain.

The team welcomed three rest days, but they would've welcomed a sporting house and a saloon with beer or whiskey even more.

While the team rested on the second day, eight men leading two wagons rode along the farm's lane seeking trade. The elder asked, "Do you have flour and dry goods for sale?"

"Of course, if you have gold," Pascal said.

They set to bargaining for the flour. The elder

shouted his outrage at Pascal's first offer for sixty-five dollars for a fifty-pound keg of flour. In the end, he paid fifty dollars a keg, ordering five kegs, plus twenty pounds of sugar, twenty pounds of dry red beans, and five pounds of bicarbonate of soda. In their bargaining, Pascal complained about the expense of buying mules and the daily cost of feeding the mules and men when returning south empty.

When the elder buying flour, sugar, and beans concluded his agreement, he paid in gold.

Another Mormon man in the group stepped forward. "If you plan to lead those mules to Mexico, what say you to an offer we buy them? We'd save you the trouble of taking them home and feeding them along the way."

Pascal argued, fussed, cussed, and complained but he sold twenty mules for $75 each, without packsaddle or bridle. The farmer paid in gold, leading Pascal to wear a wide smile, laughing for a time, until reminded there's not a saloon or a sporting house within 250 miles.

One of the men loading the kegs of flour commented when he first saw the small barrels, he thought them whiskey kegs. He hastened to say, "Not that I would imbibe in spirits."

Pascal replied, "I wouldn't carry strong spirits into yours or any community unbidden. I'm a trader. I paid one dollar for each of those kegs from a closed distillery. I loathe mealy bugs in flour and hardtack, so I prefer sealed kegs to cloth bags."

The man nodded.

A sixth of Pascal's trade load came from hand tools and dry goods consisting of bolts of cloth, thread, buttons, needles, ribbons, and lace for women's clothes. The dry goods weighed little and needed little space, whereas the hand tools weighed more and took more space. The hand tools consisted of hammers, handsaws, planes, chisels, adzes, axes, and iron farm tools like scythes, sickles, shovels, pickaxes, hoes, and rakes. None of the farm tools had wooden handles. A wooden handle made these items too awkward to pack or fasten on a packsaddle.

Pascal made a trip into Provo after the first round of food stock sold, but he kept a reserve for special trades. The local blacksmith, a clever young man, asked for a barter trade for half the hand tools. He paid two thirds the cost in gold coin and arranged, in barter, to re-shoe the team's animals.

Pascal realized the area had no shortage of hand tools. He wouldn't make a profit on these items such as he made on the scarce flour, but low profits disappointed him.

In Provo, he concentrated on the merchants who sold dry goods. The local merchants thought little of Pascal's price for piece goods. Undeterred, Pascal ordered the team into town early Saturday morning. They set up wooden plank sawhorse tables alongside the road about halfway between Provo and Spanish Fork. It didn't take long for the womenfolk to spread the word about new piece goods for sale. When it appeared they'd sell what they'd set out, Pascal sent Blackie to bring more goods from the packsaddles at Olsen's farm. In keeping with his practice, Pascal kept a few goods in reserve to have a portion to trade as he moved north.

While the iron trade goods sold well, Pascal decided they used too much space and were too hard to sell. In the future, he'd carry less bulky items that sold easily and produced better profit.

The young Ortega cousins, in the most surprising action, enjoyed flirting and flattering the married ladies. Blackie got his share of attention, as the women acted dutifully shocked to learn the lad had become an orphan when the wicked Comanche slaughtered his parents.

The next day, the road north ascending the Provo River Canyon became an easy climb into the green and fertile upper valley. The farm families on the river close to Provo had already visited the town, and with few sales opportunities, the team moved upriver without stopping. The profitable sales lightened the load and reduced the number of mules to work and heavy packsaddles to load. The daily routine grew more relaxed as they climbed into the mountains to reach the headwaters of the Heber River.

A local farmer asked Pascal, "Why didn't you continue north on the Ogden River where there are many more farms?"

"We plan to cross over the mountains to Bear River, trading at those farms before turning east to cut across to old Fort Bridger," Pascal said.

"You're a growed man, and I guess you know your business, but there ain't a dang thing up there but bigger mountains and Shoshone. Them high pastures is their summer campgrounds. I doubt they have much gold. Be right careful you don't end up as trade goods with your scalp."

"I heard folks established new settlements along the Bear River Valley. Is such true?"

"No sirree. Not the part of the Bear flowing north. It still wild up there an' clear into Ide-ho. The Bear turns around in Ide-ho and flows south into the Cache Valley and on into Salt Lake. Cache Valley is where the settlements be. If'n you want settlements, follow the Ogden north into Cache Valley. If'n you want Bridger, you can take your chances going over the mountain and trade with the Shoshone. If'n I did it, I'd follow the Ogden and use the Emigrant Trail up Echo Canyon and on across to Bear River and on to Bridger. It's by way of your elbow from here, but you'll stay clear of them Shoshone in the mountain meadows."

"I must've misunderstood the drover about the upper Bear River having settlements," Pascal allowed. *Did the friendly drover mislead me to keep me from competing with his work?*

After a discussion with Phillippe and LaFleur, the mule team followed the Provo river east to the mouth of the Heber River. They climbed higher into the mountain ridges. Phillippe rode ahead, scouting for a saddle or a break in the steep ridge near the Heber's headwaters. In two days, the team rode across a high saddle. As the team descended the next three days, they found the Bear River as a meandering stream with more beavers than bears. The team planned to ride northwest across the rugged area, expecting to find Black Fork of the Green, which would lead them to old Fort Bridger.

Shoshone scouts found the team camped alongside the Bear on their rest day. Phillippe and Pascal rode to parley in trade signs. The northern Shoshone recognized Phillippe as the grandson of Sacajawea, the Far Walking Woman. Her memory remained alive among the Shoshone. The warrior leading the small party asked in trade signs, "*Have you come to trade?*"

"Yes." Pascal nodded as he signed.

The leader signaled *come* and reined his pony to ride away.

The mule team followed the Shoshone trail signs to a high meadow on a plateau north of snowcapped mountains. Phillippe called them the Unitah mountains, for the Unitah lived south of them. It took two days to reach the Shoshone camp when dragging mules. The camp welcomed them with wild whoops and beating drums.

The Shoshone enjoy a party as much as the team did at a new town with a saloon and sporting houses. Blackie smiled at their antics and remembered flaunting his riding skills before he departed from Black Kettle's camp the last time.

The Shoshone chief, Crow Killer, sat on a blanket to trade with Pascal. The Shoshone did not have much to offer in trade. They usually traded their skins with Bridger, and Pascal didn't want to carry skins with little real value, compared to gold. The team rested several days, and in exchange for the camp's hospitality Pascal donated a mule for the feast.

"Many Shoshone understand a little French," Phillippe warned the team. "Be careful with what you say among one another in French. Don't create bad relations between us."

Phillippe prevailed in persuading Pascal to give a five-pound keg of DuPont powder and two bars of lead as a gift to the Shoshone people in honor of Far Walking Woman. Phillippe argued such a small amount of powder and shot could be only used for hunting and not to attack whites in the area, not that they'd observed white settlers in the mountains. "Who will know?"

Crow Killer accepted the gift of gunpowder as a sign of true friendship. Pascal bartered twenty-five pounds of sugar and ten pounds of coffee to the chief's wives for several prime elk hides prepared special for the chief. The women also traded white mink, white fox, and mule deer hides for the foofaraw in the dry goods.

Pascal agreed to trade since it lightened the load. The native women surprised him by showing no interest in flour but traded for a twenty-pound bag of beans.

LaFleur traded three iron hand-scythes for three pairs of moccasins, a pair of elk-hide leggings, and a doe-hide shirt the woman sewed to fit Blackie.

The women believed the scythes to be skinning knives. They chattered as one showed the others how she planned to skin hair from hides resting across her thigh with the long, curved blades.

Blackie made two friends among the young men as he learned Shoshone. He found it easy to learn because he knew Cheyenne and Arapaho. The Shoshone and Arapaho maintained peace with one another and tolerated the Cheyenne. The Shoshone culture had a more relaxed attitude of "I'll stay out of your territory if you stay out of mine" than the Cheyenne. Their traditional enemies were the Blackfoot and Crow, or Absaroka, as they called themselves.

As the team mounted to ride away in the dawn of the last day, Crow Killer rode to them with several warriors leading six beautiful silver-grey horses.

"It is our custom to exchange gifts when honored," Crow Killer said. "I must give greater gift than given by Pascal." Crow Killer swept his open hand from Pascal to six spotted Nez Perce horses with their silver-gray coats spattered with darker spots on their rumps and flanks.

The men on the team had never seen such coloring on horses before.

"Do not let anyone ride them until we leave this area," Phillippe said. "It might make Crow Killer think you didn't like them, and you dishonored his special gift to you."

Pascal glanced at the team, "You heard him. Guard them, but don't ride them."

Chapter 10

August 1856

The team arrived at Fort Supply near the Black Fork upstream from old Fort Bridger. The Mormons built Fort Supply as a new trading post to compete with Jim Bridger who the Mormons didn't like or trust. Many Mormons believed, with good reason, Bridger sold powder, shot, and whiskey to the Redman in the area. Further, many Redmen who traded at Fort Bridger thought Bridger cheated them on weights and prices. The local Redmen acted pleased to have another trading post by trading there and shunning Bridger's.

The men at Fort Supply reported Jim Bridger sold his Fort and the surrounding land to Brigham Young three months ago. The Mormons planned to use the old fort until they completed the new buildings and then move their entire trade operation to Fort Supply.

Pascal led the team to old Fort Bridger, and found it changed. The Mormons added a rock facing to the exterior walls up to a height of six feet. The rock replaced rotting bottom timber damaged over the years by runoff splatter from the roof.

The Mormon sutler in charge of the post spoke to Pascal in a curt manner. "The days of the French influence from Canada have ended. We don't want your kind and your evil spirits in our land. May God condemn you for bringing evil to the misguided natives of this land."

Pascal stomped outside. "Get mounted. We're riding to Fort Hall. Get the strings moving."

A Mormon man, named Tucker, asked, "Wait? Didn't you come to sell us your flour?"

"*Non*," Pascal shouted in French. "I won't trade with imbeciles."

Tucker had already spoken with the team and learned they carried flour and sugar. He ran inside and after another minute, the sutler ran outside.

"Are you carrying flour and foodstuff?" the Mormon sutler asked. "I thought those kegs contained whiskey. We forbid the use of stimulants and don't sell spirits to the natives."

Pascal called Phillippe to translate his exact words from French. Pascal kept his back to the sutler while speaking to Phillippe. "You are an imbecile, too rude to understand the concept of trade. We will do no business with you. We shall warn others of your hostility. We will sell our goods to any on the Oregon Trail. It will save them from riding here only to be insulted."

The team rode away without a backwards glance leaving the new sutler to deal with the people angry about losing the needed flour and foodstuff.

With so much turmoil amongst the Mormons around Fort Bridger, Pascal moved the team east to the upper Green River to the middle ferry crossing but found it busy with westbound wagons. Upstream at the next ferry, he found the operator willing to make a deal on the east-bound ferry, since most traffic headed west toward Oregon and return traffic east fell to nothing.

"The owner is away today," the ferry operator said. "If you pay in gold and ride out of sight from here tonight, I'll carry your mules across in three loads for an Eagle for each load."

Pascal's quirky ethics confused Blackie when the former Jesuit resented tolls because "they limited a man's freedom to travel," and begrudged their unseemly profits by charging high prices to cross. Blackie thought, *Doesn't he see it's the same thing as the high prices he charges?*

While Pascal resented the concept of ferry tolls, he recognized a bargain when presented. He agreed to the price. "I'll wait here and ride last, paying you an Eagle as each leaves this landing."

They completed the ferry crossing in three hours, and as promised, moved the mule train across the next ridge east before darkness fell with Pascal still muttering about paying a toll. LaFleur teasing him didn't help the situation but the rest of the team had a laugh at LaFleur's antics until Pascal chased him away, laughing as they sent one another obscene gestures.

~~~~~~

Pascal moved the team east across the upper Green River Valley and into the high desert with an extra load of water. They crossed the southern edge of the Great Divide Basin encircled with the snowcapped peaks. Pascal teased Blackie about the early days when he wondered if he'd ever visit the mountains. Snowcapped peaks rose above the barren basin in every direction.

Phillippe razed Blackie he'd sunburn his tongue by gawking openmouthed at the spectacular snow-covered peaks.

Four days past the Green River, Phillippe scouted ahead as they neared the North Platte. He returned to alert the team he'd met a large party of Absaroka, the name they called themselves, not the Crow name the whites used. Pascal and LaFleur found them earnest and honest traders. An old man, Sits-in-Saddle, from the Absaroka party spoke French and he spoke for the Absaroka in the parley. Pascal offered him a cigar and a silver cup with a splash of brandy.

The Absaroka leaders expressed their anger. They had signed treaties with the white man, and still the white man came to live on their hunting grounds. Why did they not trade like men and keep their agreements? The Absaroka knew Phillippe was part Arapaho and his grandmother was Sacajawea, the Far Walking Woman. They respected her even if a Shoshone.

Blackie stood beside Pascal and LaFleur, listening to the discussion, when one Absaroka leader pointed to him and asked, "Why is this one wearing Cheyenne moccasins?"

Phillippe stepped between them to speak in Absaroka. "We trade with any rider on the plains. When in the north, we trade with the mighty Absaroka. When in the mountains, we trade with my people, the Arapaho, or with my grandmother's people, the Shoshone. We trade with the Cheyenne at Bent's Fort. It's a trading post like Fort Hall or Fort Laramie where we ride to trade. We understand there is a truce between all people on the trading grounds."

Another Absaroka warrior said, "I visited Bent's Fort south on Cheyenne land years ago. Different people trade there. It is a gathering place for trade."

The first speaker grimaced, but nodded, and said, "Trade at gatherings is acceptable." The leader's agreement let the team avoid potential trouble with the Absaroka.

Pascal had decided days before to ride to Fort Laramie instead of north to Fort Hall where more Mormons lived, after the sour discussion with the Mormon sutler. In April 1849, the Army purchased the old private fort from the American Fur Company. The new trading post at Fort Laramie sat outside the military compound which included the adobe fort built by American Fur. A private sutler operated the trading post, still called Fort Laramie even though outside the Army Post, much to the Army's consternation. The sutler bought the remaining supplies to sell to the wagons who started late from the east or fell behind from breakdowns or illness.

~~~~~~

Settlers in Utah and Oregon territories wanted more finished goods from the East and more sophisticated farm equipment, which meant heavy and bulky trade items best carried by a large freight wagon. Dry goods, china, and iron cookware grew in demand. Pascal had inquired on what traded, what people requested, and checked prices to learn which goods gave the best profit. He knew he couldn't expect to find another shortage like flour again, but he wanted an understanding of what goods people wanted, and what they'd pay in gold to have.

~~~~~~

Pascal recognized they'd been working the mules hard through the mountains, and both men and animals grew tired. The mule sales reduced the train's size to twenty-eight and he donated one of the camp mules for the Shoshone feast. The team relaxed for three days beside mountain streams feeding the upper North Platte, where the team's men learned to hand-fish for trout.

After several water splashing episodes, Phillippe separated the Ortega cousins on different streams along the mountainside. Four had the patience to wait for the fish to pass close. Javy, Antonio,

Reynaldo, and Benito caught enough fish for a fine meal.

Two days later, the mule train arrived at Fort Laramie. Scouting east of the Army post, Phillippe came across three wagons that had fallen behind from breakdowns *en route*. They carried raw oats as feed grain for an Oregon wagon train leader who had paid them. The drovers planned to bypass Forts Laramie and Bridger to catch the wagon train by the time the train rested at Fort Hall. The drovers had yet to learn of the grain shortage farther west.

Pascal convinced the drovers, he'd make their work easier if he purchased 1,000 pounds from each wagon, which contained over 6,000 pounds of grain. The drovers accepted Pascal's offer to lighten their wagon in exchange for the weight of Pascal's gold in their pockets.

The team tied Mexican-style leather cargo bags onto the packsaddle's struts and offloaded grain into the bags in less than an hour. LaFleur carried the empty bags with the camp supplies, which were typical of the leather ones used by Mexican muleteers who couldn't afford Grimsley packsaddles with a wooden tree like Pascal used. The packsaddles let his mules carry more weight, easier, and didn't cause sores by scuffing the mule's skin raw with roped leather bags.

Pascal decided to return along the east side of the Rocky Mountains, which would be faster once they reached the Cherokee Trail south of Fort Laramie between the North and South Platte

Rivers. To keep the pace fast, Pascal loaded each mule with 200 pounds of grain. At the siesta rest, he switched the load to another fourteen mules. This allowed them to shorten the siesta break to an hour, instead of three, and allowed the train to travel an extra ten miles each day for a total of thirty-five miles per day.

The trip south across the front range passed in an uneventful seven days to Pueblo.

Pascal, Blackie, and the Vegas pair led fourteen mules carrying grain to Bent's Trading Post on Big Timbers east along the Arkansas River. Bent purchased the grain at Pascal's asking price, twenty-five cents per pound, and complained Pascal didn't carry more feed grain.

Blackie hoped to find Black Kettle and the Southern Cheyenne but found no sign of them.

"They haven't come to their winter camp this season. It's too early," Bent said.

Pascal led the mule train across La Veta Pass into the San Luis with a load of supplies for Fort Massachusetts as cartage from Bent's Post. After the delivery of Bent's cartage to Fort Massachusetts, Pascal found empty wagons lined beside a corral behind the tent saloons. He inquired about the empty wagons at a nearby tent.

The barman, who sold rotgut whiskey to the soldiers, said, "Those are from contractors' delivering to the fort. They are too cheap to pay the drover and the feed bill to return the wagon. The drover leaves the wagon on the prairie. I drag them here, so the Army don't burn 'em. If you buy one of my teams, I'll make a deal on the wagon."

"What do you charge for one of those wagons?" Pascal asked.

The barman scratched his beard, "Wagons sell for fifty dollars back in Missouri."

"True, but we are in godforsaken Colorado. I'll load the cargo on my mules. Good day."

"Wait," the barman called as Pascal reached the door. "I'll make it twenty-five dollars, but I'll drop it to twenty dollars each, if you buy three."

Pascal never slowed as he strode outside the tent to his horse and mounted.

"Make me an offer," the barman said, muttering an obscenity from the tent flap.

"I'll take my pick of three at five dollars each," Pascal said, reining his horse to turn, walking away.

"Shit," the barman said before he called, "I want it in gold or it's no deal."

"Of course." Pascal waved to Antonio, handing him a gold double Eagle. "Pick three in the best condition. If you find four decent extra wheels, pay him five dollars and find an extra front and rear axle that hasn't dried and split."

Pascal left LaFleur, Phillippe, and the three Ortega cousins behind with twelve mules to pull the wagons west into the San Luis Valley. LaFleur carried gold to the purchase surplus grain to carry south to Santa Fe. Pascal planned to add the three wagons to the Ortega Freight Company.

Antonio scouted ahead as Blackie led the empty mule train south along the eastern valley floor beneath Culebra Peak. In four days, they paralleled the Rio, entered the Rio's gorge at Red River, and exited at Arroyo Hondo. The trail had one steep ridge to cross in a zig-zag before descending to a barren rocky plateau leading to Taos. Pascal's mules followed this route often.

~~~~~~

In Taos, St. Vrain shook a finger at Pascal, "You're getting too frisky. I'll have to watch you to be sure you don't steal all my trade." But he spoke in jest. For the last twenty-five years, St. Vrain, Bent & Company had been the leader in buying and selling large amounts of trade coming across the Santa Fe Trail.

The team welcomed a few days of rest in Taos, where they found Mexican-style food, five saloons, and two sporting houses. The cousins razed Blackie and encouraged him to slip Pascal's knot for a wild night with them.

Pascal, LaFleur, and St. Vrain shared a bottle of French cognac over a plate of oysters, talked about the changing trade with the Western movement, and what trade would be in the future. Blackie sat nearby muttering about not visiting the saloons with the team.

"I'd not heard of food shortages in Utah," St. Vrain said. "I thought you'd made a mistake carrying so much bulk foodstuffs along the old Spanish Trail."

Pascal reported while he still traded with the

Redman, their skins had little value today. "I have to find ways to trade in places the wagons don't reach."

Pascal ordered Blackie and Antonio to move the empty mules south to Santa Fe, a long two-day ride without a siesta break. After deciding to spend extra time in Santa Fe, he worked on trade for next season, or future freight for the Ortega Freight Company. While Antonio and the cousins visited the saloons and bawdy houses, Pascal gossiped with the men who came around the trading areas and warehouses.

Blackie used his free time to roam the town and the surrounding area. Even though he didn't attend this church except when in town, he spent an afternoon with the local Methodist minister and his family in Santa Fe. These visits reminded him of his parents who made guests welcome in his father's small parsonage in Wales.

Much to the disappointment of the young men, Pascal sold the six Nez Perce horses for $350 apiece. Pascal reveled in how fortunate he'd been this season. They earned $8,925, and Pascal rated it as his best season in America.

Pascal awarded the Las Vegas pair their pick of saddle horses from the remuda as a bonus before they returned home for the season. Blackie received Pascal's permission to ride with the Las Vegas pair, who reassured Pascal they'd be in Zaragoza next February to work the season.

In Las Vegas, Blackie attended Sunday services at the local Methodist Church and ate dinner with one of the parishioners. The people in the congregation hadn't seen Blackie in a year and several ladies commented he'd grown into a tall and fine-looking man, which embarrassed him. He liked the hard-working, humble people at the church, enjoying their fellowship and shared their concern for the widowed women and children in the congregation. Blackie found Reverend Johnson's sermons of God's love and peace a far different message from his father's sermons of hellfire and damnation. His appeal for an offering for the three widows in the community moved Blackie. He surprised Reverend Johnson by offering a private donation of two gold double Eagles for each widow and her family.

The Reverend gave him a questioning gaze as he squinted one eye and pursed his lips.

"We had a good season. It's part of my pay for working on the mule train," Blackie said.

The Reverend thanked him for his donation. "The widow Wilson has five children, and her brother-in-law works the farm. The widow Woodruff has four children and is quite needy of our help. Widow Perkins is younger. She has neither children nor husband, and she has a small cattle and sheep ranch to run with no help. She let her hands go because she had no funds to pay them."

Early the next morning, Blackie returned on the Santa Fe Trail riding up the canyon leading to the high plateau on which Santa Fe sat. He spent one night on the trail alone. While he detected no immediate danger, it made him more aware how easily a man alone could fall prey to bandits or a party of Redmen. He carried a .36-caliber 1851 Navy Colt and Pascal's Sharps rifle in his saddle scabbard, both cap-n-ball weapons.

If more than a five attacked, he'd be in trouble. He'd hit targets as far as 300 yards in practice where he laid flat and rested the Sharps on a prop, but if the attackers rode, they'd be harder to hit. Pascal didn't advocate shooting at men, let alone at distant targets. He decided to practice the way Digging Badger taught him and learn to hit moving targets closer to him.

~~~~~~

Pascal waited until the last week of October, when wagons no longer headed east along the Santa Fe Trail to purchase five unused wagons and spare parts at ten cents on the dollar.

LaFleur, Phillippe, and the Ortega cousins returned from the San Luis with three wagons, each loaded with 5,000 pounds of maize to sell for winter feed in Santa Fe, earning $325.

Philippe decided, with Pascal's urging, to ride north to visit his grandmother's people, the Shoshone, instead of riding south with the team. He received full pay and a hefty bonus. In their private discussion, Phillippe learned his services wouldn't be needed next season.

After joining the cousins for supper, Pascal spoke in French to LaFleur and Blackie to report the Arapaho wouldn't return and included the news he'd purchased a warehouse in Santa Fe with a haybarn and a large corral for the freight line. He asked them to not speak of the purchase until he told Victorio Ortega in their winter meetings. "I must play politics with our partners."

Pascal hitched six fresh mules to LaFleur's wagons and used the remaining mules as hitched teams for the wagons he purchased. The cousins loaded the empty packsaddles and camp gear on one wagon from Santa Fe for the ride south along the Rio Grande and the *Camino Real*. They also loaded ten fifty-gallon water barrels, two on each wagon.

In his usual practice at the end of each season, Pascal bought whatever unsold goods sold cheap, for these items would find a market south of the Rio. They led eight wagons south to El Paso with the cousins as drivers. In El Paso, Pascal sold the Santa Fe goods to Señor Valencia, generating another $480 for and end of season bonanza. After a few days of partying, they rode to the Rancho in Zaragoza for the winter rest.

Chapter 11

November 1856 – March 1857

The Ortega Freight Company business grew each year with Pascal's capital investment of cash, wagons, and organizational skills. This year, they added freight wagon service between Santa Fe and El Paso to support the freight service continuing south to Chihuahua. The warehouse, corral and stock barn Pascal purchased last fall anchored their northern freight service to Santa Fe.

At the partners' meeting, Pascal said, "I suggest we develop a route with seacoast access, and we can order materials from Havana or Europe at lower prices."

Ortega countered, "The trails east of Chihuahua are too mountainous for wagons."

Rodrigo Valencia, a merchant with stores in large Mexican towns, said, "The roads through the interior south of Chihuahua are better for wagons and have less Indian fighting than in the U.S. If we send shipments to Bagdad on the Gulf at Matamoros, there are good roads to Monterrey, which is connected to the mountain route to Chihuahua. The southern route through the interior is 900 miles—the same length as the Santa Fe Trail from the U.S."

"I remind you again," Pascal said. "El Paso is only 750 miles from the Texas coast. If our shipments came through the port at Indianola or Lavaca, we can freight them ourselves to San Antonio and to El Paso." He slapped the table, "Remember, the San-San mail route to California forced the U.S. government to improve the stagecoach road to El Paso. It's usable year-round."

When the meeting adjourned, they agreed only to discuss importing trade goods from the coast after their current trade between Chihuahua and Santa Fe prospered in the coming season.

Pascal requested two more Ortega cousins work with the mule team this season to help load the packsaddles. In Phillippe's absence, Pascal planned to use Antonio and Blackie as scouts and supplement them with Nachi and Luis, the Las Vegas pair. He expected them in Zaragoza by the end of February. Pascal, LaFleur, and Antonio trained the new men, Hector Ortega and Geraldo Dominguez, to prepare them for the season, and included four men Pascal enlisted from Zaragoza to work the mule team this year in the training sessions.

Blackie became the primary hunter and Pascal assigned him to teach the new men to shoot in defense of the train. Blackie, who'd turn seventeen this season, had become the best shot in the group with Phillippe gone. Victorio Ortega assigned six *vaqueros* to take rifle practice with Blackie after observing how the cousins and local men had improved their accuracy.

Blackie instituted practicing with small-bore target rifles at fifty yards. The small-bore rifle used the same mechanics of loading, aiming, and firing, but less noisy and less tiring when firing in practice. After a man developed shooting skill and accuracy with the small-bore rifles, they'd practice firing the Sharps.

One morning after rifle practice, Pascal called Blackie aside. "We will change how we travel this season. You are the team hunter, with Antonio and LaFleur helping as needed. Antonio is the lead scout and guide and you'll second him like last season."

"Does this mean I get to have a Sharps of my own?" Blackie asked.

"When you can hit a target five times in a row at three hundred yards."

"Watch the iron target," Blackie said, hefting the Sharps. He drove a metal tipped pike in the ground topped by a metal "U" as a rifle rest. Before firing, he placed wooden plugs in his ears to lessen the ringing caused by repeated firing of the big .52-caliber rifle. Next, he withdrew five linen-wrapped waxed cartridges and a tin of percussion caps. With the smooth motion gained from hours of practice, he loaded and fired five times within a minute. Down range, the target—a chest-sized piece of iron—bonged five times after each .52 caliber lead slug slammed it.

"Do I have a job?" he asked after he jacked the lever opening the Sharps breech and blew through it to clear burnt powder residue and prevent fouling the barrel.

"Don't be a show-off," Pascal said, slapping the brim of Blackie's hat.

With a smile, Blackie strode away to clean his Sharps before he returned to work.

LaFleur nudged Pascal, pointed to Blackie and signed, *not little. Growing tall.*

"Yes." Pascal grumbled in his way. "And the bigger he grows, the more he eats. I used to buy food for an extra man, now I have to buy for two extra men."

LaFleur pulled a piece of flint from his possibles-bag to rub on his wrist, signing, *skinflint.*

"Bah," Pascal barked, slapping LaFleur's shoulder. "You two are wastrels."

~~~~~~

This year, Pascal expected to have a team of himself, LaFleur, Blackie, and the Ortega cousins, consisting of Antonio, Benito, Javy, Dom, Reynaldo, Tomas, Hector, and Geraldo, plus the Las Vegas pair of Nachi and Luis. He added four men from Zaragoza: Leon and Esteban as horse wranglers, and Jorge and Angel as cooks and helpers.

The mule-team leaders had been named and the men grew excited to get started. However, by late March, the mule train fell a month late in leaving because of delivery problems with the Ortega

Freight from Chihuahua.

The delay puzzled Blackie. Pascal never liked to waste time.

In his usual way, Pascal told the team only what they needed to know to do their work. Valencia had arranged a contract to carry a large load of cartage direct to Bent's Post at Big Timbers for wagon shipment east on the Santa Fe Trail. The shipper from Mexico City believed if he bypassed Santa Fe, he would save time and warehousing expense by going to Bent's first.

Pascal didn't like to carry cartage because when he arrived at the freight's destination, he'd have to return with empty mules to a transit point to find new cargo or trade goods to sell. Pascal often said, "Trailing empty mules across the prairie is a quick way to go bust."

Another task taking extra time came from Pascal using twenty new Grimsley packsaddles built by an El Paso saddlery. The saddles, harnesses, straps, and buckles were new and stiff, which needed more time for the team to apply. He advised the team to use an old saddle blanket under a new blanket to assure a new stiff packsaddle didn't create sores on the mule's back. This year's train consisted of sixty mules, twenty relief mules, and ten camp-supply mules. It became the largest mule train Pascal and LaFleur had attempted. This season's train required a remuda of thirty-four horses. There'd be seventeen men in the saddle and seventeen horses resting. The large remuda alone became a tempting target for the Redmen along the route.

Pascal trailed the mules in single-file line the first week, but he thought they spread too long. "If we're attacked, it'll take us too long to get into a defensive position."

Next, Pascal tried working with twenty-mule strings, three abreast, while on the open prairie. Then he decided to let the remuda and LaFleur with the camp-mules lead the way. The team agreed this formation kept them closer together, which made it harder for a hit-and-run attack to strike from both sides and separate the mule strings from the remuda during an attack.

Blackie noticed a benefit from keeping the remuda close to the mule's bell mare after a few weeks. The remuda responded to the bell mare. If Pascal, leading the bell mare, turned the mule string to rest or camp, the remuda stopped and grazed near where the bell clanged.

Pascal appointed Javy, Benito, and Reynaldo as *capataz de mula*, or foreman of mules, one for each mule string.

The mule train stopped in Las Vegas on the way to Fort Union along the Santa Fe Trail. The team looked forward to the rest stop in Las Vegas. Nachi and Luis welcomed a chance to meet with family in Las Vegas. Mateo, who provided firewood and forage last year, soon arrived to earn a gold Eagle for his work. Their favorite *Fonda* served them wonderful Mexican-style food, and nothing beat Saturday night in a town with three saloons and a sporting house. Blackie and the *townie* guarded the packsaddles and the animals while the men made sport.

~~~~~~

Blackie visited the Methodist Church in Las Vegas for Sunday services as he did whenever the mule team stopped there. A parishioner, who lived along the Gallinas River south of where the team camped, invited the church congregation to an outdoor supper at their ranch after Sunday services. The Reverend Johnston and his wife asked Blackie to attend with them.

While at the church supper, an attractive young woman spoke to Blackie. "You must have grown four inches since you visited last fall. How old are you now?" She had an oval face with a thin straight nose. She wore a white blouse with a lace collar over a green gingham skirt.

"I'll be seventeen in June," Blackie said, removing his broad-brimmed straw plantation hat. He assumed the pretty woman the wife of a parishioner at the church supper. The top of her head reached his chin. "I apologize, ma'am. I don't remember your name." Her eyes reminded him of his favorite *molé* sauce, a rich, chocolate brown.

"Oh, I doubt we've been introduced formally. Social customs become more relaxed on the prairie. I'm Mrs. Perkins, Ellen Perkins. I remember my younger brother at fifteen. He acted hungry all the time. He seemed to grow out of his clothes and shoes within weeks. He sprouted higher each year until seventeen before he quit growing, though not as tall as you. But he was hungry all the time." She laughed as she touched his shoulder, "You must be six-foot tall."

"Yes, ma'am, I am," Blackie said. "I'm hungry like your brother, too. It's why I appreciate the church family's invitation to these suppers."

"They announced your name as Blackie Wolfe, with an 'e,' but the old busybody, Mrs. Lawson, said when you visited the church three years ago, you said your name was Nigel." She loosened her sun-faded green bonnet's bow to keep it from bobbing when she spoke. "Mrs. Lawson claimed your father was a Methodist minister sent to convert the Comanche, but they killed him and your family. Is that what really happened?" Her dark brows scrunched together as she asked her question.

"Yes, my father was a Methodist minister from Wales, which is part of the Kingdom. He brought my mother, my two older sisters, and me to this country for a ministry to the Cherokee in the territories east across the prairie. Our *guide* became lost and wandered into Comanche territory. The Comanche killed my family near Bent's old Fort Adobe on the Canadian River three years ago. I don't like to talk about those events."

"I'm sorry about your family," she said, touching his wrist. "I understand what you mean. Someone killed my husband nine months ago in Glorieta Canyon as he returned from business in Santa Fe. It didn't make any sense. They guess someone tried to rob him. He must've resisted and been shot. A group of men heard the shot and rode to find him on the ground, dead. They didn't see or hear anyone ride away. They couldn't tell if the robber took anything. He lay dead." She glanced away, wiping a tear. "It still doesn't make sense to me."

"And you worry about all the things you wished you'd said to him but never had the chance." He thumped his first two fingers on the Bible in the crook of her arm. "You wonder if it's God's punishment for some terrible sin. Could you've said words or done anything to change his mind, or stopped it from happening? You might've asked him not to go and you'd be safe. You wonder if God has a plan for you, why did His plan have to take your man?"

"Yes, I ask those questions, particularly when the loneliness surrounds me. I feel as if I'm suffocating. From what you say, you must've felt this way. Is it why you changed your name?"

"Yes, I'm no longer the helpless little Nigel who let his mother and sisters be killed by the Comanche. I became a man with the Cheyenne. I decided to be called Blackthorn Wolfe now. Blackthorn after our family name. I put the 'e' on the end of Wolfe for an English spelling to honor my mother who loved England. I've asked new friends, like you, to call me Blackie."

"I'm not sure," she said turning her face away lowering her eyelids with a shy smile.

Blackie's eyebrows scrunched. "Not sure we can be friends?"

"Oh, we can be friends," she said, giving him a playful slap on the arm. "I think Nigel is a more elegant name for a dashing young Englishman like those I've read in books."

He smiled. "My sisters used to tease me like that. I learned they never meant any harm by it, only teasing for fun."

"Yes, I'm teasing," she said, "but I like you better as Nigel than as a wild Cheyenne howling like a wolf. I haven't been close enough with another who suffered such a loss to have a serious discussion about the guilt. I feel abandoned and unwanted. I don't have any close friends, or women my age, to talk about it and talk about what it's like to lose a loved one so suddenly. It feels good to talk openly about my guilt and the pain. I hope we can speak again when next you visit Las Vegas. I'm relieved to learn another felt the way I did and wondered why it happened."

"I'd like to talk again. I'll stop here in the fall. I miss my mother and sisters. If you would like to write me, you can send a letter to Pascal LeBrun at Bent's Post. He'll hold it for me."

"All right, but I'll only send you a letter if you write to me first. I can only be so bold without a matching effort on your part," she said, slapping his arm again. She smiled her lovely smile, exposing her small white teeth, before she strolled away to join the church ladies.

Blackie shifted to place his back to the group,

not wanting the church women to glimpse his face as he flushed. He continued to hold his hat at his waist. He had never experienced such a reaction before, and never in a church.

~~~~~~

Late the next afternoon, Blackie and LaFleur rode together as they approached the Mora River. Blackie told LaFleur about his discussion with Ellen Perkins, the lovely young widow.

While Blackie told of the encounter, LaFleur made silly faces, batting his eyelids, and pretending to push long hair away from his face, like girls often did around boys. LaFleur placed his hands over his heart, letting the lower one beat a fast, thumping noise. He moaned and pursed his lips as if to kiss.

He couldn't resist the mute's clowning and laughed as LaFleur joined him.

"I'm serious, LaFleur. I know she's older than I am, but you're right, my heart beat faster. At first, I thought she grew nosy, but said she wanted someone to understand her hurt and confusion. I know I wanted someone to listen and understand after my family passed on." Blackie snorted a laugh. "And I got Pascal."

LaFleur grunted and pointed to himself with furrowed brows, signing, *What about me?*

"Yes, you listen, and I appreciate it. What I wanted to ask is why do girls slap, or push, or rub against me? At times, I think they do it as a game, and they don't mean anything. But other times, their touch roused me. It grew so hard, my pants bulged. I spoke to a girl my age with her mother at a store in Santa Fe. I noticed her outside another store, and we talked a while. I saw her the next day and we talked before I bought her a treat she liked. We sat at the side of the store talking until it grew dark and she touched my arm a few times. I had to stand up and use my hat to hide the bulge in my pants. She laughed, stood, and bent to pick up her sweets and rubbed her bottom on my hips. After she stood, she gazed at the front of my pants, and said, 'You'd tempt Eve.' She smiled and strolled to the alley behind the store."

Blackie gazed across the rolling prairie before he continued. "I didn't understand what she wanted at the time and didn't follow her. A few minutes later, she stepped into sight to throw a dirt clod at me and called me 'stupid.' I think she wanted me to follow her, but I didn't know what to do."

After he glanced at LaFleur, Blackie said, "You're not helping."

The mute held a hand across his mouth to keep from laughing out loud. Tears of laughter rolled along his cheeks. He retrieved his slate and chalk, writing in French, *cherchez la femme*. He hooked his thumbs together and flapped his hands to mimic a bird's fluttering wings before pointing to the slate.

"You're saying a woman is like a bird?"

LaFleur nodded and wrote *quail* in English. He held up five fingers pointing each one and fluttering his lips to sound like a covey of quail scattering in flight, tossing his hand in the air.

"You mean women like being together in a covey, and are flighty like quail?"

LaFleur nodded, raising one finger before making a bird-in-flight sign. Next, he used two fingers in a motion like a person running along his arm. Then, he fluttered his lips making a sound like quail flying and shrugged. He pursed his lips, repeating *peep, peep* in a high register.

"One time, quail will fly, and the next time, they run on the ground. You never know when a covey will fly or run. They chatter like birds."

LaFleur smiled and touched his nose. Next, he wrote several sentences on his slate. When he handed it to Blackie, he raised three fingers.

"Three more messages?" Blackie said before he read the slate, *a woman can be a friend with the man without passion – sans joi.*

LaFleur wrote another message.

A woman of your family will touch you as a one who loves you. True love, without passion.

LaFleur wrote another message.

A woman who likes you may touch you to learn if you like her.

She may touch you to stir your interest in passion – tel joi.

"But how do I tell the difference?" Blackie asked.

LaFleur heaved an exaggerated shrug. He wrote *cherchez la femme* and laughed.

The mute man amazed Blackie by barking, laughing, making noises, and whistling without his tongue, but he failed to produce understandable speech in any language. Blackie promised himself, *One day I'll get Pascal to tell me what happened to LaFleur's tongue.*

~~~~~~

When the team reached Bent's Post, Pascal announced, "I've arranged a shipment of dry goods, china, and kitchenware for the Great Salt Basin, our first stop in the north." Despite misgivings last year, he carried bolts of cloth and women's notions. Pascal's trade goods from the East arrived a week later, on April 25 which explained the delay in heading north across the prairie.

While waiting, Pascal grumbled, "The Big Timbers' location is too far east along the Arkansas River. It's not convenient to the north-south trade route we follow along the front range. We ought to find another place along the route we travel."

After unloading the wagons delivering Pascal's goods, the teamsters loaded the freight his mules had carried for Senor Valencia, returning the cargo to Westport Landing and points east.

Bent reported relations with the Mormon community had worsened over the winter. "They've grown hostile to non-Mormons and unfriendly to wagon trains passing through Utah and refuse to sell them supplies," he said. "The Mormons have spoken of arming themselves and declaring Utah an independent country, separate from the United States. The primary reason for the separatist movement is to support their public reaffirmation of polygamy as an integral part of the Mormon belief."

While Pascal failed to grasp the full extent of the sudden Mormon hostility, he knew it'd make the prices higher for trade goods in the region. The team needed to ride across the front range to Fort Bridger with all possible speed, bringing their trade goods, work teams, relief mules, and a separate load of goods for Redmen seeking trade.

After leaving Bent's Post at Big Timbers, they returned alongside the Arkansas River to the village of Pueblo. If they tried riding northwest across the prairie from Bent's Post, they'd save a hundred miles and four days, but ride in Comanche and Kiowa's prime buffalo hunting grounds.

"We take enough risks," Pascal said. "It is not necessary to tramp across their traditional grasslands when it provokes them. Let's not make ourselves a target of their anger."

An extra four days of riding grew aggravating, but less so than fighting the Comanche or Kiowa for your life.

Chapter 12

March – June 1857

Blackie reveled in the freedom being the scout gave him even as he acknowledged the long hours spent in the saddle. He switched horses four times a day after he convinced Pascal to purchase four fresh horses when they visited Bent's Post at Big Timbers. He tied Cheyenne-style knots in their mane to mark them as his and told Antonio to use Blackie's extra horses from Zaragoza to change often. This gave each scout four horses and allowed the horses to rest every other day.

Even though scouting alone for long periods, Antonio and Blackie got together whenever in camp to exchange information and compare their observations of dangers along the route As they grew to trust one another, they agreed to alternate nighthawk supervision, so each received an undisturbed night's sleep every other day. Between the *capataz*, Reynaldo, Javy, Benito, and scouts, Antonio, Blackie, Nachi, and Luis, one always stayed mounted and alert for raiders.

After he reported the plan, Pascal said, "It's a good idea. LaFleur and I will do the same. Tell the *capataz* to rotate who stands nighthawk. We need six on watch this season with a train this large." He waved an arm north. "When we reach the Laramie River, follow it north until we're past Elk Mountain. We'll take a rest day before we cross the Medicine Bow ridge."

"I thought you planned to visit Fort Laramie this season?" Blackie scratched his horse between its ears, and it twisted its head to make it easier for him to reach the spot.

"*Non*," Pascal said. "We've a full load of trade goods for people who've settled in their new home. Fort Laramie would buy food stuffs for those in wagons, not dishware and cookpots. Study the pilgrims like you study the habits of game you hunt. Learn what they want in the different seasons, and what they want when moving between feeding grounds. Pilgrims are no different. It is how I plan what goods to carry each season."

On the way north, Pascal shifted west from the prairie and rode closer to the mountains. He stopped at the junction of the South Platte River and the Cache la Poudre River where the original buildings of St. Vrain's Fort still stood from the glory days of fur-trading. A few white settlers lived there, using the old adobe buildings to start a new settlement. Pascal told stories of the fur trade when the mule team camped alongside the river for a night.

At the siesta break the next day, Blackie said, "We have developed a nice rhythm with the three strings now. The *capataz* keep the mules moving with fewer problems." After dismounting, he unsaddled his horse, and walked it cool. He wiped its withers with a dry rag before turning it loose in the remuda, where it rolled on its back in the thick prairie grass.

"*Oui*, it will help in the mountains," Pascal said, watching Blackie saddle a fresh horse.

~~~~~~

As the team rode across Crow Creek, a hunting party of Northern Cheyenne threatened to attack. After their initial bluster of war cries, they responded to trade signs and rode close to trade hides for small metal bells, trinkets, and foofaraw for their women.

Blackie spoke in Cheyenne to negotiate the trades.

A Cheyenne warrior asked, "Who are you? You speak like a Southern man."

"I am Black Wolf, son of Yellow Blossom from Black Kettle's people," Blackie said.

The warrior asked, "Are you the one who saved Black Kettle's women from the Pawnee?"

"I called the alarm. The camp guard killed them," Blackie said.

"The tales say you attacked five Pawnee by yourself," the warrior persisted.

"No, five attacked me. I *counted coup* on two warriors. I killed one and took his scalp."

"I heard the same," said Spotted Hawk, a Dog Soldier who watched the parley from aside. "It is a good thing not to boast about your kills. Our brothers in the South spoke of you. I do not remember you so tall when you visited with our brothers last season."

"I am still growing. I don't remember you from my last visit." He understood the Cheyenne men had warrior societies, who kept their members secret. The Northern Cheyenne men called their men's society Dog Soldiers and the Southern Cheyenne called theirs Bow Strings. They had smaller groups for training young boys to hunt and older boys to prepare for their rite of passage. The men and boys worked together to defend the tribe from any enemy.

"They say you wear the eyes of a wolf. I have not seen wolf-eyes on a man before this. If you scout for the Mule Man, the Dog Soldiers will not attack if you do not make trouble for us. Do not scout for the Bluecoats. Tell the Arapaho not to scout for them."

"That one does not ride with us. He visits his grandmother's people in the Bitterroots."

"Have you replaced the Arapaho?"

"Only for this season."

"Don't trust the Absaroka and the Blackfoot in the Bitterroots to the north."

"I will listen to your counsel," Blackie replied.

After completing their trades for foofaraw, the Northern Cheyenne rode away in peace.

A day later, as they ascended to cross a ridge to the west, a small party of Southern Arapaho approached and signed for trade. They signed they wanted iron knives or tomahawks, but Pascal no longer carried such items.

"They signed asking for iron goods, but they really want firearms," Pascal said. "Have no hesitation, don't glance at me when they ask. Be firm with them. Remind them the Mule Man does not trade in weapons and spirits. They know this. They are testing you."

When they found no trade for weapons, the Arapaho wanted to trade for a mule to eat, but Blackie told them the Mule Man needed his mules to cross the great mountains to the west.

An Arapaho said, "Mule Man is strange. He has many mules, but he does not eat them."

The large mule train continued north along the mountain's base, past the Crow River, following a mountain trail too rugged for wagons to use. The mule train turned west into the foothills before crossing the Laramie River, aiming for the northernmost peak. The train crossed a high ridge using a saddle south of Medicine Bow mountain, the tallest peak in the area. They descended into the Medicine Bow River valley.

The Arapaho and the northern Cheyenne visited this valley to find young saplings for their traditional bows. Twenty years ago, trappers claimed the Cherokee created a trail by following the Arkansas River to the Big Timbers, long before Bent moved his post to there, and turned north across the flat plains to the Laramie River and west across to the Medicine Bow to gather mountain mahogany saplings to carry to their new home in the Territories west of Fort Smith.

The mountain trail west grew steep and used three switchbacks to reach Snowy Pass. After descending from the ridgeline, it brought them to the headwaters of the North Platte River, which flowed north from this point 100 miles before turning east for 260 miles to join the South Platte and form one river. Blackie and three cousins hand-fished in the streams for a trout dinner.

~~~~~~

On the west side of the Medicine Bow mountain range, Pascal called for an early rest day after Blackie reported he encountered a small party of Northern Cheyenne escorting four elders to a hot spring. The native people considered hot springs good for healing, as the team had found last year at Pagosa in the southern mountains. Most native people considered a hot spring a truce or meeting ground where all people gathered in peace.

Blackie waited a respectful distance away from The People's camp upriver from the hot springs until a Cheyenne warrior came to confront him.

When the man came close, Blackie called in Cheyenne, "I'm Black Wolf, son of Yellow Blossom from Black Kettle's clan. I'm leading the Mule Man across to Fort Bridger with trade. We conducted trade with your warriors four days ago."

"They reported the Mule Man traveled in the area." The warrior carried a flintlock rifle.

"I killed an elk this morning. It is more meat than we can use. May we share it with you?"

"How long do you plan to visit here?" he asked.

"We want to rest the mules for a day," Blackie said. "What better way to rest than soaking in the hot spring? We will camp west of the river and leave when the sun rises two times."

"We respect a truce on these grounds. Do not bring weapons here."

"I understand. If The People use the spring, we will wait."

"The elders like to come after first light and after midday. If you leave the elk where we stand, we might find a way to keep it from turning bad." The man shifted to stride away.

The men on the team visited the hot spring in two shifts, before midday and before sunset, allowing the other to guard their trade goods. The new team members hadn't visited a hot spring before and admitted their body became more relaxed after a soak. They found one end grew too hot to enter.

"*Mamacito* boiled the old roosters in a pot to make them tender." Nachi pointed at Pascal and LaFleur soaking in the pool. "There are the old roosters stewing in the pot."

Pascal barked a laugh before splashing water at the men who laughed at him.

The train continued northwest along the mountain trail where another saddle led them into the Great Divide Basin. The mule team crossed the southern end of the Great Divide Basin with four days of dry trail and cold camps before reaching Bitter Creek, a Green River tributary.

They waited until Rock Springs, another day's travel, before filling the waterskins with sweet water.

The mule train reached the Green River on May 25, 1857. Three ferry crossings operated two days ride north from where they stood, but Pascal, too cheap to pay the $12 fee for six mules to use the westbound crossing, didn't plan to ride two days north, or pay $126 for six trips across, only to ride two days south to end up across the river from where they stood today.

The Mormon church owned and operated two of the three ferries and let Mormons cross with no charge. Other pioneers paid dearly for the privilege. Pascal reported a non-Mormon Green River ferry operator made $60,000 in 1855 by charging $12-$16 a wagon to cross the river. These days, westbound wagons paid $15-$20 to cross the Green. Wagons pulled by mules paid a lower price than those with oxen because of the oxen's weight. The Green River could be treacherous where the mountain land fell rapidly as the water flowed south. It ran deep and swift with steep rocky banks, even at the ferry landings. People died crossing the Green each year, even using the Emigrant Trail ferry crossings. Upstream, they often located the ferries below a waterfall or rapids where the water pooled and slowed before continuing its rush downstream.

Rafting the Green River became a tricky maneuver and not practical for the inexperienced travelers. Pascal needed all seventeen men of the crew to make it happen. Fording a river with mules can be an adventure, and a bit dangerous. Mules can ford a river up to where the water reaches their belly, but the water makes it hard for them to keep their balance with a load on top. They can swim, as needed, but not with a loaded packsaddle.

The Green River ran more than ten feet deep and a steady current on the surface in this stretch. Pascal expected the horses, which are good swimmers, to ford the river if the current didn't sweep them too far downstream. A sandbar lay on the downstream side of Bitter Creek's mouth on the Green's east bank. On the west bank, a gentle rise led to a grassy knoll across the way. The real question became, could their horses climb the west bank after swimming across?

It appeared they must cross at this place or ride north and pay the ferryman. Downstream, the Green River's current grew swift before it dropped into a steep-walled canyon called the Flaming Gorge for the burnt-orange and sienna-colored rocks that glowed as if lit by fires when the morning or the afternoon sun reflected from the gorge's walls.

Pascal gloated over his decision to use a seventeen-man team this season. He'd need everyone to raft the Green. Pascal led one group of men to a copse 500 yards east upstream on Bitter Creek to fell four pine trees, two feet in diameter. The men divided into work groups and used long-handled, double-bladed axes to chop and trim the trees. They used mule teams to drag the logs to the Green.

While Pascal's team chopped and trimmed raft logs, men on LaFleur's team felled two trees half the diameter of the raft logs. A second team of LaFleur's men found the ground too rocky to dig a pit. Instead, they tied six-inch logs between four standing trees to form a four-foot square worktable, six feet above the ground. LaFleur unwrapped an eight-foot-long, two-handed bandsaw he carried coiled into a two-foot diameter with its wooden handles removed for packing with the camp-supply mules.

The worktable let a pair of men saw from above and another pair below with the two-handed bandsaw to rip-cut the one-foot-wide logs in half lengthwise. LaFleur's team used the long half-logs for decking to the fill the gaps between the larger logs of the raft's deck.

Pascal's team used hemp rope pieces to lash together a raft twenty-foot-long and ten-foot-wide. The two work teams needed a full day to fell the trees and construct the raft.

Years earlier, Blackie wondered why Pascal carried a packsaddle containing two ten-inch pulleys in an iron-strapped wood frame with an "eye" hook. This packsaddle also carried two, 200-foot long, one-inch-thick, braided-hemp ropes coiled inside. Today he found out why.

The next morning, LaFleur, Antonio, and the Las Vegas pair, Nachi and Luis, waded their horses across the sandbar at the mouth of Bitter

Creek and rode upstream a hundred yards. Antonio prepared to cross first by removing everything he didn't want to lose or get soaked. He removed his boots and draped them upside down from a thong around his neck, which kept them from filling with water. The other men followed his lead. He slipped from the saddle when the horse swam, holding a rope tied to the saddle horn. Antonio reached the Green's west bank without problems. The current carried him downstream fifty yards past the mouth of Bitter Creek. He reported the current held steady at medium-strong, but the banks on each side dropped steep once underwater. Antonio had carried one end of a light fiber rope across with him.

LaFleur crossed next and encountered no problems. He entered the water upstream another fifty yards north and left the water on the bank across from Bitter Creek. Nachi proved not the swimmer he had claimed. He splashed and fought the water as he crossed with his horse pulling him. Antonio walked his horse to the water's edge to rope Nachi at the opposite bank, while LaFleur roped Nachi's horse, which he'd spooked by splashing in the water beside it.

Luis showed off, floated on his back, letting his horse tow him across without a problem.

LaFleur's team pulled a thick hemp rope across tied to Antonio's smaller rope. The second hemp rope followed, tied to the first one's end. They lashed the large pulley's "eye" hook to a two-foot-thick pine tree before running the hemp ropes through the pulley wheels. LaFleur and Antonio rigged hemp ropes between two horses, so two horses pulled each rope to prevent the raft from being swept downriver. Nachi worked one pair of horses from the ground and Luis worked the other pair.

Now the hard work began.

Pascal's team, on the Bitter Creek side, loaded the raft with eight packsaddles and six men on the trial run. He'd tied one end of the inch-thick hemp rope to each of the raft's front corners. The guide ropes and pulleys worked as planned. Pascal's team pushed the raft away from the east bank into the river's current. Nachi and Luis's horses pulled the ropes through the pulleys under LaFleur's and Antonio's guidance. It swung away as LaFleur and Antonio steadied the tension on the heavy ropes connected through the pulleys, keeping the raft longwise in the current. When the raft reached the west bank, Antonio tied it fast to a rock on the bank to unload. The six men on the raft carried the first eight packsaddles ashore. Pascal's team rafted the remaining forty packsaddles and the camp gear rafted in two crossings.

Pascal instructed his team to blindfold the mules before leading them onto half-sawn plank decking atop the raft. They tied the mule's bridles to the decking with their heads held low. The Ortega cousins followed Pascal's directions, tying the hobbles to the raft with one rear-leg tied with a thong to the opposite front-leg. The cross tie allowed the mules to move their legs for balance but kept them from kicking their rear legs. Pascal sent eight mules across on the raft on the first trial run. The mules brayed their complaints on the entire raft trip.

When LaFleur's team unloaded on the west side, Hector and Geraldo herded the mules up a grassy knoll before hobbling them in a meadow with good graze. After they released a mule on the raft and led it to the edge, the mule bolted, jumping ashore to escape the bobbing raft. It brayed aloud as it trotted up the hillside, getting far away from the water. After Pascal's team pulled the raft to the Bitter Creek bank for the next-to-last-load, four Ortega cousins asked to cross with this load of mules because they didn't swim well. LaFleur, Antonio, Luis, Benito and Reynaldo returned on the raft to drive the horses and swim across again. Pascal and Blackie rode last to cross with a load of mules. After unloading the mules, they eased the raft ten feet from the west bank with men on board to lasso horses reluctant or unable to swim ashore.

LaFleur led the remuda into the river with the men driving them from behind. One after the other, the mounted horses kept the riderless horses from balking and forced them to swim the river. Several horses reached the front of the raft and acted like they wanted to climb on board, but men on the raft roped them, guiding those horses to the bank to climb from the river. It appeared like chaos until the first horse came ashore and climbed the gentle bank. After the first one, the rest formed to follow and swam to where the others had climbed out.

With the crossing complete, LaFleur used three mule-pair teams to drag the raft forty yards higher on the west bank, higher on the bank than the high-flood debris line past the trees where they'd lashed the pulleys. To the team's dismay, Pascal ordered them to untie the ropes from the raft's construction and lay the ropes aside, stretched out to dry in the sun.

"If we leave the ropes exposed to the winter weather, they'll rot and be useless next season." Pascal said, "I'll not waste rope we may need latter. We'll repack the ropes tomorrow, when dry. If we return later this year, having raft material already cut will save us a day crossing the river."

The speed with which they built the raft and arranged the pulley ropes indicated Pascal and LaFleur had used this method of fording a stream before. Rafting the Green River gave the men experience for what they might face later in rafting flooded streams too deep for loaded mules.

It'd taken three full days to ferry the mules and cargo across the Green River, but less than the expense and five days travel to a ferry crossing and return. They lost two mules who'd panicked, broken loose, and fallen into the water.

Pascal had ordered the men to make no effort to rescue any animal who fell in. He said, "We'll take our losses and pray they are small rather than risk a man's life in a rescue attempt."

Chapter 13

May – June 1855

Travelers riding east from Fort Bridger carried mixed news. The good news came in a report of winter rains followed by periodic spring rains, making it appear the drought had broken. The Mormon farmers expected large yields of grain from winter Turkish red wheat and oats in the next month or two. The better news for Pascal told of scarce dry food stocks until they harvested, dried, and processed this year's grain in their grist mills in another two months.

The bad news came in the form of the Call for Reformation issued in the previous year. It left Mormons unsettled and unsure of how they should treat non-Mormons, either residents of Utah or passing through the area. Worse news came from the reaction of Eastern voters after the Mormon Church reaffirmed polygamy as an integral part of their doctrine. The concept of polygamy created a backlash in the Eastern press, which caused an uproar in Washington.

In 1857, sugar sold for a dollar-and-a-half per pint in Fort Laramie or Fort Bridger. Flour sold for one dollar per pint and green coffee beans also sold for a dollar per pint at both Forts.

The practice surprised Blackie. "The merchants don't weigh dry food stocks." He nodded at Pascal. "They sell it by dry volume of a pint or a quart."

Pascal replied, "Accurate scales are scarcer than the flour they want to weigh, but a dry volume measure of a pint or quart is always available."

However, salted pork side meat was plentiful, and sold for a penny a pound in Fort Laramie. Pioneers on the Oregon or Emigrant Trail had grown weary of salted pork side meat by this point and wanted to sell what they carried but found few takers.

The pioneers on the Emigrant Trail to Utah, or on through to California, often tried to trade items they'd carried on their wagons to this point in exchange for food. Most found merchants or people living along the Trail uninterested in their discards. The Trail through the mountains became littered with items tossed away to lighten the wagon in order to make the trip up and across the mountain less burdensome.

Like Pascal, Blackie learned when supplies became limited, prices increased in kind. A pocket pouch of smoking tobacco, for instance, bought for ten cents in El Paso, sold for a dollar at Fort Laramie. This season, he carried cut and plug tobacco to sell around the forts. He also carried his own supply of trade cigars. He didn't have Pascal's heavy money belt, but he chose a product to sell that didn't compete with the forts or Pascal. He produced a profit from his work.

However, his "preacher's kid" mentality grew

irritated whenever he thought Pascal profited from another's hardship. However, after four seasons of day-in, day-out, dark of dawn to a darker sunset of drudgery and wrestling mules, Blackie lost many of his Methodist ideals.

Last season, he'd been shocked when Pascal charged "unfair prices" for dry food stocks, like flour, but he calculated Pascal charged a dollar a pound for the fifty-pound flour kegs, and the merchant sold the same flour for a dollar per pint, earning three times the profit of Pascal.

Blackie rode ahead to visit the Mormon Fort Bridger. He walked beside his horse as he hitched it to the rail outside. Upon entering the building, he strolled to the counter, but before he spoke, the sutler said, "Our supplies are exhausted, we've nothing for sale."

"I've come at the right time." Blackie laughed. "I'm not a buyer—I'm a seller, who leads a supply train. We offer dry food stocks of flour, sugar, and baking soda, if you're hungry, and bolts of cloth and notions, if you are bare. If your supplies are truly exhausted, we'll give you a bargain price for the entire load." He shined the neighborly smile LaFleur taught him.

The sutler's mouth gaped open, flummoxed by Blackie's offer. "I might buy some items to replenish my stock, but I can't sell to you ... in this time of trouble," he hemmed and hawed.

Blackie returned to Pascal with the news the post would welcome fresh supplies.

When Pascal entered, the sutler mumbled, "I

hope you understand my problem. I must follow instructions from the elders. I'll buy what I can with the gold I have on hand."

"I always welcome gold." Pascal nodded, smiling.

Pascal planned to offer less than half of his dry food stocks to the sutler, expecting to sell more in the towns, but the sutler lacked gold to purchase more. He didn't offer the china, cookware, bolts of cloth, and notions at Fort Bridger, but planned to ride west, following the Emigrant Trail through Echo Canyon to the Ogden River to the towns. Pascal believed he'd have fewer problems by avoiding Salt Lake City and selling to small-town tradesmen and merchants.

Blackie scouted the area while Pascal negotiated sales with the sutler. He rode sixteen miles south, following the Black Fork upstream to Fort Supply and found it closed. The Mormons had created it to provide an honest trading post for the Redman without liquor or powder available, but the pioneer wagons found it difficult to reach its remote location, forcing the Mormons to repair Fort Bridger during the winter, and close Fort Supply.

He recognized two Shoshone men from last season's trade with their leader, Crow Killer, sitting in the shade of Fort Supply's front steps. Blackie greeted them in their language and offered trade cigars. "Is there another trail west from Bridger to the valley below?"

One Shoshone man used their name for Ogden. He said he remembered the area from when Miles Goodyear, an early mountain man and trapper, had a trading post on the Ogden River before the Mormons came into the Great Basin.

"The white man have farms across the old trails," the first Shoshone warrior said. "They grow angry if we ride them into the valley. There is little hunting. We no longer ride there."

"The old mountain men tell tales of good hunting before Mormons came," Blackie said.

"The old warriors tell the same tales," the other Shoshone said. "We don't understand why the white man hunted beaver. Its skin is no warmer than a badger's and no bigger."

"Men in the East prized it's soft fur," Blackie said, "but they no longer want their fur."

The first warrior nodded.

The second warrior pointed and said, "The Utes in the south are not hostile. Farther south, the Paiutes are angry. Their hunting grounds grow smaller and provide less. Do not go there."

Blackie waved a hand north. "When we leave, we go north, upstream on the Bear, and then cross the mountains to the Snake. We might follow the Snake to the Shining Mountains."

The second Shoshone shook his head once. "Watch for the Bannocks north of the Snake. Do not bother the Lemhi Shoshone along the Camas. They are root-eaters, not fighting men."

The first Shoshone said, "Do not trust the Bannocks or the Blackfoot, in the mountains north of the Snake. Do not to trade with them." The Shoshone had warned him twice about Bannocks and Blackfoot if he rode north from Fort

Hall, following the Snake River.

"I will listen to your counsel," Blackie said. He returned to Fort Bridger before dark on the night before Pascal readied to leave for Ogden.

The next morning, Pascal called to Blackie and Antonio, "Follow the Emigrant Trail through the Wasatch Mountains and descend Echo Canyon to the Ogden River."

The mule team had no choice but to ride single-file in the steep-walled, narrow canyon, only wide enough for one wagon along the entire canyon trail. The train rode along the Ogden River to reach Kaysville, the oldest Mormon community in Utah.

Pascal offered a merchant the cookware, china, bolts of cloth, and notions, who bought them without haggling but lacked the coin to buy more. Pascal decided to ride to another town before offering the dry food stocks. Food prices had not risen as high this year as last year.

Ogden, the next community, had grown larger with more established, traditional homes. The first merchant Pascal contacted wanted everything Pascal carried and had the gold coin to buy it. Pascal hadn't intended to sell everything in one place and grew hesitant to sell without seeking to find a better price in the next town. After a deep sigh, Pascal said, "Gold in the hand is better than a promise of tomorrow," and struck the deal.

The quick sale of the trade goods left the team with thirty mules to sell or drag back to El Paso. More settled, Ogden had little demand for mules.

Pascal and four cousins traveled upstream beside the Ogden River intending to cross a ridge and descend Provo River canyon farming area to find fifteen sales at sixty dollars per mule. LaFleur, Blackie, and the Vegas pair traveled upstream beside the Bear River into the Cache Valley to sell fifteen mules where more farmers worked. The remaining men stayed with the camp supplies and horse remuda. The teams planned to meet in Kaysville in two weeks, at the latest. The mules sold in small numbers at each stop, but all fetched the sixty-dollar price without a lot of arguing. Both groups returned early.

The brisk sales became a mixed blessing. June marked the middle of trade season and they'd sold most of the trade goods, but there wouldn't be a harvest of grain or dried fruit for Pascal to buy for another month. Their choice became to wait for the harvest season and hope they could buy grain to haul south across the plains or drag the mules to New Mexico empty. Pascal hated to drag mules not earning money. He decided to ride north and told the team they would relax and enjoy the Snake River Valley and might even follow it north to its headwaters in the Tetons.

If they had time, they'd explore Coulters Hell where old trappers reported it contained boiling hot springs and gushing waterspouts. Neither Pascal nor LaFleur had visited the place but heard the older generation of trappers and mountain men exclaim its wonders.

Pascal held a reserve of 2,000 pounds of dry food stocks or eight packsaddles of food and one packsaddle of cloth and women's goods. He planned to take them north to Fort Hall and explore fruit and grain markets with the non-Mormon settlers in the Snake River Valley. As the team found last season, reducing the cargo load to the nine packsaddles, and switching the mules at the noon rest, it allowed the smaller thirty-mule train to move faster, even though still on the mountain trails. They moved north through the Cache Valley into Idaho territory.

"I spoke to Shoshone warriors at Fort Supply," Blackie reported. "They claimed the Bear River valley used to be a Shoshone hunting ground, calling it 'Willow Valley.' The Shoshone reported they hunted buffalo and elk in the valley until the Mormons came, killing all the game."

"Much has changed since the early days," Pascal said, "when the American Fur Company and the Hudson Bay Company competed to hunt in this area."

When the mule team reached the Snake River Valley five days later, they learned raids by the Redman had all but closed Fort Hall because re-supply wagons couldn't reach it without being attacked. The hostilities kept the people crossing along the Oregon Trail on edge. The team learned Fort Boise on the western Snake had closed also. After traveling upstream to Fort Hall, the team found the settlement in disrepair and desperate for food and supplies. The only merchant still in business had little money for new supplies even though it lay on the main route of the Oregon Trail. The hostile raids limited farming in the area, and no one expected a significant harvest this season.

"If'n you want grain from the summer harvest, ride up to the Lemhi Valley, northwest from here," the sutler said. "It lies west of the Bitterroot Mountains, between them and the Lemhi Mountains, past where the Birch River disappears in the sinks."

"What are *sinks*?" Antonio asked.

"Them badlands are old lava beds with a few cones to the north," the sutler said. "It appears solid ground to your eye, but it has holes beneath to swallow up three different rivers. Their water flows into the area and *sinks* from sight."

Antonio leaned away with brows furrowed, before he glanced at Pascal, who nodded.

"The Mormons have a mission up that-a-way called Fort Lemhi," the sutler said after he lit a cigar. "They done dug canals across the Salmon River valley basin and are growing crops up there. Their problem is they're too far from Utah and they can't get supplies regular. They're having problems with the Flatheads and Bannocks."

"Once those forts were company-owned trading posts for trappers," Pascal said. "Now, they serve as regional supply stores. Fort Lemhi is a recent addition by the Mormons who intend it for community defense, not trade."

"I ain't laid eyes on Lemhi, but stories say the

same," the sutler said. "They expect a fight with the Bannocks."

Pascal decided to forgo visiting Coulter's Hell since it didn't produce a profit. They'd visit the Mormon farms in Lemhi Valley to find trade to sell, and mayhap, purchase from their harvest. Pascal found an old timer and offered him a cigar before he asked questions.

"You gotta be right careful up that-a-away," the old man said. "Lots of sinks and shifting sand. It can be right dry. My druthers, I'd go way up the Snake 'til it turns east to the Tetons. Ride north two days to the dunes before you turn west. Cross Camas Creek flowing south into the sinks but ride north of the mud lake. The Bitterroots oughtta be on your right, go between Circle Butte and Antelope Butte, and you'll find Birch Creek ahead in the west. Stay north of the Creek and swamp until it's clear you're between the Bitterroots and the Lemhi range to the west. To the south, Birch Creek disappears in 'em sinks and sand, so stay outta there. There's a bunch of Shoshone up that-a-away but treat 'em right an' they won't bother you none, if you leave their camas roots alone. It's their winter feed. Trappers used to call 'em 'root-eaters,' but they're still Shoshone. Watch out for 'em Blackfoot and the Bannocks. They're tired of the white man pushing 'em from their hunting ground and killing the buffalo."

"Is the water in the Camas and the Birch drinkable?" Pascal asked. "Or is it alkaline?"

"The water in them creeks is fine. They'll be

running slow this time a year. It'll be easy to ford all 'em but the Snake. Yer young'un of a good scout for you? He been here b'fore?"

"No, none of us have been this far north before."

"Well, I don't doubt him none, but 'em sinks are tricky. You might want another man riding along behind him. If the first wanders into a sink—it's like quicksand. Damned hard to get out if'n you're alone. The second rider can rope and pull the first out quick before he sinks, if he's close. Y'all study 'em if you go there. Learn the look of 'em and then they ain't so tricky."

"Thanks for the help," Pascal said, and gave the old timer another cigar. At five cents each, cigars made a good conversation starter with men on the trail, whether white or red.

The lava beds in this area appeared different from those they'd crossed along the Santa Fe Trail's Cimarron Cut-off, or in the *Camino Real's Jornada.* They stretched for miles with black- or grey-crusted land, pock-marked, and in a few cases, small volcanic cones formed.

"I visited a dormant volcano in the south of Italy when a priest," Pascal said. "The volcano rose in a great cone as high as these mountains. It last erupted around Caesar's time and covered nearby villages with flowing lava and ash. This area is far different than what I saw in Italy. It's beyond my comprehension how and why lava forms and erupts from the earth's bowels."

Pascal didn't often speak of his time with the Catholic Church, Blackie noticed, except to admit they'd cast him out.

The team's ride up to Fort Lemhi, though not difficult, took seven days and grew quite dry between Camas Creek and the Birch River. Before reaching Camas Creek, they rode across a barren lava dome rising ten feet higher than at the edges and spread across 3,000 yards. The men spent an afternoon studying the sinks where the Birch and another two smaller streams sank and disappeared. In most areas, it became easy to spot where the sand stayed moist and unstable with water flowing into the sinks below. However, in other areas, the loose sand had dried on top, letting brush and leaves collect, which made it harder to spot the shifting sand and water lurking underneath. In areas where lava once flowed, little vegetation grew but where the sand settled, it hid small pools of sinks where the nearby rivers disappeared.

Big Lost River, Little Lost River, and Birch River truly sank into the ground in this rocky upland plateau. Another oddity came after finding sagebrush covered the upper plateau with no trees and sparse grass. High desert land formed everywhere except alongside the creeks until the water disappeared into the sinks below.

Blackie shot four sage hens, the size of chickens, thinking to add fowl to the team's boring diet of venison and bean stew but none liked its strong sage taste.

The mule team ascended the trickling Birch watershed before they crossed a high ridge to descend along the Lemhi River which, twenty miles downstream fed into the Salmon River.

The Mormons in Fort Lemhi acted cautious, almost hostile, when the mule team arrived. The missionaries didn't want to find themselves accused of assisting non-Mormons.

Brother Stephen Smith led the Lemhi mission as its captain. He understood they needed the food stocks and cookware Pascal carried but he must balance the critical approval of Mormon elders to the mission's need. Smith decided, with Pascal's quiet counsel, the Mormon leaders hadn't restricted buying from non-Mormons, only selling to non-Mormons, and referred to his sales in the Ogden area as an example. In their negotiations, Smith decided paying needed harvest workers with food didn't violate the proscription of selling food to non-Mormons.

Smith could have been a Philadelphia lawyer for how well he negotiated with Pascal and prepared to make him pay a full measure for the raw food he wanted to buy. Pascal agreed to barter for 1,000 pounds of dried salmon, fifty bushels of wheat, and 500 pounds of potatoes. In addition to giving the Mormon community the dry food stock, Pascal agreed to put the team to work in the fields to help bring in the harvest in exchange for food and lodging while they worked. No money changed hands. Smith and Pascal negotiated the arrangements as a barter.

From Pascal's point of view, he'd bartered the dry food stocks, cookware, and trade items in exchange for raw food from their crops. Pascal sold the last four bolts of cloth and notions, but the women expressed disappointment with the small selection. However, to Pascal's delight, they bought all but one bolt with gold dust their men had panned from the Lemhi River. Pascal always accepted gold, in any form, and with his big fingers, a pinch of gold dust became "a fair price." Always ready, Pascal carried a silver snuff box to collect gold dust or nuggets on the trail.

The Mormon community saw few white men during the year. While not the case in other areas, the Lemhi Mission accepted the team's men into their home because neither hotels nor eating places existed at the Fort. They'd built the Fort as a stockade for common defense and storage. It contained no living quarters within its walls. Earlier in the spring, a large party of Mormons, sixty men and women from Salt Lake City, had volunteered to work at the Fort Lemhi Mission, as the Mormon leaders in Utah called it. The newcomers had built their settlement of homes two miles downstream of the Fort since spring. The Mormons living and working near the Fort reported with pride that Brigham Young had visited them in May and blessed them for their missionary work.

While the mule team waited for the harvest to begin, Pascal told them to convert their old Mexican leather saddle bags to carry the bulk weight of 1,000 pounds of smoke-dried salmon carried on four mules, and 500 pounds of potatoes could be loaded on two mules. They lacked containers to hold 3,000 pounds of bulk wheat and it became a cumbersome load.

Pascal had one bolt of cloth unsold and he decided to use it to make sacks for the grain. They didn't need fancy sewing, or thread, but used rawhide thongs and an awl LaFleur used for making moccasins and buckskin clothes. The cloth bags didn't look pretty but lined the inside of the leather bags. The cloth liner kept wheat kernels from leaking through gaps on the leather bag's thong stitching, while the leather was strong enough to hold two bushels of wheat, or 120 pounds of wheat on each side of a mule. Pascal bought two old canvas wagon covers to make enough bag-liners to hold the wheat. Imagine how it rankled Pascal to *buy*.

~~~~~~

While they waited for the wheat harvest, Blackie rode upstream, ascending into Lemhi pass by following Lemhi Creek to its headwaters in the Bitterroot Mountains. Lewis and Clark's diary reported Sacajawea led the expedition through this pass to contact her people, the Lemhi Shoshone. While in the pass, Blackie met two Shoshone warriors. They acted hostile at first until he spoke to them in their language. As usual, Blackie carried a few trade cigars and he passed them to the men he met.

"I'm seeking he who is the grandson of

Sacajawea. He wanted to visit his grandmother's people this season. Have you seen this one?"

"He rode with others to steal a few Nez Perce ponies," one Shoshone said. "They have fine ponies and they are easy to steal."

"Such sounds like him. Tell him the little wolf came to visit and will visit him later."

"Did the grandson give you your name?"

"No. I rode with the Cheyenne one season. We hunted buffalo with the Arapaho."

"Are you with the white men in the valley across the pass?" Saying your name to another among The People is a sign of trust but this warrior didn't say his name.

"No. I ride for the Mule Man," Blackie said. "We trade goods with The People for skins along the south trails. We have not ridden this far north into the mountains before this season."

"Those whites are not to be trusted. They say they have worked to keep the Blackfoot at peace, but the Blackfoot raid us whenever they want while the white man takes away our fish and our game meat. I have heard of this Mule Man before. Will he trade gunpowder and lead to our people? He traded gunpowder to the Arapaho last season."

"No," Blackie said. "The Mule Man gave a bit of gunpowder to the Arapaho family of the grandson, as a gift to honor Far Walking Woman. The gift provided for their annual hunt to help bring home buffalo for the winter. There was no trade. If that one stood here, he would tell you we made no trade. We offered a gift to honor his people and yours. The Mule Man doesn't sell gunpowder to any people. He does not sell it to your enemies, the Blackfoot or the White Clay People. He does not help The People make war upon one another. The Mule Man is one of the black robes. He does not believe in war. He does not help the whites who want to make war on The People. He wants all people to live in peace and trade with one another."

"The white men in the valley below make war on The People. They tell lies. They don't keep their word. Will the Mule Man give the Shoshone a gift to honor that one's grandmother?"

"Such a request for a gift must come from that one. It is not the way of The People to request a gift. It would be a hard thing to honor. I speak for the Mule Man."

"We will see what that one decides when he returns with the horses. We will talk again."

Without comment the Shoshone warriors turned to ride east. Blackie continued to watch the warriors until the trail led them from sight before he descended into Lemhi valley again.

~~~~~~

Blackie reported the Lemhi Shoshone's conversation on his return. "There will be trouble. The Mormons have angered the Lemhi and the Bannocks. We shouldn't get in the middle of this."

"It's too late now, we are committed to the harvest," Pascal said.

187

"No, we should warn Brother Smith and suggest he share his bounty with the Lemhi and ask the Lemhi to share with the Bannocks. Let them settle this between them. If need be, we'll leave before the harvest to demonstrate our displeasure with the Mormons' refusal to share."

"When did you become the leader?" Pascal barked a laugh. "Your suggestion is not bad, but we are in too deep to change course now."

LaFleur whistled to interrupt, signing *leave*.

"I hope you understand, if we leave, we lose respect. The Redman places great value on not giving in. Once you do, they will expect us to give in to requests for powder and lead in the future. It spirals downhill from there. If we live to return to Mexico, we'll have no business."

After a long period of lip movements and handwringing, Blackie nodded. "I hate to admit you're correct. We will be pressured to fight or die if Phillippe returns before we leave."

The men on the mule team found working the harvest far harder than working the mules. Pascal collected his share of dried salmon while the Mormon pioneers loaded eight wagonloads to drive to Salt Lake City. The team's men carried their share of new potatoes to the Lemhi River to wash before bagging them to reduce the weight of clinging dirt clods.

The cousins had eaten potatoes after coming north of the Rio in restaurants along the trail with Pascal. They failed to understand Blackie's satisfaction with the meal of roasted venison or elk and Irish potatoes simmered in a Dutch oven buried in hot coals and its top covered in coals.

The team helped the Mormon pioneers finish the wheat harvest by the third week in August. Brother Smith admitted, without fifteen extra workers they'd have been hard-pressed to harvest it all before the weather turned cold in the mountains.

Chapter 14

Late August 1857

The team rested for two days before loading the mules for the journey to Fort Hall and south. They sat together the evening before departing to discuss Pascal's plan for the trail.

Blackie reported, "The Redmen in the area have grown angry with the Mormon missionaries because they've taken the best elk grazing areas to plant crops and shared little with the Redman. The Mormon farmers prevent elk and deer from grazing in the valley, limiting their hunting for winter foods. The Shoshone and the Bannocks, as a tradition, harvest salmon for winter meat."

"We shall move as quickly as we can back the way we came," Pascal said. "I don't recall any obvious ambush places, but we must stay alert as always, particularly at night until we reach the Snake. We'll send extra scouts around the buttes after the sinks before we pass through them. At the Snake, we'll decide if we want to follow the northern link of the Oregon Trail through the Tetons along the Snake River bypassing Fort Hall and ride the north end of the Divide Basin to Fort Laramie, or follow the Oregon Trail's southern link from Fort Hall, ford the Green again to take the mountain trail bypassing Fort Laramie to return to the Cache la Poudre."

"You want to double the scouts in the daytime until we leave this area?" Blackie asked.

"Yes, let's do that. Who do you want to use?"

"Can we alternate Reynaldo and Benito with Nachi and Luis, so they get more experience?" Blackie asked. "They are already *capataz de mula*."

"Yes, I will tell them to work with you on schedules. Assign men to stand watch during the midday rest. Be sure they change their mounts then."

Two days later, while the mule train stopped for siesta in the Birch headwaters, Phillippe fired a shot from a nearby ridge before he descended from the Bitterroot range to ride alone into their camp. Phillippe strolled around greeting everyone, including Blackie, who he called "Little Wolf" even though Blackie had grown an inch taller than the man this summer.

"The Lemhi Shoshone, my grandmother's people, and the Bannocks are angry with the Mormons at the mission," Phillippe said in French. "The Mormons promised they'd not take away the things they caught or harvested from the valley without sharing. The People have seen many wagons leave the valley and more whites come to work the fields. The Mormons have not shared with The People. The People know you traded with the Mormons and they see their game and food of their land leaving their valley. We understand you trade with anyone out here with something to trade but they see you taking away things that had been theirs."

"I don't like where this is going," Pascal said, keeping the conversation in French.

"The Bannocks are the ones driving this, not the Lemhi. The Bannocks plan to fight the Mormons. They want to know if they are going to fight you, too. If you trade with the Mormons, but do not trade with them, they will grow angry at you."

"I suppose you told them you asked me to give a gift of powder to the Arapaho last fall."

"I didn't have to tell them. You know what gossips The People are. They love to tell tales."

"And did you tell them I gave the Arapaho People a gift to honor your grandmother and her people, a gift of gunpowder for their winter meat harvest?"

"Yes. It's why they sent me. I'm asking for a gift for grandmother's people. I know what problems I've caused. Did Little Wolf report his meeting with the Shoshone's in Lemhi Pass?"

"Yes, but don't try to blame him for this."

"No. I'm not trying to blame him," Phillippe said. "The Shoshone believed they warned you not to trust the Mormons and not to trade with them. If you refuse to trade with the Shoshone but trade with the Mormons, it makes you their enemy. If you trade with them, then you are what you have been, the Mule Man who trades with all." He turned on his heel to leave but returned to Pascal. "If the Mormons had kept their promise to share, we wouldn't be here today. If you are angry at someone, be angry at them."

Blackie nodded at Pascal, who gave a curt shake of his head.

"You realize," Pascal said, "I have refused to sell the Redman gunpowder from my first day and because I never sold it to anyone, they didn't expect it. If such a trust is breached, warriors from each people will expect me to trade powder, or fight. You may as well shoot us now."

"I'll tell them you won't give me a gift of powder. I'm sorry. I'll do the best I can."

"You make it sound like we have been defeated already. Let them come."

"You might hold the Lemhi at bay for several days, but when the Bannocks arrive, they'll show no mercy," Phillippe said. "Please, I know this is my fault, but don't do this."

Pascal shook his head before Phillippe rode away.

Pascal called LaFleur and Blackie closer. "We will move into the little arroyo beside Birch Creek for a defensive position. I'd have preferred the high ground, but we can't reach it." He placed a hand on Blackie's shoulder. "Tonight, I want you to lead five Ortega cousins down the river. Slip away in the dark and walk to Fort Hall. I'll give each of you three gold coins to live on if we don't return." He glanced at LaFleur and nodded. "We'll hold them here as long as we can. If you walk through the sinks in the night, you should reach Fort Hall in four days."

"How are you going to decide who goes and who

stays?" Blackie asked.

"We will draw lots with straws, whatever they decide. It makes no sense for everyone to die when we can let a few survive. You'll have to go because you have to lead them to Fort Hall."

"If I must die, let me die facing my enemy, not running away with my back to them."

"Damn it to hell. Don't give me your Cheyenne bravado crap. Don't argue with me. You'll do this because you're the best qualified. The Ortegas shouldn't pay for my mistake."

They led the mule train and the remuda into the arroyo and set up defensive positions.

"It won't be dark for another three hours. They may strike tonight, or just make enough noise to keep us awake all night and attack in the morning. Get a fire started and cook a meal to eat while we can."

Pascal called the Ortega cousins and Las Vegas pair together. "How much of what we just said do you understand?" Several shook and shrugged to show they didn't get it.

He explained their dilemma, and said, "I intend to draw lots to decide who stays and who tries to escape. Neither task is easy."

The Ortega cousins agreed Antonio must return to the Ranchero, and Pascal agreed.

Antonio grew as unhappy with such a plan as Blackie had been.

The men drew lots using dried grass stalks. The Nachi, Luis, Javy, and Benito drew short straws to walk to Fort Hall with Blackie. The remaining ten men understood their task.

An hour later, Phillippe fired a shot before riding into the camp with a Shoshone warrior.

Phillippe signaled in trade sign as he spoke to Pascal in French.

"The chief sent Swooping Hawk with me. He said Swooping Hawk is the best at stealing horses. He said I am to make trade talk and Swooping Hawk is to steal a keg of gun powder. I am to keep you from killing him, and escape if I can. It's the best I could arrange. This way, you haven't traded gunpowder and you've upheld your honor."

"Tell him in your language to take the small keg from the packsaddle away from the fire. Emphasize he must take the small keg, not the large keg on the packsaddle. I'll tell our men to shoot high. You and I will speak before shouting and pushing one another. The other men will come to my defense. This should allow Swooping Hawk time to steal the black powder keg and escape. Blackie is telling our men what we're planning. Let's hope this satisfies them."

The plan almost worked. The men of the mule team pretended to scuffle with Phillippe.

Swooping Hawk grabbed a keg and escaped on his horse. The mule team fired their rifles in his direction but aimed high. While the team shot at the escaping warrior, Phillippe scooted to his horse and rode in the other direction to get away. It appeared the plan had worked until Blackie checked what Swooping Hawk had taken—a fifty-pound keg of flour.

~~~~~~

Swooping Hawk rode into the Shoshone camp with a loud yell. "I've tricked the Mule Man. I took the biggest keg they had instead of the little keg Phillippe said to take. Now we'll have more gunpowder than the Bannocks. They will be humbled, asking us to share."

Swooping Hawk cracked open the top of the large keg but found it full of white powder.

Phillippe rode into the midst of the gathered warriors and understood the mix-up the instant he glimpsed the large keg. Thinking on his feet, Phillippe said, "The Mule Man is one of the black robes. They can work the magic of wine into blood. He would've allowed you to steal the small keg, but you stole a large keg. You dishonored him. He turned the black powder white because of your trick, making it useless."

The Shoshone warriors muttered among themselves before they turned against Swooping Hawk. If he had not been the trickster, they would have their own powder, they said to one another. He failed them by being greedy. Now they must ask the Bannocks for gunpowder and humble themselves. Many warriors admired the Mule Man turning their trick around on them. They thought it a good trick and rode on, their anger at Mule Man shifted to Swooping Hawk.

~~~~~~

The Bannocks refused to act as forgiving and grew angry instead. They looked forward to their annual harvest of salmon. The Mormons took too many, leaving little for the Bannocks. The Mormons didn't share with the Bannocks, but shared with the Mule Man. They wanted to punish the Mormons, but first they would take gunpowder from the Mule Man before he rode south.

Blackie had told Pascal earlier, *The Redmen watch us, even when we don't know it.*

From their observations, the Bannocks understood Pascal favored Little Wolf.

~~~~~~

Blackie scouted their back trail the next morning after the team departed from the arroyo where they'd spent the night without fires. Unsure of the resolution with the Shoshone, Antonio and Renaldo rode point while Nachi and Benito rode on opposite flanks. Mounted, the team planned to swing north, returning along the path used to enter the area, taking them to the Snake.

He sat on his horse atop a stone shelf beside the trickling Birch Creek, upstream from where they camped in haste last evening. The high desert had little vegetation except for sagebrush in late bloom and edged by clumps of blue-bunch grass and wheatgrass. The sage-covered plateau descended to a level where moisture infiltrated from Birch Creek and supported grasses growing along its edges. Sage could root on the rocky plateau, but grasses could not.

A soft breeze shifted, carrying the strong scent

of sage. *Something moves higher on the plateau, spreading the scent of sage.* Blackie reined his horse east to follow the mule train.

Downstream, a dozen Bannocks rode from the arroyo where Pascal and the team had camped overnight. They spread across the stream's shallow valley from side to side.

Blackie might've tried riding south across the plateau, but the sage scent warned they waited on the plateau. He eased his 1851 Colt Navy revolver from his belly holster before pointing the muzzle skyward to fire two quick shots. A warning to Pascal and the team of trouble.

He stepped down and shucked his coat, rifle, pistol in its holster, water skin, and possibles-bag into a pile on the ground. As he straightened to stand tall, Blackie yanked loose his Green River knife in his right and tomahawk in his left. He called in Shoshone, "Come and take me."

The leader barked a laugh, pointing an old flintlock Kentucky rifle at Blackie, he said in the Shoshone language, "The Little Wolf challenges us."

"It's not a challenge. You didn't bring enough men," Blackie answered in Shoshone.

"My little brother, Tahgee, could kill you by himself," the warrior said, as he signaled his riders to surround Blackie.

"I challenge you to a fight to the death. If I win, I ride away."

"It is not your day to die," the Bannock leader said. "If the Mule Man likes to trade, we will trade *you* for three kegs of powder." He raised a thumb and two fingers. "I offer you another trade—submit without a fight—I will break your legs after we capture you."

Blackie understood he couldn't fight them, but it galled him to surrender after the threat.

The Bannock warriors gathered his weapons and removed the saddlebags, rope, and herding whip before signaling him to remount. Once remounted, they placed a two-inch thick stick behind his back and through his elbows' crook before tying the elbows to the stick, which left his hands free to hold the reins, but limited the reach of his hands.

"Don't fall," the Bannock leader said, and laughed with his men. They spoke between them.

He listened to their words, which sounded almost like the Ute language they used when trading near Pagosa last season. It helped him learn pieces of their language. The leader's nickname sounded like "Rai-ze-won," but he didn't know what it meant.

"Mule Man did not wait for you," Rai-ze-won said. "We will follow and greet them in the morning along the Camas." He waved and the warriors trotted downstream toward the sinks.

The Bannocks stopped two hours later along Birch Creek before it fell into the sinks.

After some dismounted to drink from the Birch, Blackie said, "*Pah,*" the Ute word for water.

"If you were our prisoner, and not for trade, I would put you under my horse and force you to drink its piss for your thirst," Rai-ze-won said, much to the amusement of his warriors.

This Bannocks clan lived and fought beside the Lemhi Shoshone and most understood and spoke one another's languages. Blackie figured them from the Yambadika clan, "root eaters" like the Lemhi, whose food source depended upon camas roots growing in the freshwater bogs along the Snake and Camas before it disappeared in the sinks. Other Shoshone and Bannocks clans spoke of "root eaters" as less than true warriors because they tended the bogs and cultivated the camas for their roots like farmers. These clans' winter sustenance depended upon smoke-dried salmon and camas bulbs, which explained their anger with the Mormons for hogging the salmon harvest and blocking easy access across Lemhi Pass to the camas fields east in the bog.

Pascal kept a published version of the Lewis & Clark Journals at the Rancho in Zaragoza. Blackie had read it as one of Pascal's few books in English. On this season's journey, he grew fascinated by riding across the same areas as the great explorers, and by meeting Sacajawea's clan. He admitted to being less impressed with meeting her grandson, Phillippe.

Lewis and Clark reported they ate camas root, which they said reminded them of southern yams when baked in a fire's coals and tasted sweeter than traditional yams. Unfortunately, the camas root digested rapidly in the gut, which resulted in loud farts, stomach cramps, and the "trots" among the hunger-weakened explorers. After the men recovered from their first bout of the trots, they grew fond of camas roots with their meals. Clark warned the men not to harvest the roots on their own because the white men didn't know how to tell the purple camas from the poisonous variety, known as a white camas.

The Bannocks rode north of the sinks and Mud Lake before crossing the north end of Camas Creek to camp for the night. While the warriors rested and ate their provisions, Rai-ze-won searched in Blackie's possibles-bag. He retrieved a soft leather pouch containing pemmican and dried elk strips. The pouch had three kraft-paper twists inside with the food.

"What are these?" Rai-ze-won asked, holding three paper twists in one hand.

"Those are spices. The fat one is salt. The other two, ground pepper, a spice to flavor meat."

"I will keep the salt," he said while opening one of the other twists. He raised his hand to his nose and sniffed the spice. He drew his head away and snorted twice. "You put this on meat?" He dropped the twists in the pemmican pouch and tossed it on Blackie's lap with his waterskin.

His roped elbows left his hands free to grab the elk strips and a roll of pemmican. He didn't know how long he'd be held captive and ate enough to take the edge from his hunger, but he left half for the next day. The stick behind his back forced him to lie on his side, raising the waterskin to squirt water into his mouth.

If they intend to raid Pascal tonight, they are taking their time about it. Blackie studied the raiders sitting in two groups, talking and laughing. He rolled on his side and fell asleep.

In the early morning, Rai-ze-won kicked Blackie hard in the rump to rouse him. "The Mule Man has a fire in his camp. They move around like they plan to leave without you."

"It is a rule. Don't lose good men trying to rescue one dumb enough to get captured," Blackie said in Shoshone, which these Bannocks understood.

Rai-ze-won nodded. "Will he leave you, or trade?"

"He is a trader. He will listen to a trade offer," Blackie said. "Fire a shot to alert them and make trade sign for a parley."

"Who in your camp speaks our language?"

"Me. Pascal speaks French like the old fur-trappers and he's good with trade signs."

Rai-ze-won gazed into the brightening eastern sky for two minutes. "I will take you and Snow Weasel to the trade. If you make trouble or try to escape, he will shoot you."

Blackie nodded.

Two Bannocks boosted him into the saddle while the others mounted. They rode for twenty minutes toward the Snake where it turned south after leaving the Shining Mountains. In the distance, a Bannock fired a shot to attract Pascal's attention as the sun brightened the horizon.

Chapter 15

September 1857

Pascal and Antonio rode to meet Rai-ze-won, Blackie, and Snow Weasel for a trade parley.

"I'm surprised he's not muzzled," Pascal said in French. "He gets mouthy when not fed."

Blackie translated Pascal's words from French to Shoshone.

"He is a lamb, not a wolf," Rai-ze-won said. "I will trade him to you for three kegs of gunpowder." Blackie translated Rai-ze-won's Shoshone words into French.

"I would trade with you, but I carry only one keg. I cached extra powder at Fort Hall before we rode this way. I will need ten days to ride to Fort Hall and return with more powder for you."

Blackie translated Pascal's words.

Rai-ze-won waved his rifle in anger. "You came here with only one keg? Are you a fool?"

Pascal shrugged as only a Frenchman can, with shifting his posture up and down in concert with raising his arms and hands in the air while forming a wrinkled grin. "We are traders, not fighters or hunters who need gunpowder. I do not carry things we do not need or cannot sell."

"You could sell all the powder your mules could

carry if you traded with the Bannocks and the Shoshone."

"If I sold powder to you, the Blackfoot and the Crow would attack me for aiding you. Will you protect me from the Blackfoot, or would you have me sell powder to your enemy?" Pascal held his palms forward in appeal.

"Traders speak with split tongue saying one thing but meaning another. I cannot wait ten days. The Mormons are stealing our fish and taking the harvest south without sharing."

"I will send this man," Pascal pointed to Antonio, "with two horses riding for Fort Hall without waiting for the mule train. Alone, he needs four days to reach Fort Hall and return. Bring the little wolf here in four days and I will trade you three kegs of gunpowder."

"If we must wait, return with five kegs of powder," Rei-ze-won shouted. "With fresh powder, we will need lead shot. Bring five bars of lead."

Pascal growled, glaring at Blackie with a face pinched in anger while he shook his fist at Blackie. Then Pascal's shoulders sagged in submission as he nodded to Rai-ze-won.

After Blackie finished translating, Rai-ze-won added, "By sundown in four days, or I will roast your favored one on a fire for you to listen to his screams."

Pascal scowled at the translation and nodded as he reined his horse around to ride away.

Blackie called in Spanish, "Go with haste. I will meet you at Fort Hall in two weeks or in heaven.

Via con dios, padre."

Rai-ze-won swung his rifle, knocking Blackie from the horse after Pascal and Antonio rode away. "What did you say to him? Tell me!"

"I told him to go in haste, as fast as he can to Fort Hall," Blackie said in Shoshone. "I prayed to see him again. *Via con dios* means let the great spirit, Manitou, guide you." He suspected Snow Weasel understood French, and his secondary role, after shooting him if he attempted to escape, became to tell Rei-ze-won if Blackie had translated accurately.

Rai-ze-won reined his horse around to face the warriors waiting 100 yards away and raised his rifle above his head, screaming a war cry.

The Bannocks returned to Camas Creek to wait for Pascal's expected return.

~~~~~~

At Camas Creek, Rai-ze-won spoke with different warriors before they rode away. He prowled the small camp. A warrior sent away yesterday returned, and his news angered Rai-ze-won. The Mormons moved wagonloads of salmon south. Snow Weasel sat near Blackie. In an hour, a warrior returned with a deer from hunting along Warm Spring Creek, a snow melt stream leading to a hot spring at the base of Bitterroot Mountain's southern end. It represented the closest source of green fescue for grazing game to feed. The Bannocks started a fire and settled into a camp routine before skinning and roasting the deer.

The next morning, Rai-ze-won moved his group northeast along the Camas into a ravine carved by the small stream tricking sweet water, unlike the bitter water at the hot springs west across the lava dome. In the ravine, a line of stunted trees grew beside the stream and provided firewood. It also kept them from view if local Shoshone came to work in the camas fields.

Snow Weasel decided to make Blackie work and untied the stick behind his elbows. Rai-ze-won didn't like the idea but agreed after Snow Weasel looped a braided rawhide cord around Blackie's neck. Once he collected a pile of downed deadwood, Weasel tied the cord to a dead tree leaving Blackie in the sun while the Bannocks rested in the cool shade.

I'm bored and tired of sitting on my butt doing nothing, and if I'm bored out of my mind, then the Bannocks must be, too. I must keep my mouth shut and act like a beaten dog if I want to avoid being the target of their pent-up anger. I can't afford to get injured if I want to escape tonight or tomorrow at the latest. I need to come up with an excuse for them not to tie the heavy stick behind my elbows tonight. I won't be able to escape tied to it.

Weasel ordered Blackie to wash and brush his horse in the afternoon, whacking with the stick, and pointing as if to say, "Missed a spot." Other warriors joined in the amusement, ordering Blackie to wash and brush their horses, which gave them an excuse to whack him.

As evening drew near, Rai-ze-won ordered him to stoke the fire to cook the remainder of the deer and bake a half-dozen camas bulbs for their meal. With other warriors away on errands, only six Bannocks remained in the camp. Blackie avoided eating the baked camas bulbs.

Blackie glimpsed Rai-ze-won cleaning the Colt Navy pistol and practicing with its action. He also noticed the Bannock leader carried the Sharps in place of his old Hawken. Even if Pascal returned, Rai-ze-won had no intention of honoring the deal. His behavior showed Pascal and Blackie wouldn't survive the planned exchange. Rai-ze-won suffered from the same split-tongue he had accused the whites of having. *I'll need a hell of a trick to escape from them.*

He glanced at Weasel. "I need you to cut the deer's legs for roasting," and made a slicing motion along the deer's hip and hind quarter.

Snow Weasel rummaged in his parfleche, the Redman's version of a possibles-bag, before he tossed Blackie a broken knife without a pointed tip and only two inches of sharpened blade. "Return it after our meal is cooked. You eat what remains."

Blackie pointed at the woodpile away the fire. "I need more firewood."

Snow Weasel waved a hand, signaling "away," but he rose, rifle at the ready.

Blackie slumped his shoulders and shuffled his feet, keeping in his beaten-dog pose while he gathered a large armful of wood from his earlier collection and returned to the fire.

Rai-ze-won called, "Do not use your spice on our meat. Its smell made my nose burn."

He nodded. "I will not use it," he said in Shoshone.

While cooking their evening meal, he listened as Rai-ze-won assigned a warrior to watch the horses and be alert for riders. The lava field extended northeast to southwest over a large dome, or hump, between where Birch Creek disappeared into the sinks at the dome's western edge and the camas bog where Camas Creek ended at the dome's northern edge. Although dry this time of the season, Beaver Creek's streambed ran due south from a saddle across the wall of mountains at the volcanic basin's north end before emptying into the camas bog. A low, flat-topped butte lay between the Birch Creek and the lava dome, and another butte rose east of the camas field.

From low in the ravine, Blackie couldn't survey the area, but recalled the lava field from the team's ride leaving the Snake River. He had observed two tall volcanic cones at the Snake River's northernmost point, forcing it to turn south toward Fort Hall. He'd scouted the lava field north from the Snake on their way to Birch Creek to locate the sand dunes, which indicated for the mule train to change course to due west and ride between the buttes to reach where he sat.

If he followed such a route to escape east, he'd be exposed on the lava field's hard surface without vegetation for cover. They had no need to track him across the solid rock—he'd have to make twenty miles to run from sight by morning. If he ran west, it sent him deeper into Bannock territory, and south led him into the sinks at night. He must run north, opposite of where they'd expect him to try to escape.

Created by snowmelt floodwater, Beaver Creek ran due south without the loops and twists of the Camas. It should allow him to run a long distance while hidden within its dry streambed. Two hours of running ought to place him ten miles north of where he now sat. He needed to judge time by using the stars, if it's not cloudy.

At the northernmost point, if he ran due east across the lava fields for four hours, he should be north of the sand dunes by sunrise. He must run far enough east to find shelter or he'd be visible on the barren lava field in daylight. He'd need a full waterskin for such a trek. There'd be no ground water until he reached the Snake, where it turned south at the volcanic cones.

Two, maybe three days to walk past the dunes, another day south to the Snake, and such a route leaves me five or six days walking along the Snake to reach Fort Hall. I can walk such a distance with ease. He snorted out loud. *All I need to do is escape from Rai-ze-won.*

Rai-ze-won must have told his warriors of his deceitful plan for they treated Blackie with contempt and whacked him with sticks often, ordering him to bring them more food or fill their waterskins. The chore of filling waterskins gave him the opportunity to use the broken knife to score the bottom of all their skins but one. He hoped the pressure of the water in the skin would weaken the skin, causing it to leak. He didn't score the largest skin, belonging to the youngest, who until Blackie came along had been their worker doing the tasks Blackie now performed.

He gathered their scraps to bury in the stream bank, eating any meat he found and gnawing on the bones. They'd let the cook fire burn low with bright coals, preparing to bank it before setting a night guard when they slept. Until then, they sat swapping stories and making jokes with one another.

Blackie asked Rai-ze-won, "Did Swooping Hawk tell you how the Mule Man used magic to change their black powder into white?"

"Stories to scare old women and children," Rai-ze-won barked. "They acted like fools to believe it happened." He waved a hand as if pushing away.

"If he had magic," Weasel asked, "why didn't he free you when we parleyed?"

"Magic words don't work much in the sunlight," Blackie said. "They are dark spirits and their secrets work best in the night."

"Magic words?" Rai-ze-won roared, throwing a stick at him. "You think us fools who are swayed by tricks? Say a magic word to me and make a magic happen before us."

"I will say the magic word, and I will disappear." Blackie leaped high like a dancer and swooped low with his arms extended while warbling a sharp cry. In his next low swooping turn, he tossed a kraft-paper twist into the fire containing gunpowder and a copper percussion cap before he yelled, "Abracadabra."

He swooped around in a turn ready to leap across the fire, but *nothing happened.*

The Bannocks erupted into laughter.

"You fool," Rai-ze-won shouted, as the percussion cap cracked a loud "pop" followed by the powder igniting with a loud *poof*, blowing ash and embers into a rising, spreading cloud.

Blackie leapt through the cloud as Rai-ze-won fired a shot from the confiscated Sharps. With his left hand, he flung the powdered black pepper in the Bannocks' faces before he struck the youngest brave on the temple with the butt of the broken knife. He grabbed the waterskin from the stunned youth's shoulder and freed the braided leather thong from his neck.

With the fire blown out, night's curtain fell. Blackie ran south, downstream in the Camas to the first turn east. He climbed a rocky bank when someone grabbed his leg, pulling him down. Scrambling to keep from falling, he grabbed a large rock, but it pulled loose in his hand.

Weasel swiped with his knife, but in sliding down the bank, he too lost his footing.

Blackie slid under the knife's swipe before being stopped by Weasel's leg. Slamming the rock at the nearest target, Blackie smashed the warrior's kneecap. Weasel screamed and dropped low to grab his knee. The warrior's head became the next target. Blackie struck Weasel, ending his howl, but not soon enough. Loud whoops sounded upstream—the Bannocks hunted him.

He grabbed the fallen Weasel, searching for a weapon or waterskin, when the knife's butt thumped against his foot as it fell from Weasel's dead hand. Blackie grabbed it from the ground and vaulted to the bank's top. With a real weapon and carrying a waterskin, he ran west for the camas bogs, hoping to discover Beaver Creek along the way.

Instinct slowed him from a running stride. He skidded, sliding, and dropped six feet into the Beaver's dry streambed. The thuds of a galloping horse passed to his south before it splashed. *I hope he found a quicksand sink.* He shifted upstream and stretched his stride into a ground-eating run. In a level stretch, he located the north star, fixing bright stars in rotation to track time. He hugged the streambed's east bank when thundering hoofs alerted him to a horse galloping north atop the bank, heading upstream. In the eastern distance, faint calls came between the riders.

When the star's rotation signaled two hours, he stopped running to listen, and gulped three long swigs of water from his skin. His task now became to cross twenty-plus miles of the barren lava dome before sunrise. If clever, Rai-ze-won would station men to sit quietly with their horses at intervals around their camp site. After eyes adapt to the dark, it's surprising how much a man sees in the starlight on these barren rocks. Movement catches the eye, even in the dark.

A steady pace, learned from his daily runs, becomes more useful than fast spurts and rests. Thrilled to have escaped, he let his mind open to absorb the night sounds and become attuned to what flowed around him. An hour at a steady trot soon approached two as he learned to take a sip from his waterskin without breaking stride. The lava dome's light grey surface reflected little, but it signaled subtle shifts in the surface to prevent falls, or worse, twisting an ankle or knee.

The chase wouldn't be done in a night, and he needed to conserve his strength to last another week, or more. He must not grow too excited about escaping only to let them trap and capture him again. The hunter had become the hunted. He must think like his prey and not be where the Bannocks expected to find him. *Hunger—water and food—are the controlling factors. If they lay in wait at the water holes, or on the paths to water, I'll be captured again. They know this area better than I. All they need do is keep me from reaching the Snake River.*

A half-hour after his third rest, he encountered a sand dune. He couldn't be sure in the night, but these dunes didn't stretch east for miles, as he'd expected. The southern edge curled east, and he shifted to follow it. In another half-hour, the dunes' eastern edge appeared. When he came to the end he gazed south into the dark for several minutes. Unless his eyes fooled him, a white band lay south from here another three miles. *I must have been too excited about running free and ran faster than usual to get this far north. Do I turn south into the middle of the greater sand dunes before I turn east or continue east until sunrise?*

If Rai-ze-won stations watchers at the farthest point to keep him from the Snake, the east end of the great sand dune would be his limit. *I'll continue east on this line, and rest at sunrise, when I become the watcher, not the prey.*

The sky brightened in another hour, but the sun failed to rise above the Shining Mountains for almost two hours, and the stars had long since winked out, no longer letting him mark time.

He found a rock cleft whose shadow promised two hours of sleep before the sun fell upon him. Rest, sleep, and eat in two hours before spending the day as a watcher to discover who rode this way. He'd continue east tonight, searching for Henry's Fork, which emptied into the Snake.

Pascal said it received its name from one of the first fur-trappers. Andrew Henry formed the Rocky Mountain Fur Company to compete with American Fur, which competed with the Hudson Bay Company from Canada, while French Canadians poached deep into U.S. territory.

"You may think me Methuselah," Pascal said, "but fur-trappers prowled this land forty or more years ago, soon after Lewis and Clark returned in 1806. Henry lived in Missouri. He outfitted several expeditions by longboat up the Missouri River to the Yellowstone River, due north from here. Henry claimed he built the first 'fort' in 1810 between the Camas and Henry's Fork when this area teemed with beaver. It's said he made a good profit the first few years, but after the Hugh Glass affair, and constant battles with the Blackfoot, he left it to younger men to continue. I told you Jim Bridger was a youngster with Glass when his terrible trial occurred."

Pascal and his stories. Blackie chuckled aloud.

Before midday, Blackie glimpsed movement at the great dune's eastern end, south of him. The image, or mirage, appeared like a mounted rider, but he failed to gain a clear view across two miles through ripples of heat rising from the dunes. It might have been an elk, for its size, but an elk wouldn't wander around the lava beds next to barren sand dunes in the middle of the day. He'd have wagered his waterskin the moving speck represented a Bannock warrior watching for him. Blackie planned to rest and walk east tonight until he found Henry's Fork, letting the warrior cook his brains all day while watching the sand dunes west of there.

After dark, Blackie trotted east for two hours before clouds rolled in overnight and he lost his starry compass. The cloudy overcast hid the false dawn before Blackie reached Henry's Fork.

Henry's Fork ran swift and clear to the southeast. Even though tired, he eased into the Henry to catch a trout or two for breakfast. He searched upstream for gentle falls followed by a slower pool. In five minutes, he found a promising pool with a copse of birch and larch extending to the western bank. He caught three trout in five minutes before he exited the stream to light a small fire hidden in the copse's greenery. The copse had plenty of downed wood to use with his flint striker, starting a fire in a tuff of rotted wood and dry bark. He roasted the fish on green sticks instead of waiting for coals and bake them in mud as Phillippe had done. When he finished two trout, he licked his fingers clean and saved the other one for when he awoke. With his waterskin, he washed away the fire's remains and tossed dried grass and downed wood atop to cover the spot before he built a grassy bower in the brush to hide while he slept. His hunger sated, he knew he'd fall into deep sleep and must be well-hidden to rest for four hours.

Before he fell asleep, he decided to rest beside Henry's Fork for the night, leaving the next morning. He'd scout the area this afternoon to make sure he didn't have unexpected neighbors. Fort Hall lay five or six days' walk south alongside the Snake. Before he fell asleep, he thought, *That's the easy part.*

Chapter 16

September 1857

A rifle shot roused Blackie from a deep slumber. He glanced about, judging the time a bit past midday. The shot came from upstream as best as he could piece together the sound from his memory. He eased from the bower, moving slow and cautious as not to spook a bird or game into giving away his location, easing away from the stream to better judge his surroundings in the daylight. A man whooped upstream and laughter carried on the breeze flowing along the stream.

He crept up the bank to trees marking the high-water line in the snowmelt's spring floods. With a view of the bottom lands' meadow below, his gaze searched between the trees and the Henry as he crawled upstream. In a horseshoe loop of the Henry, he glimpsed them.

A lad in a gully guarded three horses as he sat his mount. In the meadow, Bannock warriors taunted a wounded man and harassed two women, tearing their clothes. While Blackie eased lower on the hillside, the lad dismounted and tied the horses in place as if he planned to join their sport. The Bannock men intended to enjoy an evening of torment and death. Those under attack had dressed in the sun-bleached white garments of the Absaroka, called the Crow by the whites.

Blackie understood the lad's temptation as he watched one woman stripped naked and mounted roughly while her wounded man watched, disgracing both. A rock to the head worked before, and his swift blow dropped the lad without a sound. To his surprise, and delight, the lad carried a fine bow and a quiver with ten arrows, a bit light for a man's arms, but serviceable.

Alone and without firearms, he stood no chance against three Bannock warriors using only a knife and a light bow. He rushed to set up a diversion while the men enjoyed the sport of chasing two naked women around the meadow. Time worked against him. He grabbed two braided rawhide ropes from the Bannock's horses.

An arrow plunked into the chest of a naked warrior standing over a woman on the ground before Blackie stood to wave with one hand and the other as he called in Shoshone, "They are here." As he waved each hand, he yanked a rawhide rope, which released a peg holding a bent over sapling. Each sapling held a three-foot long log, six inches in diameter. When released, the sapling tossed the log forward to appear like a man crawled forward in the grass. At opposite ends of the meadow, the objects rolling in the grass beside waving saplings, attracted the warriors' gaze in a diversion and allowed Blackie to run closer and loose another arrow.

The trick worked for a moment when the two Bannocks' gaze sought to find who joined the attack. He aimed his second arrow at the Bannock to his left. It struck home, killing the second warrior as the last Bannock's rifle shot missed. The woman on the ground helped by kicking the third warrior as he stood to shoot at Blackie when he loosed the second arrow. The last warrior didn't have time to reload his cap-n-ball rifle as Blackie charged, stolen knife at the ready. The Bannock swung his rifle by the barrel like a club waist high, expecting to swat Blackie aside.

Blackie slid on the grass under the rifle's swinging arc and through the Bannock's legs as he did with Luke last season. This time, Blackie's knife slit open the warrior's bare inner thigh from groin to knee, to leave blood pulsing. The warrior spun around as Blackie scrambled to his feet, dancing to one side. The last Bannock raised his empty rifle above his head preparing to club his opponent on the head, but the rifle grew heavier each second until Blackie pushed the Bannock over backwards—he'd bled dry. Blackie failed to recognize him as one from Rei-ze-won's raiding party, but who knew how many Bannock hunted him.

A weeping woman crouched on the ground staring at Blackie for a moment before she turned away to hide her naked body.

He grabbed a woven blanket from the ground to wrap around the crying woman's shoulders before he helped her stand. After guiding her to the wounded man, he shifted to seek the other woman. When he came close to the other, she screamed, "Stay away from me," in Arapaho.

"I mean you no harm," he said in a soft voice, speaking in Arapaho. Only after he came close did he realize she sheltered two children, a girl of ten and a boy a few years younger. If captured, the girl would have received the same brutal treatment as the women before becoming a slave, and the boy, if lucky, integrated into the tribe to become a Bannock warrior.

"The wounded man needs help. Can you help me speak with him?" Blackie asked her.

"Turn away. Go to him. I will help after I dress." She turned to hide her naked body.

After a flash from memory of a naked Morning Star in Black Kettle's camp, he stared at her before moving away. Upon returning to the injured man, Blackie dropped to a knee beside the wounded man who blinked twice and muttered a word before a long sigh rattled in his lungs and escaped from his throat.

He glanced at the first woman with the blanket around her shoulders. He spoke in Arapaho because the woman with children spoke it. "I sorrow with your man's death."

She nodded but said nothing as she took the dead man's hand.

"Did you ride with more of your people?" Blackie asked. "Are they nearby to help?"

She shook her head before wailing and laying her head on his chest.

He glanced at the second woman as she approached. "What name may I call you?"

"I am Fawn Hiding in the Chokeberry of the White Sage People. You may call me Fawn."

"Are other of your people with you?" he asked.

She shook her head as she comforted the first woman who appeared not to speak Arapaho.

With the blanket over her shoulders, the first woman continued to moan and wipe her face with dirt and cut hanks of her hair with the warrior's knife.

"I need two blankets to wrap him for his long sleep." Blackie said to Fawn, "Do you want to cover him with his white robe before I wrap him in blankets?"

After Fawn spoke to the first woman, she nodded, and rose to search through their goods, scattered in disarray by the Bannock. "We will prepare him in his robe," Fawn said. "We didn't bring his finest robe."

While the first woman hunted blankets, he turned to Fawn who took a knife to her hair. "I am Black Wolf. What is her name? You know we must leave here before others find us."

"Her name is Pretty Eyes. She was Mountain Elk's first wife. She didn't want him to come with me or allow me to return to my people. She will blame me for his death, and she is right," Fawn said as she cut another hank of hair.

Pretty Eyes returned, dressed, and carrying blankets. He took the blankets. "We don't have time to build a bier for your man in the traditional

Absaroka manner. Do you want to select a tall tree to serve as an altar to keep animals from his resting place?"

With a glance at Fawn, Blackie said, "I know you want to honor your man with a period of mourning, but we must move away from the dead Bannocks if their people hunt for them."

Pretty Eyes wandered away wailing in a rhythmic fashion.

"I escaped from the Bannocks," he said in Arapaho. "I've walked far. I'm hungry. Have you any food? Can one prepare meat to eat while the other prepares your man for his sleep?"

"I fed what food remained to my children. I told them to hide. I didn't want them to watch what the whites or Bannock do to women. They wanted my daughter. I fought them to save her." Fawn glared at him, knife in hand. "I will not let you have her, either."

"When a boy, your daughter's age, the Comanche killed my father and took my mother and sisters in the way the Bannocks took you. I hid and cried, doing nothing to help my family. I refuse to take a woman in such a cruel way. Your daughter is safe from me."

She snorted aloud. "I saw your wolf's eyes gaze at my naked body. I saw your pants bulge."

"Yes, I am a man stirred by a beautiful woman's naked body, but I do not take a woman in anger or unbidden. Right now, we need food, and we must leave this area before dark."

"Hunting is the man's job. I will cook what you bring." Her lips formed a straight line.

They stared at one another. Blackie broke the stare, muttering, *"Cherchez la femme."*

"I'll catch fish after I wash. You will cook the fish I catch. I will place your man in a tree."

Pretty Eyes walked close and nodded as she pointed into the grove.

"You've found a tree?" he asked. She pointed again. He said, "Show me."

While Pretty Eyes showed him the tree, Fawn covered her man with his white robe before she stitched a thong to hold the blankets around their man's body in their custom. Pretty Eyes returned to help Fawn prepare the body. The women worked on the body, chanting, and crying.

Blackie found a quiet pool below a series of rapids. In thirty minutes, he caught six fat trout. He gutted them away from the stream banks in the trees and ran a leather thong in their mouths before he returned. He gave Fawn the fish. "Call your children home. I am no threat to them."

The women had worked on their dresses in his absence. They wore tan buckskin dresses, stitched with thin thongs made from cleaned and dried animal sinew. The women had repaired ripped seams, and donned long sleeve shirts to cover the gaps in the stitching. Both wore knee-high leggings and buckskin moccasins with a Bannock belt and knife at their waist.

Blackie dragged the Bannock bodies downstream with one of their horses. He rummaged through their parfleches to gather items of value. He kept an iron, trade tomahawk, a small powder horn with a measuring cup lid, and seven .54-caliber balls. The leader carried a well-used U.S. Army issue1841 Mississippi cap-n-ball muzzle-loader from the Mexican-American War.

After he hid the Bannock bodies, he sat cross-legged by the fire to eat. Fawn's children sat behind her, devouring the fresh-cooked trout.

"What are their names?" he asked.

"Why do you need their names?" Fawn asked, her face twisted into an angry mask.

"I escaped from the Bannocks two days west of here. The Bannocks are searching for me. Others may find us. If we are chased, I need your children to do as I ask for their safety. I will call them 'girl' and 'boy' in Arapaho. They must do as I ask if we are attacked."

The boy dressed in hand-rubbed smooth buckskin, wearing trousers with slits for a thong drawstring, a long-sleeved shirt reaching past his butt, leggings below the knee, and plain moccasins. He carried a buffalo hide vest with the hair on it. The Absaroka didn't believe in cutting their hair. The boy wore a strap around his forehead to keep the hair from getting in his face and tied the long hair with a thong at the neck's nape.

"Do not order my children about," Fawn shouted. "They are not your slaves."

"No, but thanks to me, they are not Bannock slaves, or dead."

Mountain Elk's family stood in silence with tears flowing as they watched Blackie place the Absaroka warrior's body in a tree roost. He used the Bannock's trade tomahawk to fell and trim five saplings eight feet long, tying them in place between two adjacent forks in the tree using one of the Bannock's leather thongs from creating the distraction, and, with the other thong, tied the blanket-wrapped body atop the saplings. The man's feet faced east in Absaroka tradition. He gave the family fifteen minutes of grief and wailing before he spoke.

"We must ride. We need to move faster than we can walk. Since I found no horses, I assume your family walked as the Absaroka often do, planning to *find* horses on your return. The Bannock gave us four horses. I want to reach the Snake by this time tomorrow."

"Where are you taking us?" Fawn asked, as she stepped away from him with arms crossed.

"You asked a fair question," Blackie answered. "Can you find the trail across the northern mountains and return to the Absaroka alone?" He pointed at the mountains in the distant north.

The two women glanced at one another before they shook their heads.

"I scout for a mule train bound for Fort Laramie. It's a fourteen-day journey to the Fort from here. In the middle, there is no water for three days. If you follow the Oregon Trail past South Pass, the Mountain Arapaho live north into the Wind River. The trail across this area has been picked bare of firewood and game. If you kill two elk, make their stomachs into waterskins, and cook the meat to preserve it, you can reach the South Pass by following the Trail east."

"You will ride away and leave us alone on the Snake?" Fawn said tight-lipped, her arms crossed over her chest. "How does such a thing help us?"

"I helped you more than I should have. I could have stolen the Bannock horses and ridden away while you and your daughter amused them. I killed the Bannocks to stop them from hurting you. You have been nothing but angry at me. I didn't know the Bannock rode nearby until they shot your man. I'm not responsible for his death. I will carry you from harm's way to the Snake."

"It doesn't help us. I must get to my people, the Arapaho in Wind River mountains." She took his hand in hers. "I will lay—." She stopped when Blackie placed a finger on her lips.

"I am unworthy of such an offer from an honorable woman of the Absaroka," Blackie said. "I am bound to Mule Man for work. He does not allow women and children on the mule train."

"Please. Anything. I'll do anything to find the Arapaho again," Fawn pleaded.

"What is it? What is so important a great warrior like Mountain Elk left his people to return you to your people? What words did you say to cause him to attempt such a journey alone?"

She turned away. The wind in the trees and the rapids failed to hide her crying. She faced him, wiping tears. "I will not see the snow fall. An evil spirit lives inside me, eating its way out."

He enclosed her in his long arms holding her tight while she buried her faced and sobbed.

"I loved Elk with all my heart," Fawn sobbed. "Pretty Eyes grew jealous of our love. I hate leaving my family behind with her, letting her raise my daughter."

"I'm surprised Elk would let you take his son," Blackie said.

"He didn't," she said. "He came along to bring his son home after I die. I want my mother to raise my daughter, not Pretty Eyes. I want her to know a loving grandmother, not raised by one who hated her mother and caused her father's death. Pretty Eyes would make her life miserable."

He glanced at the girl. *When she's grown, she'll rival Morning Star's beauty.* She wore a sun-bleached, pullover jumper reaching to her knees. It had beadwork and berry-stain patterns on the shoulders. Under it, she wore a hand-woven soft shirt, he guessed. Her leggings and moccasins lacked adornment. *If the Absaroka women are like the Cheyenne, they wear nothing under their long buckskin dresses. She'll be taller but fair-skinned like Fawn.*

"I will ask Pascal. We will wait on the Snake for his answer. We must ride."

Fawn released her embrace, and, in a moment, he released her as they parted.

"Do you and the children know how to ride?" Blackie asked.

"Better than you, white man," she said and laughed.

"Don't be clever. The Cheyenne taught me how to sit a horse."

She snorted aloud. "Sitting a horse is not how you are known, wolf-eyes. In the Absaroka camps, they laughed at tales of a wolf-eyed Cheyenne whose dragger frightened the buffalo."

He admired her spirit as he settled them on their mounts. Once ready, he led them into Henry's Creek to make it harder for others to follow where they rode. When the stream crossed atop the lava bed's edge, he led them west on the hard base for a mile before turning south.

Blackie called a rest break for the horses when they reached a swift-running stream, waving for the women to come close after they dismounted. He pointed to a pair of volcanic cones to the southwest. "Those hills mark where the Snake turns south to Fort Hall. Across from here is the place where I am to meet my people. If I send them a message to ride north and follow the Snake to where it leaves the Shining Mountains, they can join us at the gorge."

"Mountain Elk spoke of a trail south where the river splits the mountains," Fawn said. "There are two small rivers entering from the south. He planned to follow the second one south into a narrow valley. After the valley river turns east and then south like an elbow, climb the second mountain stream from the east to the top. Then—"

"Wait," Blackie interrupted. "If you know the

way, take the horses. Go without me."

"Six moons ago, I would have caught more fish and had them cooked before you left the creek," she said. "It's good we ride. I cannot walk as much as I did."

"Will you make it there?"

"It will be easier for us if you hunt for food and elk stomachs to carry water across to what whites call South Pass and north to the Wind River."

"I do this in memory of my lost sisters," Blackie said. "I failed to rescue them—I won't fail your daughter. Children should not suffer for their family's mistakes."

They reached the Snake before the sun touched the western mountains. He found a small copse of trees seventy yards from the water. Camping beside a river let others find you too easy.

The next day, he rode away to hunt before the first light, bringing a second horse to carry his harvest. He carried the Bannock lad's light bow and had recovered two arrows for a total of nine.

As the sky brightened, he dismounted and tied the horses. From his mount, he glimpsed a small island in the Snake appearing to hold a grassy meadow with deer grazing among a dozen small trees giving them shelter during the day. He crawled through the greasewood and bunch-grass brush beside the river and hid in a clump of small hackberry trees. He wanted to crawl closer, but he'd expose his movement in descending the bank. He decided to risk an arrow shot at the deer thirty yards away. He loosed his first arrow. It struck home in the chest of a medium-sized doe, which fell after running thirty-five feet. The others fled, swimming across the Snake.

Blackie waded the shallow river section closest to the bank to reach the island. He slit the doe's throat to bleed it before he dragged the doe across to the north bank. He field-dressed it, separated the hind legs at the knee joint to remove the scent glands, and turned it head down to drain while he returned to bring the horses to the river.

The sky brightened as he rode toward their camp with the doe's carcass limp across the other horse. On the western side of the Shining Mountains, they would not have sunlight for another hour. As he trotted along, ducks scattered from the Snake west of where they camped.

Bannocks? Blackie wondered. *I hope it's not the Bannocks.*

He dismounted and tied the horse to a chokeberry bush. After listening for three minutes, the only sound from the camp came from the children talking to one another. The camp hadn't been attacked yet, but who scared the ducks from the river? He scooted around the brush towards the river and glimpsed someone coming. He dropped low to catch the one walking toward him. In a minute, given the casual manner, he guessed it one of the women from his camp.

He rose from a squat, startling Fawn.

She gasped for a moment, "Quit trying to act like one of us—you will always be a white man. I will have a meal ready soon." She raised a thong strung with six trout.

"I have a doe for you to roast. While—" He grabbed her arm, yanking her to her knees.

"Two warriors coming from the river," he whispered in her ear. He held up the bow, pointing at her, and mimicking shoot it.

She stuck out her tongue and grabbed the bow as he slid the quiver from his shoulder for her. She nocked an arrow in a practiced smooth motion and crept into the brush like a panther.

Blackie glimpsed the movement of a warrior ahead of him and in two running steps, leapt on the man's back, his left hand over the Bannock's mouth and his right driving the knife into the heart from below the breastbone. His over-the-shoulder thrust allowed the blade tip to rise inside, ripping open the Bannock's heart. He rose, grabbing the dead man's rifle before continuing toward the camp. He didn't recognize the weapon. *It must be a French rifle the Hudson Bay people traded to the Redman for furs. I'll give it to Pascal, if we ever meet again.*

He froze in place as if an icicle had plunged into his heart.

Rei-ze-won held Fawn's naked daughter with a knife at her throat.

"You didn't think a white man could fool us and escape across land we hunt, did you?" He grabbed a handful of her hair lifting and stretching her neck while he wove his knife as though he sawed across her neck. "This one and her mother," he nodded at Pretty Eyes, "won't make up for losing the powder, but I'll stake you out to watch us use them. We will—"

An arrow zinged past the top of the girl's head, penetrating Rei-ze-won's throat above his breastbone, but his knife slid to slit her throat.

"Nooooo," Fawn screamed from behind Blackie.

Even his great leap wouldn't get him there in time to stop Rei-ze-won before his last gasp slit the girl's throat.

The man holding Pretty Eyes shifted to shoot Blackie, and in doing so, pushed her away— toward Rei-ze-won—where she lowered her shoulder to ram his back, knocking the knife hand aside. As he fell, the girl twisted away, shrieking as the dying man yanked a handful of her hair.

The last Bannock's bullet buzzed between Blackie and Fawn, singing like a bumblebee, as Blackie crouched to raise the stolen rifle to his shoulder. The French rifle fired true, knocking the last Bannock to the ground.

In a rage, Fawn raced across their small camp, slowing but a moment to grab Rei-ze-won's knife from the ground before plunging it into the downed Bannock, again and again, screaming incomprehensible words while she vented her fear and anger.

To avoid the wild swings of her knife, Blackie booted her hip, pushing her from the dead Bannock. "Care for your daughter," he said, "Look who tends her."

Pretty Eyes held the trembling girl, stroking her hair and crooning soft words.

"Ride my horse to the river and wash the blood away before greeting your children." When she sat in shock at what had occurred, Blackie scooped her into his arms, carrying her in five long strides to his horse and set her atop.

"Go to the river. Wash. I'll follow with your children." He swatted the horse's rump.

"Boy, find a blanket for your mother," he called as he strode to Pretty Eyes holding the girl. "Mother and child have been frightened by an evil spirit. They need to hold one another to seal their bond again." He laid a hand on Pretty Eyes' head, "She may never thank you, but we are in your debt for stopping the evil one. We honor you for being a true sister."

She nodded but when a horse whinnied, she glimpsed the doe astride the spare horse. She pointed to herself, "I cook," she said in Arapaho. Pointing toward the river, she said, "Wash."

In an hour, Blackie led the horse with Fawn and her daughter mounted while the boy strode beside him. The lad hung his head as they approached the camp.

With a hand on the lad's shoulder, Blackie said, "When younger, your size, the Comanche attacked and killed my father and mother, and I grew so frightened, I wet myself. Remember as you grow to a man, you knew fear as a child, but you did not wet yourself."

The lad held his head high and called to Pretty Eyes.

I don't know Absaroka, but I'd wager the boy

said, *'I'm hungry. When do we eat?'*

After she dismounted, Fawn and the girl stepped to Pretty Eyes. Fawn bowed, wringing her hands. Too far away to catch the words, Blackie made no effort to intrude. He did, however, slice the top layer of the doe's haunch cooking over a small fire. He left the fire to tend the horses.

Horses' hoofs pounded, charging into the camp from east and west.

A tenderfoot mistake, leaving none on guard while we ate. I hope I live to learn this lesson.

A warrior leapt from his horse, a stone-head war club raised to strike, but he leapt too late.

Blackie grabbed the war club hand and spun, letting the man's weight add to the momentum as he struck the ground. Blackie shifted, grabbing the war club when a passing horse butted him from his feet. As he tumbled, another rider's war club struck a glancing blow, and sunlight faded.

He awoke with his hands tied behind by leather thongs. He rolled aside and an Absaroka used a foot to push him flat again. Blackie glanced at the warriors, counting a dozen in view, which meant three or four more with the horses. He hoped to find them friends of Fawn.

As he gathered his wits, a rough, gravel-voiced man barked angry words at Fawn while she knelt in front of him in a submissive posture with her head bowed. Close by, with her head bowed, Pretty Eyes sat erect and cross-legged with an arm around each child.

Gravel-voice glanced at Blackie, barking a command. The warrior who'd held his foot on him yanked Blackie to his feet. He growled a question, but Blackie touched his mouth and spoke in French, "Great warrior, I do not speak your language."

Another man stepped forward, "Many Bears asked, 'Why do the Bannocks chase you?'"

"I serve the Mule Man. We traded with the mighty Absaroka last season when the grandson of Far Walking Woman scouted for the Mule Man. The Mule Man was a black robe. He wishes peace among all men, Red and White living in peace. He never trades in spirit water or weapons. He wants peace for all. The Bannocks broke a trade-truce to capture me, demanding Mule Man trade them all the gun powder and lead he carried in exchange for me alive. The Mule Man said he was not a hunter and carried little powder but cached more powder at Fort Hall. He said he'd return in four days with many kegs of powder, but he never intended to return."

"He would let you die?" the French speaker asked unbidden.

"It is a matter of honor. He would not trade powder to the Bannocks to let them attack the Absaroka. The Mule Man is sad white men have lied to the Redman. He is a holy man, a man of peace but not the leader of the white men, and the whites do not listen to his words of peace."

Many Bears spoke and the French speaker said, "Where is the Arapaho grandson?"

"The Mule Man wanted to save the cost of paying the Arapaho."

"He wants to know where he is today," the French speaker said.

"He is in Lemhi Pass with his grandmother's people," Blackie said.

Many Bears spoke many words. The French speaker said, "The Bannocks and the Lemhi made war on the Mormons. The white leader in the east will send many bluecoats. The Bannocks have made trouble for all. We ride north to protect our land from the bluecoats when they come."

"The Mule Man does not control the blue coats," Blackie said.

"Many Bears says he is angry with you. If you had not come this way, the Bannocks would not have ridden to find his brother."

"The wind blows a leaf from a tree. Where it falls, no man can tell," Blackie said.

"And still, his brother is dead, and his brother's children have no father."

"I alone avenged Mountain Elk. If not for me, his children would be Bannock slaves, or dead," Blackie said.

"Many Bears will think about what to do with you." He paused while Many Bears spoke. "If you escaped, how did you have weapons to fight when they attacked his brother?"

"I stole a knife when I escaped from the Bannocks. When I attacked those holding Mountain Elk, I gathered more weapons from the Bannocks as I killed them."

Many Bears grunted before he stood, marching to the women.

The Absaroka warriors made the fire larger and roasted the doe. They made no effort to feed him or give him water as he sat cross-legged. He studied their routine, noticing Many Bears had ordered scouts from the camp to prevent being surprised as Blackie had failed to do. Many Bears also spoke to the women separate from one another before he spoke to the children.

After an hour, Many Bears and the French speaker walked close, with the latter carrying a water skin. The French speaker spoke to the guard, who sliced the thong holding Blackie.

While Blackie stretched his arms and rubbed his wrists, the French speaker tossed the waterskin in his lap. He stood before taking a drink.

Many Bears spoke and the French speaker said, "The women say Mountain Elk killed a lone Bannock four days earlier. Two days past, Bannocks shot him from hiding while Elk walked south. They say you fought the Bannocks alone with a Bannock bow and knife. You lifted Mountain Elk to his resting place with honor and respect. I save my anger for the Bannocks."

Blackie nodded.

"Many Bears asks for you to sit and eat with him. He will speak of what to do with Mountain Elk's wives," the French speaker said.

"I would be honored to have Many Bears'

counsel," Blackie said.

As they sat, Pretty Eyes and Fawn served them roasted meat. Fawn interpreted Many Bears words into Arapaho. "A warrior said Mule Man traded with our people on the Green River where we used to rendezvous with the fur-trappers. They called you 'little man' for your size as a boy, now they call you 'tall man.' They believe your Cheyenne name is strong. It fits a warrior."

After she translated, she said, "I told him you earned your name by standing against five Pawnee, protecting Cheyenne women. I didn't have to tell him about the other name."

Blackie laughed and stood to remove the front shoulder from the roasting doe with a twist before he bit into it like a coyote eating a hen's leg.

Many Bears spoke and Fawn said, "Mountain Elk's son and Pretty Eyes will ride north with Many Bears. He will raise him like his own son to become an Absaroka man. If I did not have a sickness, he would carry us home, but he will honor Mountain Elk's agreement to return with my daughter to die with my people. He loved his brother. He is saddened by Elk's death, but he will not blame you."

"I am surprised he'd let your daughter go," Blackie said.

"Many Bears plans to punish the Bannocks and the Lemhi by stealing many women and horses to teach them to stay home and guard what they have."

"The whites have a saying, 'Don't poke a bear in

the ass,'" Blackie said.

Many Bears barked a laugh when she translated. He nodded, and Fawn translated, "True."

"Many Bears wants to know how you plan to cross the shining mountains," Fawn asked. "I told him the route Mountain Elk planned to follow."

"We have not ridden in this area. If a man can tell me a trail, I will follow his advice."

Many Bears called to the French speaker and another warrior, who strode to the fire and sat. After a discussion with Many Bears, the French speaker said, "My name is Sits Tall on Horse. I will lead you south into the pleasant valley as Fawn described and across the mountains to the Green River rendezvous gathering place."

"Thank Many Bears," Blackie said in French, "but I need to ride south to Fort Hall and gather the Mule Man, bringing him here to ride with us."

Sits Tall spoke with Many Bears and the second man before he said, "Snow will come if you wait too long. Fox in the Night will ride to Fort Hall and lead the Mule Man across the middle mountains to meet you in the pleasant valley below the Salt Mountains."

"The mules are slower than a man on a horse. We may wait many days for the Mule man."

"It will save ten days going across the mountains," Sits Tall said. "Fox will leave today. We will hunt for meat and leave in two days for the pleasant valley. Many Bears will wait with us."

"I am grateful for your help." Blackie nodded to Many Bears.

In two days, Many Bears departed with Pretty Eyes, Elk's son, and the other warriors.

Sits Tall led them to the Snake where they swam their horses across from the island. The Snake ran cold and swift, carrying them downstream before they reached the other side, soaked and chilled. The fall sun offered scant warmth.

Blackie rode alongside Fawn as her daughter buried her face in Fawn's blanket. "Will I ever learn your daughter's name?"

"She is still young and innocent of men's way. The Bannocks' attack frightened her. She didn't speak for several days. I expected to explain what men do to make babies in a loving way when her time comes. I didn't want her to learn it this way or from another woman."

"Is she too young to enter her moon?" Blackie asked.

Fawn scowled at him. "Do not speak of this in front of her. She is terrified and wakes in the night in fear of men attacking her like she witnessed with Pretty Eyes and me." She glanced away. "It's not your fault, but you represent large, strong men who have their way with women. She fears you. I have tried to explain, but in her fright on that day, you became her night terror."

Chapter 17

Late September 1857

Pascal and LaFleur hooted on sighting Blackie in a small camp above the stream along the bottom of the pleasant valley. Most of Pascal's team spoke enough French to welcome Sits Tall, but none spoke Arapaho save Blackie who informed Fawn of the occasion.

Pascal and LaFleur dismounted to hug Blackie and slap his back. LaFleur kissed his cheeks.

"You had us worried," Pascal said, shaking Blackie's arm. "People nearby reported many sightings of Bannocks north of the Snake. We thought you escaped, but feared they recaptured and killed you when you didn't appear." He spoke in Spanish for the cousins.

"Let's us speak in French so we include our guides in what we say," Blackie said.

"Of course." Pascal boomed his laugh. "I only speak *Anglais* to humor you."

Fox pointed to a mule deer on one of the spare mules. "We need to quarter the deer and roast it for our evening meal."

Sits Tall glanced at Fox, asking, "Ready to ride across the mountains tomorrow?"

"The mules find their own pace," Fox said. "It

243

may take them six or seven days to cross."

Sits Tall nodded at Blackie, "Will you be ready to ride tomorrow?"

Blackie glanced at Pascal, raising an eyebrow.

"They lazed six days at the Fort and grew soft." Pascal boomed his laugh again. "We'll ride at first light on the morrow."

With a wide grin, Blackie nodded to Sits Tall. "The Mule Man says we ride at first light."

Pascal and LaFleur led Blackie aside as the men settled in camp to enjoy their meal.

"How do you get entangled in such events?" Pascal asked as his brows furrowed.

Blackie reported escaping from the Bannocks and running north and then east to elude them, followed by fighting other Bannocks who killed Mountain Elk. "I never intended to carry her along," Blackie said. "I only wanted to keep the Bannocks from hurting her."

"And then you killed Rei-ze-won and more Bannocks." Pascal slapped a hand on his cheek.

"We had no choice by then but to fight for our lives. Fawn's arrow killed him."

"You say such as if it makes things better?" Pascal barked. "I doubt we'll trade with the Bannock or the Lemhi Shoshone again."

"Fawn's brother-in-law came after we killed the Bannocks at the Snake. I expected I'd be killed after they captured me. I think the Absaroka men wanted her away from their village. They believe she carries death. Many Bears sent the two scouts to make sure she doesn't return."

"I will admit they showed us a path across the mountains to here I never knew existed, but what will we do with a woman in our camp? An Arapaho woman no less."

"Tell the team the truth. She's dying and wants to go home to her mother. She's frightened she'll die and leave her daughter unprotected. It's all that keeps her alive—going home."

"What do we do in the meantime?" Pascal asked.

"We ride with deliberate haste to reach South Pass," Blackie said. "Ten days, two weeks at the most. You'll be six or seven days from Fort Laramie at South Pass."

"What languages does she speak? Only Crow and Arapaho?" Pascal asked.

Blackie nodded.

"How will we communicate when you are away, scouting?" Pascal grumbled.

LaFleur grunted aloud and signaled with trade signs, pointing at her.

Blackie called to Fawn.

When she glanced at them, LaFleur signed in trade, *Have skins to trade.*

She stood, shaking her head.

Pascal groaned aloud, but LaFleur whistled when she signed, *Trade a necklace.*

"I don't want her distracting the men," Pascal said, but LaFleur elbowed him hard.

He wrote on his slate. *They are curious. Tell them she is sick. Leave her and girl alone.*

"I can tell I'll not win this argument. Two weeks, no longer." Pascal stomped away.

LaFleur wrote on his slate, *Saved God's children. You will receive His blessing.*

Blackie strode to Fawn, explaining she'd ride with them through South Pass and he'd take her north alone to the Wind River to find her people. She held the girl close to her side.

Fawn reached to squeeze his hand, and asked, "How long?"

"Ten days. Maybe as many as fourteen," Blackie said in Arapaho, and she nodded.

"We will ride at first light. Do you need anything? Food? Water?"

She smiled before glancing down. "Men are bad cooks. Beans and meat can taste good. Not yours. It burns my tongue. Give us meat cooked over fire and corn meal, if you have some."

"We have both. The man who does not speak words knows trade sign. Ask him what you need." He shifted to turn away. "It'll be cold in the mountains. I'll bring you blankets and an oiled canvas ground sheet. Lay it–"

Fawn interrupted, smacking his arm. "I'm not a child. I know how to sleep on the ground."

The men roused in the dark to make the mules ready while LaFleur and Tomas fixed *café* and a light morning meal. Out-of-sorts in the morning, the men groaned and grumbled.

After the sun brightened the sky, the mountains loomed like a wall above them. A tall peak anchored the northern end, a massive peak so solid it forced the persistent Snake River to turn west and carve a steep-walled canyon, splitting the Teton Range. Pascal claimed the northern peak's name as Hoback, so named to honor a fur-trapper with John Jacob Astor's Pacific Fur before it merged with Rocky Mountain Fur Company.

"During such time," he said, "a young Jim Bridger, David Jackson, Jedidiah Smith, Lucian Fontenelle, Joseph La Barge, and John Grey trapped furs in this region. They stuck their name on the stream they trapped to tell others to keep away. No doubt the local Redmen have their names for these places before the fur-trappers came. The native people called the Green River the Spanish River, because it led south into Spanish territory."

"How long have you lived in the west?" Blackie asked.

"The Jesuits sent me to proselytize the Redmen as a punishment in hopes the Pope would not excommunicate me for my sins of the flesh in 1843."

"And why did LaFleur come with you?" Blackie asked.

"LaFleur came because he's my friend and didn't want me exiled alone. He is the son of the estate's vintner. We grew up together and my father let him attend my tutor's lessons to keep me settled and paying attention to my studies. LaFleur's presence forced me to study hard to beat him on tests. He has a fine mind."

"Did you preach here?"

"We came west to a mission with the Mandan on the Canadian border, leading two mules with our gear and food. Within a month, news came the Pope excommunicated me. The Jesuits ordered me to return. I loved the native people and the prairie, and with nothing to return to, we wandered with our mules. When we needed money, we'd carry food and supplies to the trappers. As the fur trade died, we continued to drag our mules seeking cartage or trade. It became our way of life."

Pascal glanced at the mountains above. "Stop asking questions. Save your breath for climbing. I fear we have three or four days in this climb, and descending will be no easier."

The mule train stopped in place along the narrow path beside the mountain stream before sunset. The mules suffered in the climb along with the men. The *capataz* teams, with a string of ten mules, walked along the line, removing the packsaddles to allow them to rest overnight. LaFleur didn't set up the usual camp, but he created a fire to cook the bean stew for the men. Hector scavenged driftwood beside the stream and assisted LaFleur with meal preparation.

"Before it's completely dark," Pascal called, "check the backs of your mules to make sure the packsaddles and rigging are not rubbing them raw." He told Blackie to post guards at the bottom and Antonio to post guards at the upper end where the horse remuda foraged.

The Absaroka warriors strolled higher to camp away from the mule train's smell. When Fox passed Blackie, he grumbled, "Guiding mules is worse than guiding women and children."

Fawn and her daughter kept from the men's way and Blackie had little time for them.

At the midday rest the next day, fog and mist settled along the mountain's upper ridges. While not rain, the fine mist coated everything. The men's oiled canvas dusters didn't keep the mist from soaking their cotton clothes. The team grumbled and griped the next two days with cold, wet camps. Their guides grumbled, "The mules walk too slow." All grew unhappy.

Fawn and her daughter wore soft deerskin caps to keep their heads dry while Fawn's buffalo robe shed water naturally. Their soft, tanned deerskin dresses didn't absorb water like the men's cotton clothes did. All in all, Fawn and her daughter remained dry and comfortable in the mist.

The mule train crested the ridge in the sun before midday on the next day and continued ahead to bring the entire team on top for the midday rest. To Blackie's surprise, the top lay in a broad knob covered with fir and pines leading to a grassy meadow on the eastern edge, which dropped at a steep angle, too steep to ride down. It required the mules to cross at an angle.

While on the knob, Sits Tall and Fox led Antonio and Blackie south to reach a promontory with a view east. "Across the valley is the Wind River mountains. They are steep and cannot be crossed from the Green valley. The steep mountains end at South Pass. Cross the Green River before you ride south, or you must pay the Mormon ferry to cross. Ride half east and half north close to mountains to find South Pass. On the rise above, follow the wind to find the Wind River. It has three small forks but all lead to the main river and flow north. It is where the mountain Arapaho live. The Shoshone live there, too. You will find those you seek there."

"You speak as if you are leaving us," Blackie said.

"No, we will guide you across the Green River. It is as far east as we ride. Too many whites with their wagons on the other side."

"We are grateful you have led us across. I'm not sure we'd have made it across without your help. *Merci*," Blackie pointed east. "I glimpsed elk below. After we ride lower, can we hunt for elk and have a feast in the valley?"

"You can hunt, but can you kill one?" Fox asked.

Blackie hefted the Sharps from the crook of his left elbow.

Fox huffed his disgust. "Any pilgrim on a wagon can kill from across a meadow with such a great rifle. Sneak close and capture its spirit with your arrow."

"I think the Bannock lad's bow is too light for an elk. It's all I carry."

Fox flicked his fingers, signaling *give it here.*

Blackie slid the bow from his saddle scabbard before he notched the bowstring.

Fox drew it twice, extending it to its limit. "Yes, it is a lad's bow, but it will test your skill as a hunter. You must get close. Close enough to hear it break wind. Do not shoot from front or rear. With such a bow and shorter arrows, you must strike behind the shoulder where the ribs spread the widest, or you'll not penetrate to the heart. Ride ahead, have an elk waiting for us."

Blackie accepted Fox's challenge, riding ahead after the four men returned to the mule train.

Sits Tall led the mules north across the ridge to the next valley with a stream running east, offering a less steep decline and a worn path beside it. "The white men called it Horse Creek."

The team complained about unloading in a line along the creek. One of them said, "We may as well be in a cold camp when we sleep beside the animals along these mountain streams."

Even descending, the mule train needed another two days to reach the broad basin below.

Pascal announced a rest day after they reached the valley floor. With plenty of firewood from downed trees, LaFleur and Hector promised a hot meal and a warm fire tonight.

Blackie trotted on his horse, calling across the meadow, "I have an elk, but I'll need two mules and three or four men to load it and carry it here."

"*Non! Non!*" Pascal called. "You are to carry it home on your shoulders. What weakling can't carry home his catch?" Pascal and men on the team laughed, remembering Pascal's earlier challenge for Blackie to carry home a deer he killed on his shoulders.

Fox rode along with the men and the mules to examine the carcass. Although Blackie had gutted the bull elk, its organs remained in the upper chest. An arrow shaft protruded from its right chest, two inches below the ideal place to penetrate to the heart. Fox reached inside with his knife, separating the pierced heart from its vessels and held it up to Blackie, who leaned forward with his mouth open and bit hard, pulling loose a bite of heart meat. Fox bit into the heart. Blood dribbled from their chins as they ate raw heart, believing they'd gain the bull's great strength.

"Our people do not like the Cheyenne who help the Lakota," Fox said.

"I came from the Southern Cheyenne. We do not like the Lakota or the Comanche."

Fox nodded.

Blackie turned to skin the hide from the carcass before they quartered the bull.

"It is a woman's work to skin a hide." Fox turned away with a sour grimace.

"You don't like her, do you?"

"She carries an evil spirit inside her, eating her from within. We do not wish to be near when she dies, and the evil spirit is set free. When she first became Elk's woman, she laughed and danced with spirit in our village. Our people loved her spirit. As she grew weaker, the village suffered with her. Our village will miss her, but it is better she dies among the Arapaho."

"You will ride north after we cross the Green River?" Blackie asked.

"Yes." Fox gave a quick nod.

The mule team reached the Green River one day

after their rest day. Pascal wanted them rested and ready to ford the Green River. Good news came after they reached the Green. This late in the season, it flowed ankle deep. The far side had overhanging banks where, loaded with a packsaddle, the mules needed a less steep bank to climb from the river without stumbling and losing the cargo.

Pascal sent one Absaroka scout with Blackie and one with Antonio, one to search upstream and the other downstream to find the best place to cross.

At the evening meal, the mule team men said their goodbyes to their Absaroka guides who rode into the dark, preferring to camp away from the smell of the mules and the team.

The next morning, the mules forded the Green upstream, entering a meadow across from the mouth of Horse Creek. Pascal sat in the meadow lost in thought for a long while, while the *capataz de mula* formed their ten-mule strings and Esteban, the horse wrangler, pushed the horse remuda ahead with LaFleur leading the camp mules.

Blackie returned to the meadow but approached Pascal quietly.

"Who walked across your grave?" Blackie asked. "You're as pale as I've ever seen you."

"A true act of contrition does such to a man if he's honest with our Father. I rode here in 1843 but I missed the true Black Robe, Pierre-Jean De

Smet, a Jesuit who converted many Redmen to the way of Christ. His converts said he delivered his first communion in this meadow in 1840 or '41. Dates get lost here. It's said Captain Bonneville, a misguided fur-trapper, intended to create an outpost in this meadow. His cabin stood when De Smet visited."

"Did you know the man?"

"*Non*. I would have liked to have spoken with him, but he heard about me from the Redmen and considered me a fraud, even though I never sought to convert or offered communion. Like many Jesuits, a man of principles, but those principles failed him when he encouraged the Redmen in the north to come together and sign the 1851 Peace Treaty at Fort Laramie. He trusted the U.S. government to honor its agreement. The Federal government never paid the Redman the agreed payments nor kept whites from trespassing, hunting, and mining on their treaty lands but punished the Redman whenever *they* didn't abide by the agreement."

"Did you attend the treaty meeting?"

"*Non*, they did not invite me. I feared what would happen under the treaty and moved to Mexico to be gone from here. It saddens me to see such great intentions undone."

"I'll keep the mules moving." Blackie reined his horse away. "We won't be hard to track."

Pascal heaved a long sigh. "I'll ride with you if you stop asking questions."

Blackie nodded, gigging his horse southeast to

follow the mules.

The mule train reached South Pass five days later.

Blackie, Fawn, and her daughter rode with the train for another day, which saved them climbing a steep ridge to reach the Wind River plateau higher above them.

Chapter 18

Late September 1857

Blackie led a mule with Fawn and her daughter on horses from the camp after promising Pascal to return in three days, five at the most. "Ride to Fort Laramie in five days. I'll meet you there."

"Bah!" Pascal replied. "You said such when you rode away with the Bannocks."

"You'll not be rid of me so easy." Blackie laughed and waved goodbye. "By the bye, when do I get paid? I'll need new clothes when we reach Fort Laramie."

"Pay! Pay!" Pascal shouted. "You wastrel, you have to work every day to earn your pay, but you're away chasing skirts again." He still brayed his loud laughter as Blackie rode north.

Mounted on the Bannock horses and dragging a pack mule, Blackie led Fawn and her daughter from an Oregon Trail campground north, ascending Rock Creek canyon until it turned west. They followed Smith Creek north before turning west to cross Little Beaver Creek.

After they topped a ridge, Fawn said, "The white-faced bluff ahead has two gaps, like missing teeth. The north gap is easiest to climb. Beaver

Creek runs along its base."

He rested the animals at Beaver Creek and unwrapped roasted elk for the midday meal. After their rest, he led them up the steep gap dismounted to make sure the animals didn't stumble and get injured. At the top, Fawn pointed northeast across a wide expanse of bare rock. By mid-afternoon, they crossed a rocky ridge, climbing higher before glimpsing red-stained bluffs to the northeast and a longer red bluff running to the northwest.

"A creek runs along the base of the red canyon," Fawn said. "It has firewood and water for a camp. Can we stop when we reach it?"

Blackie nodded. "These mountains are more rugged than I expected. I hadn't anticipated climbing stretches of hard rock." He rubbed his horse's neck. "It's hard on their legs and feet."

Blackie got them mounted and moving at first light the next morning, riding northwest along the base of the red bluff rising over 100 feet above them. He halted before midday after they crossed the Little Popo Agie Creek. They rested the animals for an hour and ate a cold meal.

"Popo Agie doesn't sound Arapaho or Shoshone."

"It is an Absaroka word from the time when those people lived here," Fawn said. "It is pronounced as two words, 'Puh-Poe Zha,' and means 'water that gurgles.'" She shrugged. "We want to go west around the flat-topped mesa ahead. A larger fork of the Popo Agie runs downstream to the northeast into a broad valley. My people lived there ten years ago."

"We met men from the Mountain Arapaho south of the Unitah Mountains last spring. Runs-After-Antelope told the grandson of Far-Walking Woman they used the Wind River valley for a summer camp, but their winter camp is east along the Powder River, west of the Pumpkin Buttes. They hunt buffalo in Thunder Basin with the Southern Arapaho and the Northern Cheyenne."

"We will need to ask the Shoshone, if we meet them first." Fawn raised an eyebrow. "Do you speak their language?"

Blackie nodded. "I glimpsed two wooden buildings west upstream on the Beaver, but I've seen no sign of either the Shoshone or the Arapaho. Their absence worries me."

"Do you have good standing with the Arapaho?"

"We did six months ago," Blackie said.

When he found a place to camp for the day, he first helped Fawn's daughter from the horse. Fawn didn't dismount and held a hand to him in a silent request. Her usual vitality slipped away since leaving the Oregon Trail to ride into the mountains. When he lifted her from the horse, she winced in pain. She appeared unsteady when he set her to stand. He scooped her into his arms and carried her to a place where he planned to build a small fire.

Before he returned to the horses, Fawn said, "Do you have a blanket? I grow cold."

At the mule, he retrieved a blanket from the

pack and tossed it to Fawn's daughter.

Mother and daughter sat together wrapped in the wool trade blanket, while he unsaddled the horses and removed the pack from the mule. After he picketed the animals in tall grass, he glanced at the camp to find the girl gathering firewood. He moved the cooking gear near Fawn and broke the wood into smaller pieces, and added shavings with this knife to build a fire.

Fawn and her daughter argued about something. Her daughter kept shaking her head. Both had tears flowing as Fawn pleaded with her. He understood how weak she'd become when she let him prepare a meal from a cooked elk haunch as big as his thigh and reheated beans without any seasoning but rinsed side meat. She didn't like the Mexican spices used by the mule team.

When he returned from cleaning their pie tins and wood spoons, Fawn beckoned him to sit by the fire. "My daughter's name is Chattering Squirrel. You are the first white man she's met."

While gazing at her, Blackie said, "We'll ask your grandmother to give you a new name. I haven't heard you speak once."

"You frighten her. She's never seen men at war. Until her father fell, she didn't understand death. Then you came alone and killed four, then killed more at the river camp. She fears you because you bring death. She doesn't understand why Many Bears didn't slay you when he had the chance. What the Bannocks did to me and Pretty Eyes terrified her."

"I only fight my enemies," Blackie said, "The Arapaho People are not my enemy. She is safe with me."

"I told her the only way she'll be safe with you is by blood bond. A wolf pack will not kill one of its own. Give me your hand," Fawn held out her hand, fingers beckoning.

"Please don't fill her head with this. I'm not a death bringer. I fight to defend myself."

"She's a child and frightened. Do you fear a child?" Fawn said. "Give me your hand."

Blackie sighed. "This is not the way."

She signaled as if she grabbed for something, before he stretched his hand to her. Fawn whispered to her daughter wrapped in the blanket with her.

Chattering Squirrel crept from the blanket and knelt in front of Blackie, raising her hand.

Fawn sliced a small cut on Blackie's thumb and one on Squirrel's thumb. "Press your thumbs together so the blood mingles. Press hard. Tell her she is your sister and you pledge your life to carry her safely to her grandmother."

"I would protect her and carry her home without this ceremony."

"I believe you would, but *she* needs to believe she is safe with you and do as you bid her without arguing. The ceremony is for *her*."

Blackie took Squirrel's hand, licking the blood from her thumb three times before it quit bleeding. He paced his hand on her head. "Sleep safe, little sister."

Squirrel grabbed his hand and licked the dried blood from the cut before she shifted to snuggle in her mother's blanket.

After Squirrel fell sleep, Blackie asked, "Is your time near?"

Fawn nodded. "Have you ever been around a childbirth or spoken to women about it?" She continued as Blackie shook his *no*. "I loved birthing. The great pain ended with a wonderful new baby." She lowered her head, whispering, "There is no baby this time, only pain."

The next midday, they followed a well-worn trail through the rocks. They ate a light meal while resting the animals beside a large pond whose overflow became a Popo Agie fork. After he mounted the women, he led them through a shallow canyon opening into a wide valley ahead.

"You are not welcome here. Ride away," a Shoshone warrior called from atop a ten-foot tall boulder beside the rippling creek. To convey his meaning, he fired into the ground near them.

"I ride with the Mule Man," Blackie said in their language. "We are friends of the Shoshone. I don't intend to stay. I want to visit the Arapaho, Runs-After-Antelope. Is his camp nearby?"

"They rode to the Powder River eight suns past. Leave now." He waved to signal away.

"We have been friends with the Shoshone for many seasons," Blackie said. "We traded with, Crow Killer, smoked a cigar, and sat to eat together. Friends do not shoot at one another."

"You chose the Absaroka as friends against the

Lemhi Shoshone and the Bannocks. You carry an Absaroka woman into our land. Does a friend do these things?"

"She is an Arapaho, stolen by the Absaroka. She wants to find the White Sage people."

"They are not on the Wind River. You fought the Lemhi. Go away."

"I am saddened to report the Bannocks, acting for the Lemhi, broke a trade truce. Rei-ze-won kidnapped me, holding me hostage. He demanded three kegs of gunpowder and bars of lead in trade for my life. You know the Mule Man never trades in powder or whiskey. He rode away, forfeiting my life rather than break his oath. I did not fight the Lemhi. I fought the Bannocks, who are weak. I escaped from the Bannocks. I found this Arapaho woman seeking to return to the Wind River and carried her home."

"The Bannocks are allied with the Lemhi. They fight alongside the Lemhi."

"They are weak. I escaped. Those hunting me found her. I killed four with my knife. With the dead Bannocks weapons, I fought eight. Rei-ze-won acted the coward. When he feared I would beat him, he grabbed the young girl." He pointed to her daughter, as he continued. "He used her for a shield to run away. The woman killed him with an arrow from a Bannock bow she'd taken from a dead Bannock. Rei-ze-won died a coward's death with her arrow in his back. Do you want weak friends like the Bannocks, or strong friends like the Mule Man and me?"

Another warrior appeared nearby. He called in Arapaho, "Who are your mother's people?"

"My mother is Little Sage Hen from the White Sage People," Fawn called.

"I sorrow, sister," the Arapaho warrior said. "That one passed to Chebbeniathan last winter."

"Friends don't bring a dead woman into another friend's winter camp," the Shoshone called.

Fawn gasped and moaned behind Blackie.

Blackie said, "Keep quiet, or we'll die." He called, "She sits a horse fine for a dead woman."

"She has an evil spirit inside, eating its way from inside her. When she dies, it will escape and eat the Shoshone people nearby. Send her away, or burn her, so the evil spirit can't escape."

Blackie rolled from the saddle at the same moment the Shoshone warrior on the boulder fired his rifle. As Blackie rolled to kneel on one knee, he shouldered his Sharps, firing at the warrior in the act of reloading. The heavy .52-caliber slug knocked the warrior from his perch.

Two Shoshone warriors ran across the Popo Agie but never reached the near bank as Blackie fired his Colt from the ground. As he rose to mount, two events pulled him apart. Fawn reined her horse about and, leaving her daughter's horse, galloped upstream. He had no time to seek where she rode, because two Shoshone warriors rode around the boulder to attack.

Blackie swung into the saddle, shoving the Sharps into its scabbard and, as his boot slid into the off-side stirrup, he switched the .36-calibre

1851 Colt Navy to his left hand and yanked his long, heavy Walker Colt from its pommel holster before charging the attacking Shoshone.

A Shoshone bullet swept his broad-brimmed hat away. Another tugged at his possibles-bag.

Blackie alternated firing between left hand and right. In a matter of ten seconds, the fight ended when the last Shoshone warrior fell. He reined his horse about to find Fawn.

"Follow me," Blackie shouted to Squirrel as he rode past. "Fetch my hat and the mule."

He glanced past another huge boulder, catching sight of dust raised in Fawn's passing. After rounding the boulder, he glimpsed her 200 yards ahead, dismounting to enter a cave.

She should know better than hiding in a dead-end cave. I'll have to get her mounted again.

His horse skidded its rear legs to stop in the streambank's pea gravel as he leapt from the horse before it stopped. "Fawn! Fawn!" he called but failed to glimpse sight of her.

The cave's mouth confused him. At first, he thought water gushed *from* the cave as he strode toward its mouth, but he jerked to a stop. The water gushed *into* its mouth—and disappeared!

"It's a sink," Blackie gasped aloud. "It's swallowing the whole creek."

Two heartbeats passed before he realized what Fawn had done.

Open-mouthed in horror, he screamed, "Nooooooooo!" He drew another breath and howled, long and loud. It echoed from the cave entrance. He sank to his knees and howled again.

Despair—after holding on for so long to return to her people, only to find her mother dead, with no one to care for her daughter, and rejected by the living as dead, she ended her pain.

Raw emotion swept over him in torrents like the Popo Agie had swept her over the edge in torrents, carrying her into the flooded caverns below. He wept while he covered his face with his large hands.

"Has mother joined Chebbeniathan?" Squirrel asked beside him.

"Yes, little sister," Blackie said. "May he grant her peace and end her pain." He pulled her close and hugged her. "Your mother was a strong woman. You have her beauty. I hope you find her strength. We must ride until dark. I have angered the Wind River Shoshone."

Nearby, the animals grazed on the lush grass watered by the mist from cascading water falling into the sink, never to be seen again.

Hunger growling in his stomach forced him to stop before darkness fell. He unsaddled the animals beside a trickling stream and set the gear on the ground. "I'll not make a fire tonight." He unwrapped the remaining elk and sliced it into bite-sized chunks, offering it to Squirrel.

Squirrel sat crossed-legged, wrapped in her mother's wool trade blanket. She rocked and moaned, refusing his offered food.

Blackie tossed a ground sheet beside her and spread it on a smooth spot, before fetching another blanket. "We'll ride by first light. Sleep now. I'll catch fish in the morning."

Squirrel continued to rock and moan as he hugged her.

"My mother died four years ago, and I still miss her. The loss never goes away. We learn to live with it to honor the one gone. We'll ride toward the Powder River to find your people."

Stirring in the night he sat up, glanced at the stars, before he howled in loss and defeat. His sudden scream spooked the horse Fawn had ridden, sending it galloping into the dark. As he laid back, he sensed if he made another sound, he'd be afoot, abandoned by his animals.

Chattering Squirrel reached to hold his hand, and he didn't know who comforted whom.

The sun had yet to brighten the sky when he rose again. He remembered the deep ache after his family died, but Fawn wasn't family, and yet he ached deep inside. Had he failed, as he'd failed his mother? Could he gain a deeper commitment, learning to protect those in his charge?

Commitment. He had a commitment to rejoin Pascal in another week, but he had another to return Squirrel to her people. The team could move to Fort Laramie on the Trail without him.

Is this loss and worry what makes Pascal grumpy and irritable? Pascal has a commitment to the men on the team to get them home safe at season's end and have gold in their pockets, and his. Pascal and LaFleur have a life-long commitment bonded in friendship. *Who are my friends? What are my commitments? I'm Pascal's apprentice on a mule train. Is such the sum of me?*

Blackie snorted, thinking he must not vent his despair on Squirrel or the animals. He had glimpsed her stroll upstream, away from the camp, thinking she went for her morning necessaries. After five minutes, he wondered where she went and strode upstream to search.

"Mother said you couldn't catch fish." She held three nice trout on a rawhide string.

After barking a laugh, he said, "I suppose you want me to build a fire and cook them."

"She didn't think much of your cooking, but at least you could make a fire." She gutted and cleaned the fish, slicing each side from the bone but leaving the skin. "Where is the fire?"

With his small firing growing, he cut green sticks to hold the fish for roasting.

She cooked the fish, turning them often as they browned. "Mother said you must be a good hunter to find food to fill such a big stomach. She said you must eat much food to grow as tall as you are." Squirrel handed him a cooked fish. "You get one now and one at midday."

I understand how she got her name, but I'll let her speak of her mother as she mourns. After eating, he wet and scattered the fire ashes before packing the blankets.

Blackie mounted Squirrel on her horse before glancing about to find his landmarks and recognized the red-stained canyon as the route to the Oregon Trail and Fort Laramie. Instead of riding to catch up with the mule train, in five days he'd turn north to the Powder River.

With the pack mule's pace, he rode at a brisk trot with periodic stops to rest. Despite her name, Chattering Squirrel remained silent. Descending across the rocky plateau made the trip faster. He expected they'd camp tomorrow night along the Overland Trail.

Chapter 19

October 1857

Blackie departed the Rock Creek campground on the Oregon Trail at first light. He said to Squirrel, "I'll follow the Trail for six days east before turning north at Independence Rock. I will get you home in ten days. Let's try to travel fast with few stops on the Trail."

"Do you know the way?" Squirrel raising her eyebrows.

Blackie barked a laugh. "The Trail is marked well enough, so I won't go too far astray. I ought to have killed a deer before we left the mountains. We won't find much game near the trail, even this late in the season. Keep your eyes open and alert me if you notice any game."

In an hour, she called, "A deer rests under a pine on the rocks above."

After she spoke, he reined his horse to stop and turned it beside her. "Don't look at it. Many game animals watch another's eyes to sense a hunter. Glance at it and drop your gaze. Describe the tree it lays under."

"It's a pine with two forks half-way up. The deer's head is on the right side of the trunk."

As if speaking to her, he raised his arm to point

ahead and lifted his head to glimpse above. "I'll have to shoot from the saddle. I can't see it from the ground. Hold your reins tight to keep your horse from bolting after I shoot."

He reined the horse forward is if he moved to ride away, but instead withdrew the long Sharps from its scabbard. In a smooth motion, he shouldered the rifle as he cocked the hammer and fired when the deer's head appeared in his sights.

Two hundred yards away, the deer spasmed and fell still.

"Now I have to climb up and get it," Blackie said, glancing at a twenty-foot cliff. "Follow me across to the rock's base. We'll rest and unsaddle the animals until I finish butchering it."

"I told mother you bring death." Squirrel's brows and mouth drooped.

"Would you prefer to eat grass?" he asked. "Did your father never hunt game for food?"

"You do it so easy. Bang, and dead things fall. A deer today, five Shoshone warriors yesterday. How many Bannocks at the Snake River before then?"

"I'd let you pluck out my shooting eye to have your mother ride beside us so I might return both of you safe and whole to your grandmother's people. It's beyond my power to create life, but if Chebbeniathan gave me the power for only one, I'd have saved your mother."

Two hours passed for him to climb the cliff, butcher the deer, wrap it in its own skin, lower it below, and tie the quartered deer onto his mule. "We'll lose a travel day if we roast it here. Let's ride and cook a quarter or two this evening when it's too dark to travel."

Chattering Squirrel remained quiet while they rode though the day, but she helped in the camp, gathering wood, and marveled at the iron grate and spit rods he carried on the mule.

"If we encounter a store along the way, I'll buy a supply of dried beans. They're more filling." He sliced thin strips of meat from the back strap. He roasted the back strap first because sliced, it cooked faster, while left the rear haunch cooking on the spit through the night over a small fire. He cat-napped and tended the roasting meat to avoid dreaming about Fawn's death.

Squirrel laid on her blanket to sleep without his urging.

In the morning, he offered her mashed beans cooked with a bit of rinsed pork side meat. She cleaned her pie tin and ate a few pieces of roast venison.

The next day on the Trail passed without problems and they made good time, covering more than thirty miles.

Three freight wagons approached late on the third day. Blackie decided to ask if they'd passed a mule train headed east. He waited beside the Oregon Trail for the lead wagon to stop.

When it did, he removed his broad brimmed hat, which hid his Colt Navy in a belly holster. "I ran an errand while my friends kept moving. Did you notice a large mule train headed east?"

The drover on the nearside said, "Yeah, passed

them five or six days ago."

"Thanks, neighbor." Blackie reined his horse to back away before noticing Squirrel had closed behind him.

A large, whiskered man with a bent nose, sitting on the offside, raised a clay jug by its finger loop. "I'll trade this here jug a corn liquor for a spin or two with yer squaw. I ain't—"

From his belly holster, Blackie drew his Colt Navy and fired, shattering the clay jug, and leave Bent Nose holding the clay finger loop and cork-stoppered top. "Take care how you speak of my sister. Ride on before I teach you better manners."

Bent Nose wore an angry snarl on his lips as his eyes glared at Blackie.

The drover snapped the wagon's reins, causing the horses to strain forward to get rolling.

Blackie leaned forward and removed the Walker Colt, to carry a cocked pistol in each hand.

The men on the offside of the next two wagons had grabbed rifles and held them with muzzles raised as they passed Blackie. He said, "Bent Nose in the front wagon made an ill-considered comment about my sister. Keep rolling and mind your manners."

The last guard spit from his side, but Blackie's cocked Colts suggested he hold his tongue.

After the wagon passed, Blackie returned the Walker Colt to the pommel holster and the Navy to his belly holster before he withdrew the Sharps. He kept his eye on the spitting guard in the last wagon who returned a glance at the far range of

Blackie's Navy, but when "Spitter" glimpsed the Sharps, he snapped his head forward. The wagon picked up speed to move away.

He glanced at Squirrel. "What do you think?" He nodded at the wagons on the Trail.

"I don't understand the white man's world," she said. "They carried hate in their eyes."

"Next time we encounter men like those, don't ride so close behind me," Blackie said. "If they had chosen to fight, and they acted angry enough to fight, you might have been shot by a bullet aimed for me."

"I wanted to run," she said, "but I knew they would attack like a dog after a rabbit."

"Or a squirrel." Blackie smiled. "Good thinking. It might have sparked a shooting."

Squirrel glanced west along the trail, toward the dust the wagons kicked into the air.

"We'll ride an hour longer in case Bent Nose and his spitting friend want to try this again."

Squirrel glanced behind again, kicking her heels to urge her horse to ride beside Blackie.

~~~~~~

In two hours, Blackie said, "Like you, I don't trust the men from those wagons," as he reined his horse from the road into a glade between two huge boulders Oregon Trail's north side.

"That man frightened me." She shuddered in an involuntary shiver. "His eyes searched my body. It made my skin itch like ants crawled on me."

"We will set up camp with a small fire before dark, but we'll wait atop a boulder and be ready for who visits in the dark. If those men are innocent travelers who continued on their way, they are miles away, and we worried for no reason."

"Will you kill them if they come?" She glanced down after she asked the question.

"If they come, they are not innocent. I say this to warn you. Men like those are rabid skunks—a threat to everyone they meet." He shifted his gaze to check the trail. "My godfather, and my true father, believe Chebbeniathan tells us not to judge one another, but I believe evil must be destroyed whenever it's encountered." He glanced at Squirrel. "Do you understand?"

"You are the death bringer," Squirrel whispered.

"I did *not* kill your mother." He closed his mouth in a thin flat line.

"She trusted you. You should have ended her pain. We could have taken her body to grandmother who would have given her a proper ceremony and joined us in mourning."

"Fawn wasn't mine to take. Mountain Elk should've held her in the final moment, not me."

"Mountain Elk refused her request. He wanted to keep her with him to the end and refused to shorten her time."

"Our loved ones do not want to become a burden for us, but we refuse to let them go."

"Am I a burden for you?" She glanced away as if afraid to catch his response.

"You are a flea who bites me and jumps to hide." He pounced on her, tickling her ribs, and ruffling her hair. "This time, you didn't jump fast enough."

She giggled before she twisted away. "I need to gather wood for our fire. It must burn into the night." She rose, their play forgotten, and gathered sticks from the drainage ditch nearby.

"Use the extra saddle blanket to cover your sleeping place," Blackie said, laying a log her height as if one slept by the fire. "Don't use anything you don't want holes shot into."

"You believe they are coming?" Squirrel asked while she spread the saddle blanket on the log, adding the black rag he used to wipe the horses, to appear like her hair in the dim firelight.

"I humbled them. They believe killing me will prove they are men. You will become a trinket to boast about, proving they bested me. You are their imagined reward." He placed his hand on her shoulder. "Their final reward is the long sleep." He built the campfire higher.

A half-hour later, as darkness descended, Blackie settled her atop the boulder, away from potential stray shots. "I don't want a word from you," Blackie said, pointing at a sleeping pad with a wool trade blanket. "Not a sound until this is over."

Squirrel nodded and stuck out her tongue before grinning.

Near midnight, Squirrel clicked twice in her cheek like a real squirrel.

Blackie, stretched flat on the rock's southern

edge, twisted and placed a finger on his lips.

In another moment, she threw a pebble at him.

He rolled, ready to say an angry word, when she twisted, jabbing east along the hillside.

Blackie lay unmoving, letting his gaze search where she pointed for movement in the dark. He glimpsed a shadowed form slide between two large rocks beside the drainage ditch.

Squirrel turned to point at the approaching figure, trying to get Blackie's attention, but he didn't lay there. She jerked and gasped. Across the quiet night, she trembled, expecting the dark figure to attack. A soft whisper fluttered, almost a loud sigh followed by soft, wet gurgling that soon fell silent. She jerked in fright when a shadow passed, and Blackie's hand patted her head.

"Little sister, you have the eyes of an owl. You saved us," Blackie whispered before he stretched flat again.

In five minutes, an owl hooted from the Oregon Trail below.

Blackie stood at the rock's edge and waved the hat he recovered from "Spitter," the dark stranger lying dead in the rocks behind them, as he called, "Come get 'em."

"Thanks, Henry," Bent Nose called when he stepped into the fading firelight and shot into the blanket-covered log where he expected Blackie to lie next to the smaller mound.

"Bent Nose!" Blackie called as he shot the man

in the chest with his Walker Colt in his right hand and followed with a shot through the man's bent nose with the Colt Navy in his left hand as the man fell backwards. He fired the right- and left-hand pistol again, striking the man on each side of Bent Nose as they turned to run.

He slid down the front side of the rock and rolled to the right as his feet touched the ground. *There had been six men at the wagons. Where are the other two hiding?* His Cheyenne training led him to slide his knife under the breastbone of each man to make sure they never rose again.

"Help me down," Squirrel called with a soft voice from above.

"Not yet. Two are missing," Blackie whispered. "I'll hunt them and return before the morning star rises in the east. Stay quiet and rest until I return."

The Oregon Trail, wide and dusty, made an easy route for running. He hadn't run since Fawn joined him, and he enjoyed stretching his legs. In a half-hour, judging by star movement, he almost passed the wagons parked under a grove of trees south of the trail near the river.

I didn't expect those lazy turds to walk three miles to kill me and take Squirrel.

"It's Henry," Blackie called into the night. "Where are you cowards? The deed is done."

"Tol' ya," came a soft response. "We want no part of killing and raping a little girl. Why I'd wager she ain't bled yet."

"Why did you wait here then?" Blackie asked.

"We want our share from selling the whiskey," a new voice said. After the man stepped close, he gasped, "Ya ain't Henry."

"I am Black Wolf." He killed the two greedy men for trying to sell liquor to the Redman.

He detached the rear gate on the nearest wagon, tossing it toward the road. He stripped the weapons from the downed men. As he searched the wagons, he found two double-barreled shotguns and an old cap-n-ball rifle. He doubted Bent Nose would leave any cash or coin with these two, but he found a lantern and lit it to aid his search. In five minutes, he released their mules and piled their shoddy camp gear beneath the wagons. He stood on the wagon's seat to blast the clay jugs in each wagon with the shotgun, shattering most of them. Before he trotted east to rejoin Squirrel, he tossed the lit lantern into the middle wagon. With a whoosh, flames leapt high, spreading to the other wagons.

In his earlier search, he had found a used can of red paint in one wagon's foot box. He worked in the firelight, painting a warning on the wood tailgate he had set aside for this purpose.

Death to those selling Indians liquor.

He led four mules by their bridles in his return. In a half hour of steady trot, he returned to Squirrel. He loaded the dead on the mules and returned to the burning wagons to dump their bodies alongside the last two. Fueled by alcohol, the fire reduced the wagons to glowing embers except for the axles and wheel hubs in two hours.

Driving them toward the river to drink, he removed the mules' harnesses and reins before he trotted east along the Trail in the dark.

Upon return, he climbed the drainage ditch to the rock and lifted Squirrel into his arms to carry her. She wrapped an arm around his neck. He placed her on the saddle blanket pad.

She rolled over and slept.

The sun brightened the prairie before she rolled over again, glimpsing him squatted by the fire, sipping a tin cup of coffee. "I expected fresh fish this morning, Little Sister."

"You camped too far from the river," she replied, grinning.

"What? An Arapaho maiden can't walk a half mile?"

She leaned close to grab three slices of roast deer and "accidently" bumped him hard enough with her hip to knock him from his squat to land on his side with a thump, making him laugh.

"I witnessed your bonfire last night," she said, as she took his hand. "Thank you for carrying the trash away." Blood had stained his shirtsleeve cuff and remained on the back of his hand and wrist. She rose to return with a water skin and poured water on the black rag from last night. After scrubbing the blood from his hand, she poured more water to rinse it from his cuff.

While she worked, she said, "The Arapaho and Absaroka do not often use 'black' in peoples' names because it also means 'death.'"

"The Cheyenne have the other meaning, too," Blackie said.

"To name a young man Death Wolf is a terrible burden."

"Black Kettle, and his advisors, believed such is true."

"I will never call you Death Bringer again, my brother." She gazed at his face.

When they reached Independence Rock a day later, they strolled into the general store. Squirrel wandered about inside, eyes wide, mouth gaping, while Blackie approached the counter.

"I'd like a twenty-pound sack of dried beans," Blackie said.

"I have it in twenty-five-pound sacks," the counter man answered.

"That'll do. You the owner?" he asked.

After the man nodded, Blackie said, "Night riders struck three wagons of freebooters selling liquor to the Redman four nights past on the Trail east of Rock Creek. Six bodies and a warning sign lay beside the burned wagons." Blackie glanced around as people in the shop stood stunned into silence. "What gets into a white man to sell them liquor?"

The owner and the customers wagged their heads but remained a shocked silence.

An Easterner in a suit and silk hat broke the spell after he bustled inside and spied Squirrel walking toward Blackie. "Dear God! What's a savage squaw doing in a civilized store?"

In a step, Blackie pushed the man against a post and inserted his shiny Green River knife into the man's mouth. "Retract your foul oath about my sister, or I will remove your tongue."

The Easterner whimpered, afraid to move his tongue with the blade inside.

Squirrel tugged on Blackie's pants leg and spoke soft words.

"My sister is correct. She says, 'Forgive them for they know not what they do.'" Blackie set the man free, patted his chest, and whispered, "A Christian should know to keep a civil tongue in his head. If you refuse to act Christian, I'll feed it to the dogs if I catch you flapping it again."

Blackie lay a gold half Eagle on the counter. "What do I owe?"

"Two dollar an' a half," the owner replied, rattling in a drawer to pass him the remainder.

After he stepped away, Blackie glanced at Squirrel, and stopped. In Arapaho, he asked, "Is there something you'd like?"

She nodded and pointed along an aisle as he followed her.

Squirrel touched an iron grate, a twelve-inch heavy iron skillet, and a gallon pot with a lid.

"We have those, Little Sister."

"Grandmother doesn't."

Blackie nodded, grabbing one of each and added a set of three iron rods forming a spit.

The counter man said, "Iron costs more to ship than the metal does. Those items are pricey."

"How much?" Blackie asked, laying the coins

from his first purchase on the counter.

"It's based on weight. The grate is ten, eight for the skillet, six for the pot with the lid, and six for the spit." The man pulled a pencil from behind his ear, preparing to calculate the total.

"It's thirty dollars," Blackie said as he swept the loose coins from the counter. He tugged open a leather pouch with a thong drawstring, dropping the silver inside before extracting a gold double Eagle and an Eagle. As he gathered his goods from the counter, he handed Squirrel the spit pieces. With the twenty-five-pound sack of beans balanced on one shoulder, he placed the grate under one arm and gathered the other cookware in his hands to carry outside.

"Hold onto my coat," he said to Squirrel as they strode to the mule to load the cookware. Once mounted, he rode less than a few paces, when a man dressed in buckskin shirt and cavalry blue twill trousers called as he stepped off the store's porch, "Wait a minute, neighbor."

"You know of a trail over those hills north to the Powder River?" Blackie asked, pointing at a low range of hills brooding in the north.

The man glanced where Blackie pointed, before he glanced at Blackie. "I'm Ward Perkins. I work for the Indian Agent at Fort Laramie. We got word some men carried liquor to the Indians. Bossley, in the store, said you reported the wagons burned. Want to tell me about it?"

"I need to reach the Powder River. You guide me to the trail north, and I'll answer questions while we ride. Otherwise, the Lord says sitting around gossiping is a sin."

"Give me a minute to fetch my horse," Ward said.

"Catch up," Blackie said, trotting north as Squirrel and the mule fell into line.

"Why don't you like him?" Squirrel asked.

"Have you heard of your people being held in an iron box with bars?"

"As punishment?" Squirrel asked.

After he nodded, he said, "A man such as him takes people to the iron box. Say nothing."

"Wait up," Ward called as he neared. "What's the rush?"

"It'll snow in six days. I must be away before it does."

"What did you see out at Rock Creek?" Ward asked.

"Masked riders came in the dark. They did a lot of shooting. Twenty minutes after the shooting ended, it erupted in flames. Whatever those wagons carried, it burned high and blue, but died to embers in thirty minutes. Six bodies and a painted sign laid on the ground the next day."

"What'd the sign say?" Ward asked.

"Death for those selling Indians liquor."

"Did you see them?" Ward asked.

"Heard them ride past. We doused our fire and hunkered 'til sunrise."

"Who is the girl?"

"My little sister." Blackie stared hard into Ward's eyes. "I'm taking her to her grandmother with the White Sage people, where I'm told they are in their winter camp on the Powder."

"It's dicey for a white man to ride alone to the Powder River."

"It's dicey from here to the Lemhi and the Bitterroots. The Bannocks and Lemhi Shoshone attacked the Mormons in the Lemhi valley. The Wind River Shoshone are upset. The Mormons have raised militia, but it appears more like they're bracing for a fight with the *Yanquis*."

"It's not like them to go to war at the start of winter." Ward pursed his lips.

"The *Yanquis* have to stop poking them in the ass."

Ward wagged his head. "Follow the Trail after the Sweetwater joins the North Platte. In twenty miles, a stream joins from the northwest. In another ten miles, a stream flows from due north. Follow the second stream due north climbing a ridge, cross over and ride north for sixty miles. The Powder flows north up there. Pumpkin Buttes will lay to your northeast. If they don't want her, you're a long way from home." Ward touched his hat brim. "Thanks."

"Thanks for what?" Blackie opened his eyes wide with innocence.

Ward grinned. "If nothing else, for reporting it. Keep your hair." He reined his horse away.

Three days later, Blackie roused Squirrel from her buffalo blankets on a frosty morning. "I'll build a fire up on the knob and we'll wait to find who visits. You want beans or venison?"

"Both." She stretched once she stood. Her shaggy-haired buffalo coat hung below her knees.

In an hour, the mule carried a pile of firewood to the knob. Blackie stoked it to get a good blaze going before tossing on an uprooted creosote bush, which burned fast with a heavy grey smoke. The fire's heat carried the smoke high. They took turns leading the mule to gather creosote bushes from the plain and kindling from along the riverbank.

"A man watches from the ridge toward the buttes," Squirrel said, late in the day.

"We'll stop for the night. We'll start again in the morning, if no one is here."

"I would welcome a different meal," Squirrel said.

"I remember an Absaroka girl telling me I didn't know how to fish. How many fish have you caught, Little Sister?" Blackie raised his eyebrows.

"This river flows too fast and has few rapids and no pools to encourage fish to rest."

"If we stayed longer, I'd build a fish trap they could swim in but not out to escape."

After reheating venison strips and mashed beans for the third night in a row, they settled together in the dark as he taught her simple arithmetic. "Time for sleep, Little Sister."

"Are you going to keep a night watch?" Squirrel asked.

"Of course."

"Then let me stay up with you, please."

"A squirrel chatters too loud, and I'd fail to

catch a stranger sneaking close. Sleep."

"Can I sit with you until I fall asleep?"

"Of course." He ruffled her hair. "You know, I can take you with me if you don't like your new grandmother."

"When I asked at first, you said Godfather Pascal wouldn't let me ride on the mule train. No women allowed."

"It's not the best place for a young girl to live, but I want you to know you have a choice. I'm not leaving you because I don't want you. I'll remain faithful to my promise to carry you to your mother's people, but they must welcome you."

"I'm frightened. I never knew another home but with Mountain Elk. The Bannocks scared me. They hurt mother." She buried her face in the blankets. Her little shoulders shook with her sobs. "Until you helped mother, I'd never seen a white man." She held her arm next to his deep tanned arm. "How can you be a white man when your arm is darker than mine?"

"If I opened my shirt, my belly is whiter than a fish's belly." He laughed.

"What will I do there?" she asked. "I don't know anyone there. What will happen to me?"

"They will love you as much as I do and make you an Arapaho princess."

Squirrel stuck out her tongue.

"Sleep little one. A new adventure begins tomorrow," Blackie said.

When no riders appeared the next morning,

Blackie rekindled the fire, letting it grow hot before adding a creosote bush to begin the smoke.

Before midday, two riders trotted toward them from the north, on the river's east side.

Blackie knocked the smoking creosote bush from the fire with a stick and kicked the heavy base logs apart, reducing its heat and fire. While they waited for the riders to come close, he emptied his water skin on the base logs and refilled it at the river, returning with a gallon pot of water. The fire's embers grew cold before the two riders rode close enough to call.

"You don't belong here," one warrior called. "What do you want, white-eyes?"

"I'm not white-eyes," Blackie called, "If you rode close, you'd learn I'm the Cheyenne with wolf-eyes. I've smoked and eaten with Runs-After-Antelope. I am carrying a lost daughter home to the White Sage People. This one seeks her family, the sisters of Little Sage Hen."

"Have you heard?" the speaker called.

"That one has gone beyond, but she had many sisters. This child needs her own family to teach her to become one of the Hinono'eiteen, as the Arapaho People call themselves. The Absaroka stole her Arapaho mother. Her mother went beyond on the journey to find her grandmother. Chattering Squirrel wants to come home. To live with her mother's family."

The speaker turned to his companion, and after a short discussion, the companion rode south in a gallop. "The village will send a signal by sunset if she has family. If not, leave with her."

A column of smoke rose in the late afternoon. Blackie had the animals saddled and ready to ride. As it grew dark, he twisted to the Arapaho behind them. "Do we camp for the night?"

"There is an arroyo ahead to camp hidden from the wind," their *guide* said.

The guide joined them in the camp, watching as Blackie heated a venison roast and beans, he had cooked with the signal fire. Squirrel served his meal on a pie tin with a wooden spoon.

After Blackie checked the animals picketed in grass by the river, he said, "We'll rise early and be ready to ride at first light. Unless you want the fire, I'll bank it to use in the morning."

"That is good. Sleep well."

Blackie led Squirrel into a small village sheltered from the north wind by a rocky bluff layered with a ten-foot-thick black stripe in the rock's middle.

The Arapaho village turned out to welcome a lost sister. Two of Sage Hen's sisters came forward, each hugging and welcoming Squirrel. One aunt told her another aunt lived in a different village and would visit after the snowstorm expected in two or three days.

The village leader, Climbing Bear, offered his tipi for Blackie's shelter. He tended to his horses and the mule. Before entering the tipi for the evening, he carried the gear from the mule into the tipi. To make a sleeping pad, he unrolled a buffalo robe he used for a winter coat and his wool blankets from the pack. At the bottom, he yanked loose one of Pascal's flannel shirts, too large for him, but a layer of warmth if the predicted snow arrived on his journey south.

The next morning, Squirrel and her aunts visited Climbing Bear's tipi. After ten minutes of ceremonial greetings, they sat round the fire in the tipi's center. Bear asked, "Have you agreed to accept this lost girl into your family?"

Squirrel's aunts laughed before the older sister, Winter Berry, said, "Each wants her to live in their tipi. We will share her between us. Her return brings great joy to our family."

Blackie touched Squirrel's shoulder. "Have I fulfilled my promise to your mother?"

Squirrel rushed to hug him. "Please don't leave. Stay the winter."

"Little Sister, my heart breaks to leave you, but I have offended friends of the Arapaho. This village might suffer if I stayed here. They see me as the name you once called me."

"No," Squirrel cried, "You are not like that. You protect those you care for."

"I will be your brother always." Blackie kissed her forehead. "Snow comes, and I must ride to Fort Laramie. In the night, when a wolf howls, remember your brothers, Little Elk and me." He rose with a wolf's smooth economy of effort. "The horse you rode is yours. Please share the mule and gear with your family. Chebbeniathan's blessing on you and your grandmothers."

None ventured outside to watch him leave where

he traded his cook pot for roasted bear shoulder and pemmican rolled in a two-inch-thick buckskin. *Food until I reach the Trail again.*

A cold northwest wind swept across the western mountains, scudding clouds carrying the scent of snow. He followed Pascal's practice of ride an hour and walk or rest the horse for fifteen minutes. Without the sun, he judged time from the habit of riding with the team. When it grew dark, he stopped by the river to let the horse drink and graze for an hour. He led the horse by its reins as he walked for another hour, in case someone watched and planned to visit in the dark.

He awoke before the sky brightened to gather his hobbled horse from its graze. Last night, he wrapped the horse blanket across his chest, under the buffalo coat, and warmed the saddle blanket before tossing it on the horse's back on the cold morning. With similar reasoning, he led the horse by its reins as he trotted south beside it for thirty minutes, allowing each one to warm muscles and joints before pushing one another hard today. When the sky brightened, he surveyed the Powder River Valley to the north. Overhead, the clouds tumbled in the color of molten lead, but in the north, white clouds touched the ground—snow fell fifty miles north.

The early winter storm blew itself out in two days by the time Blackie reached the North Platte, but the cold northwest wind persisted for two more days it took to reach Fort Laramie.

Chapter 20

October 1857

When the mule team arrived intact at Fort Laramie, reports followed claiming the Mormons required prior approval for non-Mormons to travel into or across Utah. The Mormon militia also required a written pass for non-Mormons traveling to Utah, but the territorial government only issued such a pass in Salt Lake City.

People fleeing the area reported the Mormon people had grown less friendly and agitated about the increased flow of settlers traveling through Utah, which the Mormons considered *their* "promised land," the new Zion. New arrivals from the East reported President Buchanan had sent the U.S. Army to Utah "to quell a budding insurrection."

Part of the problem came from the Mormon Church not wanting to recognize U.S. law or the power of Federal judges appointed for Utah territory. Mormons believed all law came from God. Therefore, only a person appointed by God could administer the law—that is, only appointed Mormon apostles could administer God's justice, not secular judges. The appointed Federal judges fled Utah territory under duress in May 1857, adding fuel to the insurrection fire reported blazing in Utah. The President decided to act, and the U.S. Army marched toward Utah.

It came as no surprise to Pascal to find Jim Bridger at Fort Laramie. Bridger bragged to any who'd listen that he'd become the lead scout for the U.S. Second Dragoons, and when the Dragoons arrived in force, he'd lead them to Fort Bridger and reclaim his property.

Pascal offered his entire load of foodstuff to the Army quartermaster at the military's tent camp beside the old adobe stockade of Fort Laramie. The military had done nothing to improve the original fort. Even though cut lumber grew scarce and expensive, the Army constructed eastern-style, wood-frame buildings for the headquarters and officers' quarters. The new troops bivouacked in tents arrayed between their camp and the old Fort buildings.

A new lieutenant in the Quartermaster's tent treated Pascal with brusque rudeness. "Your proposed prices are outrageous. The U.S. Army is not so desperate as to succumb to such."

Pascal muttered a few unkind words in French, before saying, "I believe Bonaparte said such on his jaunt to Russia. 'There will be plenty of food in there. We will travel light and fast and dine in Moscow.'" On departing, Pascal said, "Warm your feet by the Mormon fires."

An older officer with a great coat draped around his shoulders strolled past and listened to Pascal's comments. In passable French, he asked, "You believe they'll burn their outposts?"

The great coat hid the older man's rank, but his sophistication, and the fact he spoke French, convinced Pascal the man represented a senior rank.

"I returned from there this day. They denied food to wagon trains on their land. I bartered for this load at a remote outpost before word came to gather in Salt Lake City. Heavy snow will close the mountain passes before you can reach there *en force*. If you left today, and didn't dawdle on the Emigrant Trail, you might reach there before snow. If you wait another week, you may as well stay the winter here. You're not equipped for a winter campaign in the mountains."

"I tried to tell them such. Command believes we can march across and wait out the winter in *their* city," the officer said in French. "Can you imagine? They sent a captain, *a captain* mind you, to give Brigham Young a letter from General Harney ordering him to furnish food and quarters for an occupying army. You know how much food and shelter such a letter will get us?"

"I will bid you *adieu*, my good sir, and wish you well." Pascal barked a hearty laugh.

"What load do you carry?" The older officer asked in English tainted with a Southern drawl.

"I've a thousand pounds of dried salmon, five hundred bushels of wheat, and five hundred pounds of potatoes. I'd planned on hauling the wheat to Santa Fe to get it milled into flour."

"Smoke dried salmon? How much do you want

for the lot?"

"For the smoked salmon, $600. For the potatoes, $150. For the wheat, $500. A total of $1,250 in gold. I take neither script nor promissory notes."

"I doubt the Quartermaster has such an amount of gold on hand as of yet," the senior officer said. "They issued supply contracts in July, but I don't expect to have a bit of it before next July. Damned Army contracts." He snorted his contempt.

"*Bonjour*," Pascal gave a jaunty wave as he stepped to stroll away.

"What do you want for the mules, if we buy the entire load?" the officer asked in French.

"You know those mules will be more valuable than food, once you ride into the mountains?"

"I'm aware of what a mountain campaign will be like, particularly in winter. How much?"

"For each, $75. If you make it $100 each, I'll include the Grimsley packsaddles and bridles."

"By God! You are a scoundrel to ask those prices while at war," he continued in French but laughed. "Are those really Grimsley packsaddles? They'll be worth having in rough country."

"*Oui*, they are Grimsleys," Pascal said. "It pays well to be such a charming scoundrel. I don't trim tails, but these mules are three-bells. They're trained to follow a lead and work daily."

"I must send to Fort Kearny for such gold. It may take a week or more to get gold to here."

"I can be patient for gold." Pascal smiled. "If you are sending for gold, I have another twenty

Grimsley packsaddles. I will give you a bargain on those, only twenty dollars each."

"Why not, indeed. In for a penny, in for a pound," the older officer replied. He extended an open hand, "Lieutenant Colonel Albert Sidney Johnson, Commanding Officer of the Second Dragoons, at your service."

~~~~~~

Blackie arrived before dark, ten days later. The team members whooped and hollered, calling for a celebration of food and drink.

Pascal rushed to hug Blackie, but with a glance at his face, Pascal asked, "She died?"

Blackie nodded, "Let's not speak now. Let me talk with you and LaFleur after we eat."

Blackie apologized to the team for both his absences and for not appreciating their party. After eating his fill, he begged their pardon before he withdrew.

Pascal and LaFleur spent the night and most of the next day consoling him. He understood he had done all he could to save Fawn, and the decision to take her daughter to the Arapaho winter camp was his alone. He fulfilled his promise. Delivering Squirrel had buoyed his spirits, yet the feeling of loss and not "saving" Fawn haunted him. He cried tears he hadn't shed over the loss of his own mother.

LaFleur wrote, *The Crows called her dead woman. It's why others shunned her. She knew her death sentence. She knew it before you came along. We are but shepherds. Some sheep are taken no matter what we do. You did all she asked of you. Accept her decision as you accepted your mother's decision to save you. It's a mother's choice, not yours. None of us like it, but she chose it.* He pointed to each one. *It rips us apart. Pray God grants her absolution and peace.*

Pascal wrapped his arms around them both, saying, "Let us pray," as they knelt together.

~~~~~~

Blackie accompanied Pascal on his next visit to the Army camp. While Lt. Colonel Johnson spoke in French, Blackie stood beside Pascal. He nodded once to a question, and Johnson glanced at him, asking in French, "*Parlez vous?*"

"Of course. You think me an ignorant savage?" Blackie said in English.

Pascal slapped his arm.

"I heard a few of the native guides spoke French," Johnson replied. "What local dialects do you speak?"

"There's been a misunderstanding, sir," Blackie said, with a sharp nod. "I'm Welsh and the Queen's English is my mother tongue. I speak fluent French and Spanish. I also speak Cheyenne, Arapaho, and Shoshone. I use trade hand-signs with the Redmen along the front range and across the mountains of Utah and Idaho."

"I apologize for my error. My lead scout said our

Pawnee guides don't like you and called you the 'Cheyenne wolf killer.' I mistakenly believed you a Cheyenne."

Blackie and Pascal snorted aloud. "If you mean Jim Bridger," Pascal said, "keep in mind the Redmen in this area don't trust the man because he is not an honest trader. He cheats them."

Before Johnson responded, Blackie said, "Pawnee are what you call them. They call themselves the Wolf People. Bridger's translation is not correct. I'm told they call me the Cheyenne who kills the wolf people. It's not a compliment." Blackie smiled at Johnson.

"I gather you and the Pawnee don't get along," Johnson said with a twisted, wry smile.

Blackie's eyebrows rose as he shrugged.

"What would it cost to hire you?" Johnson asked.

"Again, a misunderstanding, sir. I am part of Monsieur LeBrun's Company. I promised many Redmen across the mountains I would not scout for the Army, and in return, they let our mules pass and trade with us when the mood suits them. If I give my word to a man, I keep it. The Army should remember such when signing treaties and making promises to the Redmen."

"The Pawnee are unhappy this far west," Johnson said, ignoring the comment. "They admit they do not know the mountains or the passes. Are there reliable scouts for the mountains?"

"If asked to arrange for scouts, I'd speak to the Absaroka. Their enemies call them 'Crows.' Don't make such a mistake. They are a proud people," Blackie said. "Many Bears is a war chief. He's at odds with the Bannocks and the Lemhi Shoshone. Overall, the Absaroka are unhappy with the bluecoats for failing to abide by the 1851 treaty agreeing to keep whites from invading their land. If you send a man, send a seasoned officer who speaks French. They would attack a column of bluecoats but may respond to trade signs for a parley by one man. It's worth a try."

~~~~~~

The gold arrived two days later, and Pascal couldn't stop smiling at $4,650 in Army gold. The sale of the original cargo and the mules in Utah netted almost $6,000. It'd become another successful season. By October tenth, the team rode south with the camp pack mules. Pascal said, "Without cargo and pack mules, we should reach Santa Fe before the end of October." He maintained a brisk pace.

~~~~~~

Once again, Pascal's luck held. The Army paid him gold two weeks before the Fort's Quartermaster received a report of three large freightwagon trains scheduled to arrive at Fort Laramie in two weeks. The Army planned to march to Fort Bridger.

In late October, the Second Dragoon infantry marched west alongside three heavy-ladened freightwagon trains, eighteen wagons in each train. Pascal needed twenty mules to haul what one of these freightwagons carried. The Army followed Sweetwater Creek, leading to South Pass. With few mounted scouts and no cavalry protection, the Mormon Militia outmaneuvered the Dragoon's infantry with mounted hit-and-run attacks. The Mormon Militia burned fifty-four freightwagons loaded with the Army's entire winter supply of food, gear, tents, and blankets.

The Army refused to pay the contractor's loss for the burned supplies because civilians drove the supplies in private wagons. A Washington lawyer decided the Army had not yet accepted the supplies, as evidenced by civilian drovers in civilian wagons, and the loss was not the Army's responsibility. The fact that the Army had neither the wagons nor the drovers to deliver the goods west never entered the discussion. The disaster led to the bankruptcy of the Russell, Majors, and Waddell Freighting Company, then the largest freighter in the West. It also left the Army perilously short of supplies, mules, and equipment for the winter campaign.

The Mormons burned Fort Bridger and Fort Supply on October 27, 1857, to prevent the U.S. Army from using it as a winter camp.

The U.S. Army arrived at the ruins of Fort Bridger on November 15, 1857. Unable to mount a winter campaign across the mountains and reach Salt Lake City, the troops suffered without adequate food and clothing in a long and bitter winter beside the remains of Fort Bridger.

~~~~~~

On the ride south to Santa Fe, Blackie asked Pascal about the morality of buying and selling with the Mormons one time and selling to the Army the next time when the two sides would do battle with one another soon.

"They will do battle with one another whether we sell them our goods or not," Pascal said. "It's like I've said, 'water flows downhill.' You cannot change the nature of things. The Mormons want to proclaim independence from the union of states. The U.S. President cannot allow such an event. So, he sent his Army. You and I cannot change their actions or prevent the war. We will sell where we can to make a profit, or someone else will in our place."

During the return trip along the Front Range, Blackie met Running Elk, now an adult by Cheyenne custom. The meeting became a little awkward because they were men now and should act more serious. As it grew dark, Blackie and Running Elk strode away to talk alone. They spoke about how hard actions had become between the Cheyenne and the whites. The two young men came to understand how difficult it'd be to maintain their friendship in the future.

"I remember the one who was my mother. I think of her often, remembering her counsel," Blackie said. "I had a good time living with you.

You will always be my brother."

"She speaks of you often. She will be happy we've spoken. The white chiefs want Black Kettle and White Antelope to sign a new treaty. The People do not trust the whites to honor one."

"I will look for you when I scout for the Mule Man," Blackie said before they parted.

Pascal stopped for a day in the little village of Pueblo. He planned to ford the Arkansas and lead the men and camp mules along the west bank of a tumbling stream emptying into the river.

"What do you suppose is the name of this creek, Javy?" Pascal called.

"Pah," Javy said, drawing laughs after he used the common Redman word for water.

"The early fur-trappers called it *Fontaine Qui Bouille*, another creek with a French name," Pascal said. "It means 'fountain that boils.' Do you suppose they thought the water tumbled over rocks looked like a pot boiling? The locals call it Fountain Creek."

After the team set up camp beside the Arkansas, they drew straws to see who watched the camp. The next morning Pascal commented, "If this village had a sporting house to go with the cantina, I might stop here more often."

When the mule team crossed La Veta Pass headed for Fort Massachusetts, they found the Army working on a fort to replace Massachusetts. The troopers said the new Fort would be ready by next year and be called Fort Garland. It did not appear they had much territory to protect, but it did place the new fort closer to La Veta Pass to deter the Comanche raids into the San Luis.

~~~~~~

On October 29th, while the team rested in Santa Fe, news arrived announcing Mormons had massacred a wagon train of people from Arkansas, killing over 120 men, women, and children. The slaughter occurred at Mountain Meadows, a rest stop on the old Spanish Trail to California. The first reports blamed the Paiute for killing the settlers on the wagon train, but no one in Santa Fe placed a bit of stock in such a rumor.

"The Mormons acted foolish to do such with the Army at Fort Bridger," Pascal said. "It'll be interesting to see what happens in the spring. War makes profitable trading." He smiled.

While Blackie didn't like Pascal's comment about profit and war, he grew even more offended by the religious aspect of Mormons killing people solely because they weren't Mormons. Blackie had listened to people in the West complain about Mormons. From his experience in trading goods there the last two seasons he found them hard-working farm people who looked after one another. Their hostility to other religions disappointed him.

As Catholics, Pascal and others on the team avoided discussions on the concept of polygamy, or what the Mormon Church called plural marriage. Blackie's strict Methodist upbringing prevented him from being objective. He didn't care what the Old Testament said, Christians followed the New Testament. Jesus married one man to one woman at Canaan. Jesus spoke of no other wives.

~~~~~~

Pascal followed his usual practice of buying whatever products remained at the season's end and sold cheap in Taos or Santa Fe. Once again, he bought used wagons and surplus goods to load on the wagons before the team rode south in the fall to El Paso for the winter rest.

Sheep topped this year's surplus list in the Santa Fe stock corrals.

LaFleur argued by stomping his feet. He drew a line in the dirt with his toe. *No sheep herd.*

He wrote, *If you cannot sell this winter, you will try keeping them at the Rancho. They will be the ruin of our pastures, and without the pastures, the ranchero is worthless. No sheep!*

After four days of eating, drinking, and sporting, the Las Vegas pair discussed returning home. Blackie expressed the desire to ride with them to Las Vegas and visit the lovely widow Perkins. Pascal wanted to visit St. Vrain and insisted Blackie come with him. Frustrated, Blackie sent a long letter to the widow, hoping she wouldn't be gone or have forgotten him by spring.

Luis said, "I promise to deliver the letter in person. I shall tell the widow how you longed for her and howled at the moon every night."

Nachi and Luis laughed and wrestled with Blackie as he grabbed one in each arm.

"I hoped you'd ride with us to Las Vegas," Nachi said. "I'd have introduced you to the lovely *señoritas* at the sporting house in Las Vegas without Pascal knowing."

While they laughed and slapped one another's arms, Luis said, "If you visited those *señoritas*, you'd be prepared to satisfy the widow when your time comes."

Blackie thought he ought to have been offended by their crude language and gestures, but they read his thoughts. As he learned with his Cheyenne family and friends, they know the difference between good and bad, but the concept of "sin" and "sinful thought" didn't exist in their life. He wanted to lie with a woman like Morning Star or the widow Ellen Perkins. Blackie knew such thoughts or actions formed a sin in the eyes of his father's church, but he dreamed of Morning Star and Ellen Perkins in the night.

Blackie continued to run daily and to shoot often, but most often, he shot game for food.

He had grown into a tall, gangly young man. The daily lifting of packsaddles loaded with 250 pounds of cargo developed the muscles in his chest, shoulders, and arms to match his well-developed runner's legs.

He prayed for his last family less often these days, not from loss of religious fervor but more so from fatigue from long days at work.

It shocked and troubled him when he thought of

motherly love, Yellow Blossom's image came to mind as often as his mother's fading image. He held scant memory of his two sisters.

He thought of his father when he listened to another's sermon and compared those he remembered his father delivering. What came to mind from Wales these days became a rolling green hills of peaceful, rural countryside and frequent rains.

He understood he'd changed and it became more than growing tall.

The cousins treated him with deference.

Pascal would ask him for his opinion about things. *Not that it ever changed his mind.*

No longer did he act like a whiny Welsh brat who acted so helpless.

Only Pascal called him *Noir.* If he had his tongue, so would LaFleur.

He had become Blackthorn Wolfe – Black Wolf of the Cheyenne.

Blackie to his friends on the team and to people on the trail.

Tomorrow, the mule team would ride to Mexico—south in the fall.

FINI

Dear Reader:

I appreciate you taking your precious quiet time to read North in the Spring, Part II in the *The Apprenticeship of Nigel Blackthorn* series. I hope you'll look for Part III "South in the Fall" in April 2020.

In the Western tradition, one cowpuncher going along the trail talks to the next puncher, spreading word by the moccasin telegraph. If you liked our story, please tell your friends—the old moccasin telegraph, word-of-mouth, is the best advertisement. Amazon and browsing readers rate a book by the number of reviews. I'd appreciate a review if you have the time, a few lines will do. The link to submit an Amazon review is below. (or visit the book page on Amazon and scroll down to existing reviews and click button :Submit a Review.)

Thanks
Frank

amazon.com/review/create-review/B07Y5JFWDM/

Historical Note: The "sinks" described in the book are in Idaho. They are on Federal land controlled by the Dept. of Energy, Idaho National Laboratory. The "sink" on the Popo Agie is in the Sinks Canyon State Park outside of Lander, WY. It is a unique natural phenomena, as described in the book.

For your reading enjoyment, I've attached the first two chapters of California Bound.

Description

In a Union POW camp, Jeb & Zach struggled to stay alive while they dreamed of finding California gold, but the road West leads Jeb past his sister's home in Texas. Jeb finds her dead.

A border war rages along the Rio near Eagle Pass with cattle rustled and ranches burned.

Innocents are killed or kidnapped and Jeb's fourteen-year-old niece, Becky, is missing.

Texas lawmen refused to go get Becky. The U.S. Cavalry can't cross the Rio.

The Cavalry officer said, "Cortina has an adobe-walled fort in Mexico. My cavalry company couldn't take it without artillery. What chance do 2 men have?"

The two Civil War veterans wade the Rio to rescue a stolen girl—or die trying.

Jeb and Zach plans to carry a case of dynamite to Cortina's fort.

Zach will sneak Becky from inside before Jeb blows-up the fort.

What could go wrong?

The Jeb & Zach series collection of
all 3 e-books is available on Amazon.

Excerpt from

California Bound

Chapter One

1866

"Is that a ... a lynching?" Jebidiah Benjamin whispered over his shoulder to his partner, raising an open hand head-high. The two Confederate veterans knew military signals all too well, using them without a second thought. Obscured riders in the woods ahead alerted Jeb, who reined his sorrel gelding to a stop. "Dismount 'til I can figure what's happenin'."

Zachariah Daughtry followed Jeb's lead, as usual. Once on foot, they slid between tall pines, letting their horses and pack mule trail behind. Thick layers of pine needles carpeted the ground, creating a silent footpath. Jeb halted their advance creeping a dozen yards ahead to peer around a thick pine trunk, returning to Zach in a flat-out sprint.

"Tie the pack mule to a tree. Mount up. Them rascals are tossin' a necktie party."

"Whoa." Zach grabbed Jeb's arm. "You're inviting *us* to a hanging?" Zach shook his head.

"Let's ride around. We don't need this kind of trouble."

"Somethin' don't seem right." Jeb spat tobacco juice, a habit he acquired while in the Union POW camp. "Can't let it go by." He rubbed the stubble on his chin. "We'll stop to say howdy … get an idea of what they're doin'."

"That your entire plan?"

"Yep." Jeb nodded, as certain as if General Bobby Lee had handed them written orders.

"Not much of a plan."

Jeb lifted his sweat-stained gray hat to wipe his brow. "It's all I got right now. We'll see how they play it."

"That's what I'm afraid of." Zach grinned, giving his head a shake. He eased his riding jacket forward in a half-hearted effort to hide the two Remington pistols he wore in shoulder holsters. In the war, the military holster with flap delayed his reaction to hostilities or ambush. As former scouts and skirmishers, both shunned holsters strapped to their legs.

Mounted again, Jeb led them into a clearing created by a spreading live oak. He wore a cartridge-converted Colt Navy in a belly holster, but kept the fifteen-and-one-half-inch-long converted .44-Walker Colt in a pommel holster close at hand when riding.

Four mounted men faced a rider who wore a rope noose dangling from a massive oak limb. The soon-to-be-hanged man's expression conveyed he needed an answer to his mumbled prayers.

Resurrection ferns living on the oak limbs reminded one of salvation, leading the man's eyes to flicker with hope when the two riders approached.

"Have we done missed the trial?" Jeb called after Zach and he rode close to the men astride their horses. "A trial's more entertaining than a circus." His distracting, and often annoying, chatter rivaled a mockingbird.

"Ride on, strangers," a heavy-set, chin-whiskered man growled. His fat belly strained the buttons on his red vest when he hiked a thumb over his shoulder toward the trail west. "This here's none of your concern. We're ridding the world of a horse thief." Sunlight filtering through the oak leaves caused shadows that hid his face, but his eyes shined as if lit by lanterns.

"I've told you, Mr. Dawson. I got me a bill of sale," the roped man pleaded.

"That's a Ferguson brand on the hoss he's straddlin'," a tall, skinny, scarecrow-looking man said, his large Adam's apple bobbing with his words. "I ain't known Ferguson to sell no horses these days."

Scarecrow and the two other riders dressed like working cowhands—dungarees, cotton shirts, and neck bandannas. Jeb thought Dawson dressed like an eastern dandy, or worse, a carpetbagger.

The bearded Dawson jerked his reins and kicked his horse's flank, moving it to face them. "I done told you two to move on. Unless you intend to join him, you'll heed my words." He shifted his right hand to rest on his pistol butt.

While Jeb gigged his horse toward Dawson, Zach moseyed left, placing the four men between them—into crossfire. The veterans had made this move so often during the war one needn't check where the other had positioned himself. The pair eased along using nothing but "good ol' boy" guile due to Jeb's way of distracting folks with his chatter.

"Have you checked the man's bill of sale?" Jeb asked, pointing a finger at the roped man but he rode toward Dawson, figuring the fat man's loud mouth showed him as the lead bully of this rag-tag mob. Jeb shifted his weight in the saddle, signaling his horse to stop.

The portly carpetbagger spat, curling his lip in a snarl. "You deef or something? I tol—"

Before he finished his threat, Dawson and his men faced Jeb and Zach's drawn pistols—two pairs of Remingtons and Colts. Eyes widened. Jaws gaped. Eyebrows rose.

Silence.

"I hear you well and good, stranger," Jeb said, baring his teeth in a grimace. "But you see, I'm a curious cuss. I'd like to see this here man's bill of sale—it'll take but a minute. If he's a sharper or a blackleg, I'll leave you to your social."

While pointing his pistols at the lynch party, Jeb pressed his knees into his mount's ribs, guiding it behind Dawson before reaching the roped man. "Where you got the paper, neighbor?"

"It's in my right shirt pocket. Inside an

envelope," the roped man said, his quivering voice betraying his fear hidden in his quiet, defeated demeanor. Sweat dripped from his baldpate. His hat lay on the ground, tossed aside for his hanging.

Jeb slid his Walker Colt into its pommel holster, using his right hand to tug a paper from a half-folded envelope. After scanning it, he said, "This bill of sale is signed by Matthew B. Ferguson. Any of you gents recognize the name?"

Scarecrow gulped aloud. "I'll be danged. That's how Ferguson signs his papers." The skinny man whipped his head around, glancing at the two cowpunchers alongside, who stared at one another, eyes wide, while color drained from their faces.

"Sounds like a piss-poor excuse for a lynching." Jeb eyed each cowhand before he returned his gaze to Dawson. "You gents gonna ride on ... or do y'all want to make somethin' out o' this?"

Dawson grumbled aloud. "It's *you* who better keep moving. We don't like your kind around here." He leaned aside to spit, but his weight shift caused his horse to sidestep, letting the spittle dribble along his chin.

Like I thought, a carpetbagger—a Southern man woulda said "we don't cotton to your kind." Damn Yankees.

"Is that so?" Jeb said. He eyed Zach, motioning toward Dawson with his head. "You hear him? We ain't wanted hereabouts." He rested a forearm on the saddle horn, smiling tight-lipped. "And just what *kind* is that? Law-abiding honest folks?" Upon straightening, he drew the Walker Colt, cocking the hammer, and aiming at Dawson's chest.

Zach motioned Jeb with his head. "Let me take care of this." With his Remingtons in hand, he gigged his horse next to Dawson's. While glaring into Dawson's serpent eyes, Zach's face flushed crimson with anger.

"What?" Dawson shouted, his lips forming a snarl.

In a flash, Zach cracked his pistol alongside Dawson's head, spilling the fat man from his horse, plopping him on the ground. He slapped his hand to his gashed head with groan.

"Is that clear enough for you?" Zach said. "I don't cotton to murdering an innocent man." He glared at Dawson. "Get on your horse while you still can."

Dawson pushed himself from the ground, grabbing a stirrup to stand wobbly-legged, and then struggled to mount his horse while blood oozed from the gash above his temple.

Jeb held his Colts on the other men.

Veins on his temples throbbed while Jeb spoke. "Now I'll say it a'gin. Slower this time so you understand it. I'd take it right kindly if you rode east a while."

Dawson glanced over his shoulder, seeking to gain the support of the other riders to back his play, but his companions whirled their horses, trotting east.

"You 'deef or somethin'?" Zach shouted, mocking Dawson's voice, while motioning with his Remington. "Go on—get."

Dawson grimaced, his face flushed in rage. While holding a kerchief atop his head wound, he reined his horse in a circle before he galloped east, following the other riders.

"Love it when a plan works," Jeb said, holstering both Colts before reining his horse next to the almost-hanged man, removing the noose from the man's neck. It swung loose beside them as a reminder of a future that could have been. He loosened the roper's knot holding the man's hands behind his back.

"You call *that* a plan?" Zach leaned from the saddle to retrieve the almost-hanged man's fallen hat from the ground in the practiced way of the men in the Tenth Texas Cavalry, holding the pommel to fetch something from the ground, which they often did on the run, to save time and effort.

"If it works, it's a plan," Jeb said.

"Hard to create a ruckus when your head's bleeding like a stuck hog," Zach said, trying not to laugh aloud.

"Indeed it is." Jeb's smile grew wider, his teeth showing. "Got to admit, my plan worked pretty well, didn't it?"

"The no-plan plan?"

"No, the plan that worked."

"What would we have done if they'd drawn on us—"

"Quit your gripin'," Jeb said, dismissing the argument with a sweep of his hand. "I'll take tried-and-true over new-and-dead, any day. That carpetbagger's lucky to be alive."

"As am I," the almost-hanged man interrupted.

Jeb and Zach quieted their banter.

"I'm John Cavanaugh," he said, reaching to clasp Jeb's hand. "I feared I was a goner before you gents rode in. I sure do thank you." Cavanaugh rode close to shake Zach's hand while collecting his hat.

"We're heading to San Antonio," Jeb said. "Although I think it unlikely, you might want to ride with us for a spell to prevent those jaspers from circlin' to try this stunt again."

"I'd sure appreciate it. My spread is twenty miles southwest of here. If I can ride west with you 'til near sunset, I can be home by morning."

~~~~~~

The two veterans stood six-foot tall, broad shouldered with narrow hips. While Jeb denied it, Zach edged a smidgen taller. Folks often assumed them kin, but neither thought he resembled the other. Jeb kept his light-brown hair trimmed— barbered, when he could find one. Zach wore his dark locks long and combed straight back, using a leather cuff to gather it into a pigtail at his collar. Jeb wore a simple mustache on his upper lip while Zach sported a Van Dyke darker than his hair. Jeb's hazel eyes expressed his every emotion, changing from light to dark with his mood, but Zach's chocolate-brown eyes betrayed no secrets.

They rode along for thirty minutes before Zach nodded to Cavanaugh. "Why'd you buy a horse this far from home?"

"Ferguson trains horses to push wild longhorns from cane breaks and heavy brush. He breeds 'em from wild mustangs. They're smaller, short-coupled with strong hips—turn quicker. Longhorns grew wary and mean in the brush during the war. If you drive them from the thickets and cane breaks, they're yours."

"What's that carpetbagger Dawson's gripe with *you*?" Jeb asked.

"His cousin has a spot of property near me, and I mean *a spot*," Cavanaugh said. "He ain't got but six cows. I found him 'checking for unbranded calves' on my spread. Told him if I catch anyone taking a calf off my land, I'd shoot 'em."

Jeb considered his answer. "So Dawson figured why bother with calves—he'd grab it all after hangin' you as a horse thief." He scratched his stubbled chin. "Somethin' about the whole scene struck me as outta kilter."

Zach harrumphed. "Jeb says he has a special gift. Even found him a fancy French name for it, but I just call it 'clear annoyance.'" Zach rolled his eyes, smirking.

Jeb lifted his head, laughing. "You done yet?"

"I thought that *clear annoyance* of yours would let you know when I'm done." Zach laughed a short bark before he dropped behind on the narrow trail through the piney woods.

The men rode the next few miles in silence, crossing a shallow washout before snaking around wild brambles. Pileated woodpeckers hammered nearby while calling with a stuttering wuk-wuk-wuk.

Zach pointed at Jeb as he nodded at Cavanaugh. "I been wondering … did them Yankees return your sergeant stripes?"

"What'd you say?" Jeb didn't bother to glance behind when they left the trail to ride around a tall pine's deadfall.

"You know," Zach continued, "back there in Ill-a-noise, 'fore we slipped past the fence to sneak away from that damned Yankee prisoner-of-war camp?"

The men rode along for a minute before Jeb shook his head. "Did I ever tell you I use to have me a long-haired, black puppy? That dog yapped if I petted him. Yapped if I stopped petting. Any stray dogs or critters came near the yard, he yapped. Yapped all the dang time—same as you."

"Hey, I had a dog like that once … a playful pup. You're right, *just* like me." Zach beamed a smile. "My dog died 'fore the war started. Whatever happened to your dog?"

Jeb broke trail as it narrowed in an area overgrown with blackberry brambles while Zach guided the pack mule carrying their gear, Cavanaugh following behind.

"Ma caught him in the henhouse sucking eggs—shot him on the spot." Jeb said, "She had a smidge less tolerance for an egg-sucking dog than she did for a yapping dog." He twisted his shoulders to glance behind, beaming a big grin.

"Tough woman," Cavanaugh said.

"She was that, all right," Jeb said. "Cured *me* from suckin' eggs."

Zach tilted his head aside. "If you're gonna be like that, I won't yap—I'll shout." He hollered, "When do I get to rest so I can fix some eats, Sargent?"

"Yap, yap, yap." Jeb chuckled. "I can't savvy how a man as tall an' rawboned lean as you can be so dang hungry all the time." *Maybe three years in the POW camp left him haunted by hunger.*

Cavanaugh pushed his hat back, laughing aloud at their teasing banter.

"You know this area, Cavanaugh?" Zach asked.

"Been through it."

"Any campsites nearby?"

Cavanaugh stroked a hand on his cheek. "I think there's a small stream ahead ... maybe four miles."

"I'd hoped to find a sweet water creek," Jeb said, "might be we can find decent wood to build a campfire. Only downed wood hereabouts is pine. Burns too hot and fast."

"Cooking sounds good," Zach said. "I've got a mess of black-eyed peas soaking in a water-tight pouch. If we make camp before dark, I'll boil them with sliced pork belly."

Jeb snorted as if expelling a gnat from his nose. "There's somethin' different."

"I'm as tired of eating my cooking as you are." Zach raised an eyebrow at Cavanaugh. "Ain't there no towns in these parts where we can find a bite of another cook's grub?"

"Few and far between," Cavanaugh said, shaking his head.

"We'll leave these woods tomorrow or the next day, before we join the El Camino Real to San Antonio," Jeb said.

"None too soon for me," Zach said.

"Nor my stomach," Jeb said with a belly laugh.

Near sunset, Cavanaugh thanked them again, parting with a wave before trotting his horse south into the fading light. Meanwhile, Zach built a growing fire, waiting for it to become hot enough to simmer his iron pot full of water and black-eyed peas.

Jeb moved his saddle near the fire before grooming his horse, wiping its back with a frayed saddle blanket. He brushed his horse whenever he unsaddled it, but never ran a brush through his own unruly brown hair. Afterwards, he sat on a deadfall log to rest before he fished a letter from his jacket pocket, reading it over again by the firelight.

Zach watched as Jeb finished, and with deliberate care, folded the letter, returning it to his jacket.

"We'll get there soon enough," Zach said.

"I know," Jeb replied. "It's just ... I don't know. Somethin' about it worries me."

"We'll be there in ten days or so," Zach said. "Your family will be fine. We'll visit for a spell before we ride to California—all that gold is waiting for us."

After Jeb patted the letter in his jacket, as if to reassure himself of its presence, he spat tobacco juice into the fire, where it sizzled and flared.

"You acted kinda chancy today. You gonna do this all the way to California?" Zach asked, without giving Jeb a glance.

"Just didn't seem right. That's all." He spat another stream of tobacco, missing the fire. "Didn't have the look of a horse thief." He rose to attend his horse.

"Neither do we." Zach resumed cooking, stirring the pot with a foot-long wooden spoon.

"What? Was you worried we couldn't handle four conniving blacklegs?"

"Not hardly," Zach said. "No, I'm talking about our history of riding borrowed horseflesh." He moved the boiling coffee pot aside, letting it cool for a minute or two before adding a cup of cold water to settle the grounds.

"Pshaw. These horses got a bill of sale from the Union Army," Jeb said.

"A worthless bill of sale is what we got. It ain't even for these horses. Hell, it's not worth the paper it's printed on," Zach replied.

"It's a government document, ain't it? Of course it's worthless." He spoke over his shoulder as he gathered tin-plates and spoons for their meal.

Zach smirked, then caught Jeb's eye, nodding. "You got a point there."

"Indeed I do."

Chapter Two

"These long rides, rough bivouacs, and short food rations have me thinking I'm still in the Texas cavalry, Sar-gent." Zach called "Sar-gent" in a mock bray.

"Will you stop the sergeant crap," Jeb said. "If I recall, they promoted you to sergeant at same time they did me." The pair had forded the Colorado River the day before, while Jeb expected to cross the Guadalupe River later in the afternoon. Low water in the rivers, not even getting their boots wet, indicated a dry winter season, which forecast poor grass for grazing this summer.

"Oh, yeah, I forgot. Reckon I got busted to the ranks within the month when they caught *me* helping *you* pull one of your Johnny-jump-up capers."

"It was a good plan," Jeb said. "It just needed a ... a rigorous execution."

"A plan?" Zach laughed. "Making it up as you went along, if I recall."

"And you learned a valuable lesson—don't get caught."

"You ought to run for governor the way you dodge the subject," Zach said. "We've spent a dozen days on the trail, but we ain't no closer to your sis's ranch, let alone San Antonio."

"That ain't so. San Antonio's jus' over the next hill," Jeb said, motioning with his finger.

"That so?"

"Mebbe."

Jeb lifted his hat to wipe his brow. "I expect we'll be in San Antonio tomorrow before dark, if you ride as fast as you complain. Are you in such an all-fired hurry to get to California you'll gripe about resting for a day or two?"

"A two-day pass?" Zach feigned surprise. "Mighty generous of you, Sar-gent."

"We've been pushing these horses pretty hard. They need to rest and eat decent oats," Jeb said, ducking as Zach swatted with his hat. "It's rest the horses or buy fresh ones. And you know how I hate paying cash money for someone else's horseflesh."

"Ain't done much of that lately," Zach said.

"Indeed. Sally's ranch is six, maybe seven days farther south, along the Rio Grande. Don't 'xpect another couple of days restin' here will make much difference."

~~~~~~

San Antonio de Bexar had once been the capital of Spanish Tejas with an old and storied history, and in 1866, it's the largest city in Texas. Unlike the cities Jeb and Zach visited in the East, San Antonio had no paved streets. Two sturdy cypress-log and timber-planked bridges crossed the narrow river flowing through the middle of the city. Wagons, ox carts, carriages, cattle herds, and mounted riders churned its thoroughfares into wagon-rutted, dusty streets.

After renting a room in a quiet *mesón* across the river from the Alamo, Jeb and Zach decided to enjoy a special treat. They strode across a pontoon footbridge over the river to reach the Menger Hotel, the fanciest hotel in the Southwest. The Menger's restaurant maintained the old Southern tradition of white linen tablecloths, a complete silver service, imported bone-china place settings, and crystal stemware at each meal.

"I want the biggest beefsteak you have," Jeb said.

"Our best steak is a porterhouse served on the bone, sir. We prepare it rare, serving it with a bowl of red potatoes, boiled spinach, and pole beans."

"How big is it?" Zach asked, raising an eyebrow at the black-frocked waiter.

"It's larger than a dinner plate, sir," the waiter said. "It's this thick," holding his first three fingers close together to demonstrate.

Jeb figured the waiter must suffer from a cold, because he lifted his nose to sniff after each of their questions.

"That's what I want," Zach said, pounding the heel of his fist on the table.

"By the by, is somethin' wrong with your eyes?" Jeb asked.

Startled, the waiter answered. "No sir, why do you ask?"

"Seems you keep rollin' 'em each time we ask somethin'."

When finished with the sumptuous dinner, they ambled outside to walk along the street, planning to visit a nearby Victorian house serving hard liquor and easy women.

The next morning, after a breakfast of biscuits and side meat, they rocked in cane-bottom chairs on the sporting house porch.

Zach studied a fancy carriage leaving the Menger Hotel, rattling along Crockett Street past them. "Reckon after I gather me a wagon load of California gold, I'll buy a gilt-trimmed carriage like that one, where I can sit on a soft cushion, fluttering a hankie at my Mexican driver like that fat swell." He scratched the stubble under his chin whiskers.

"Nah, I expect you'll piss it away on cheap whiskey and cheaper women," Jeb said.

"This house don't have no cheap ladies. Paid two dollars for her. I figure for about a thousand dollars a year to have me a different one every night." Zach smiled like a pig in the feed bin. "May even have *two* on Sunday."

"Mighty religious of you."

Zach placed his hat atop his heart, in mock reverence. "Just paying my respects."

Moments passed in silence as they rocked on the porch.

"Plan to find me a place on a mountain meadow, say in the Sierra Nevada, or the Rockies western slope," Jeb said. "You ever seen Appaloosa ponies? Like blue roans but with spotted rumps. I'll breed and then train the most easy-riding horses a fella ever sat."

"Why, you'll need a troop of guards to protect such fine horses." Zach feigned a surprised, wide-eyed face. "Oh, shoot, I forgot—you won't worry none about a low-down horse thief stealing them ... 'cause *you* already own them."

After he swatted Zach with his hat, Jeb leaned close, to say in a low voice, "I know you're joking, but you ought not to talk so loud 'round strangers. One of them might take you serious once they get to thinking about a reward for reportin' us to the law."

"Ain't no reward offered for us skedaddling 'fore we got parole papers," Zach replied. "They never even wrote our names right."

An older gentleman, broad in the shoulders, narrow of waist, strode from the sporting house wearing matching black corduroy riding jacket and pants with his pant legs stuffed into shiny, stovepipe boots. The blunted rowels on his silver spurs jingled when he stopped at the stairs, waiting for the house's Mexican lad to fetch his horse from their stable. His trim Van Dyke beard shined silver-white on his weatherworn tanned face.

"Fine morning, ain't it, sir," Jeb said, smiling.

The tall, lean man shifted to study each of them with the squint-eyed gaze of a judge sizing up scofflaws. "You two serve in the Texas Cavalry?" He pointed at Jeb. "I seem to remember a sergeant with the scouts or skirmishers. Did you serve with the Seventeenth Cavalry?"

The men stood to attention as Jeb said, "The Tenth. I apologize, sir. I don't recollect you."

The older man extended his hand, "Colonel Sebron Noble, Third Battalion Commander with the Seventeenth. We fought alongside the Tenth often enough for me to recognize your scouts and skirmishers from ours in the field."

He glanced at Zach, studying him for a moment. "Were you a sergeant?" His brow furrowed. "Wait, now I remember. You whitewashed a bull's-eye on the rump of an officer's mount." A smile spread across his tanned face. "We laughed about it in the Seventeenth's Officer's Mess, but I'd have broken you to the ranks if you'd been in my command."

"Who, sir? Me, sir? No, sir. Not I, sir," Zach replied without a stammer.

"If I remember the officer from the Academy, he *was* a horse's ass." The Colonel clapped Zach's shoulder, smiling at the joke while he slid a finger along the gold chain across his buckskin suede vest to pluck an engraved gold watch from its pocket.

"I don't often imbibe before supper, but I'll stand you two fine skirmishers to a drink." He pointed to the Stockman's Saloon across the wagon-rutted street.

~~~~~~

After the barman set fresh glasses on the bar, he reached under the counter for a bottle of red-eye whiskey, but Colonel Noble wagged a finger. "Ollie, go to the backroom. Fetch us a bottle of the fine Tennessee bourbon your boss keeps for special guests." He glanced between Zach and Jeb. "Where are you two headed? You looking for work?"

"We're gonna visit my sis's ranch in the Rio Grande valley for a spell," Jeb said. "Later, we're riding to the California gold fields."

"You're late getting home," Noble said.

Neither Jeb nor Zach responded.

"The Yankees did parole you after the war?" Noble asked.

"No, sir," Zach said. "Kept us 'til they closed Camp Douglas then we sneaked through the back door." Zach smirked, biting his lower lip. "Not exactly paroled with paper, but we got gone."

Jeb coughed into his hand while Zach glanced through the saloon's front window, scratching the back of his head.

The colonel puffed his chest, his face tightening. "I gather there's a story behind your stalling."

The barman uncorked a labeled bottle of Tennessee bourbon before he filled their glasses.

"We got captured by Sherman's cavalry at the north end of Missionary Ridge on the day Bragg's center fell apart in Chattanooga." Jeb's voice grew softer, halting.

"Son, we all had to surrender at one point or another. It's no disgrace."

"It became a little more complicated than that, sir," Zach added.

After a nod at Zach, Jeb said, "The cap'n sent my squad to reconnoiter if Sherman planned to flank the ridge or move against the railroad tunnel to cut off our supply lines. A danged sharpshooter shot Zach's horse from under him. I couldn't leave him behind."

Zach shrugged, wrinkling a frown, as if to say, "*Nothing I could do.*"

"I sent my scouts hightailin' to report that Sherman himself led a reconnaissance-in-force near the tunnel. I sneaked into a woody ravine trying to locate Zach, finding him before we galloped toward the tunnel to escape." Jeb heaved a deep sigh.

"His favorite horse stepped in a hole," Zach continued. "We flew ass-over-teacart. In the fall, we lost our rifles. Nothing to do but shoot the poor animal with his pistol." He glanced at Jeb. "I don't think he's forgiven me yet."

"Yeah, I kinda have," Jeb said. "We were afoot, with Sherman's own guard hunting for who fired the shot. The damned Yankee fool done captured the wrong hill—we didn't hold it, or want it.

"Zach pointed at mounts nearby. An aide-de-camp, outfitted for a dress parade in front of the officers' wives, held two horses whilst the General strolled around munching blackberries in the midst of the battle." Jeb spat tobacco juice in the dented, brass spittoon beside the bar's foot rail. "I would've shot the twitchy-eyed runt, but I used my last bullet on my horse."

"I slipped behind the fancy-pants lieutenant, smacking him with my pistol," Zach said. "While I mounted one horse, Jeb took the other one. We learned later, Jeb *borrowed* Sherman's personal horse—a coal-black Virginia jumper, black to his skin and hoofs. While we spurred the Yankee horses to skedaddle, the General shouted for his guards.

"Lordy, how that twitchy-eyed man cussed." Jeb's cheeks glowed hot as he bragged. "He could out-shout an' out-cuss most sergeants—and then some."

Colonel Noble stood open-mouthed, his eyes wide. "You ... you stole General Sherman's horse?" The man's stiff bearing relaxed as he arched his neck to guffaw. "You came close enough to see his twitchy eye?" He gasped, "Oh, dear Lord," laughing.

"I picked the best horse. Didn't know it was *his*," Jeb said, as if apologizing.

The Colonel gripped Jeb's shoulders, giving a strong shake. "By God, I love skirmishers. The tip of the sword—leading the battle." His eyes glistened.

"Yeah, them Yankees thought it so funny, they gave us three years in that danged prisoner-of-war camp for 'misappropriating Federal property,'" Zach said.

"Damned Yankees," the Colonel said.

"Amen," Jeb and Zach replied in unison.

The three men grew silent for a moment, each lost in his remembrances.

"What happened with you, Colonel?" Jeb asked before spitting in the direction of the malodorous brass spittoon beside the foot rail.

"Stories for another day," the Colonel said, lifting his glass. "To lost battles."

"To lost causes," Jeb responded.

"To lost friends," Zach added.

They touched glasses before swallowing the Tennessee bourbon, ending with a flourish by slamming their glasses on the bar in unison.

The senior officer flicked a finger along the chain to retrieve his fancy gold watch, flipping open its engraved cover. "Sound Boots and Saddles, Sergeant."

"Sir," Jeb replied with a salute, while Zach rushed to open the saloon's door.

A stout man wearing a brass-buttoned Yankee dress-blouse with sergeant stripes blocked the doorway. He asked over his shoulder to a grizzled ne'er-do-well behind him, "These the Rebs you reported?"

"Shore 'nuf," came the reply. The ragamuffin pointed a crooked finger at Jeb. "Thas th' 'un wha' claim'd he done stole the gen'ral's hoss."

"All right, Reb, you're under arrest for horse thieving. That's a hanging offense in Texas." The sergeant stepped away, beckoning Jeb to step onto the boardwalk. Pointing to two blue-coated men with him, he said, "Blake, you and Wally clap him in irons, while I question the other Rebs for seditious behavior."

Zach opened the door wide to step outside in front of Jeb. Instead of a cross-draw, he hooked the trigger-finger of each hand into each pistol's trigger guard, easing them from their shoulder holsters, presenting them butt-forward to the sergeant.

"I suppose you'll want these?" Zach said, offering his pair of Remingtons.

"Watch out, Borden. He's doing a—" Blake said before Jeb grabbed his extended arm, twisting it around behind his back while kicking his right boot from under him. Blake found himself resting on his knees, dazed with Jeb's cocked Army Colt pointed at his head.

As Blake tried to warn, Zach performed a Border roll, swiveling the pistols around his trigger finger, the butt of each pistol resting in his hands, cocked and ready. Borden and Wally stared open-mouthed at the reversal.

"Stand down," Noble bellowed. "Return your weapons to their holsters. I'll not allow unruly behavior from either side." Colonel Noble stepped in front of Sergeant Borden. "Take me to your senior officer. I'll vouchsafe these men."

Borden bared his teeth in a twisted snarl. "There ain't vouchsafing for Rebs. We're the State Police—what we say is law. You best get used to taking orders."

"I doubt you earned those stripes in the U.S. Army, Sergeant, or you'd never argue with a field-grade officer. Take me to your commanding officer, *now*," Noble barked.

After the four men entered the provisional Military Headquarters, the Command Sergeant Major bellowed, "Ten-hut." Officers and enlisted men snapped to attention with the appearance of the Commanding Officer.

"Sergeant Major, clear the room of enlisted men and civilians, except those two men with Colonel Noble," General George Armstrong Custer said before he crossed the room to clasp Noble's right hand.

"Seb, why didn't you send a note about visiting San Antonio? We could have had supper together. Is Nancy along? Elizabeth is starved of companionship."

"I'm passing through on the way to my ranch," Noble said. "Nancy is in Memphis with her family until it's safe on the Brazos. I heard Washington assigned you to head the Western Command. I hoped it meant the Army planned action against the Comanche in Texas."

"I requested permission to bolster the number of troops in the frontier forts, but the Army is reducing to peacetime numbers. Shepherding reconstruction of civilian operations is not my idea of proper duty for a cavalry officer," Custer replied, clapping a hand on Noble's shoulder.

He glanced at Jeb and Zach, but addressed Noble. "I understand some serious charges have been leveled at these two. Let's continue this in my office." Custer waved an arm for his senior staff and the other men to follow.

Three senior officers from the Western Command sat to one side of Custer's office. Jeb and Zach stood at parade-rest behind Noble. Custer's aide-de-camp, a young shavetail, stood at ease behind Custer, who sat at his desk.

"I encountered two scouts from my command this morning," Noble waved a hand over his shoulder at Jeb and Zach, "I offered them a drink at Harrison's Stockman Saloon. They reported serving three years in Camp Douglas for misappropriating Federal property—they stole General Sherman's horse at Chattanooga."

Lieutenant Colonel Johnson barked a laugh, pointing at Jeb and Zach. "You two did *that*? I served on General Sherman's staff before his march to the sea. He ranted for weeks about losing his horse."

"Sherman dismounted in the midst of a battle?" Custer asked with furrowed brows.

"His mounted guards found a blackberry bramble with ripe berries. He stopped for dessert—his favorite." Johnson shrugged while spreading his open hands wide, as if saying, "*Who am I to question General Sherman?*"

Custer interrupted the joking banter. "How does this relate to the sergeant's complaint of 'armed insurrection'?"

"Sergeant Borden attempted to arrest these two men all over again, assuring they'd hang, when I interrupted. I demanded to speak to his commanding officer, expecting to find a rosy-cheeked plebe." Noble chuckled, waving a hand at Custer and Johnson. "Instead, I find two old classmates from the Academy."

"Seb," Custer said, "friendship aside, Texans are resisting the Reconstruction Act. It doesn't look good to have a well-known Confederate officer resist lawful orders." Custer glanced at his adjutant, Lieutenant Colonel Johnson. "Fred, did the U.S. Army convict these men in a military tribunal and pass sentence?"

"As far as I know, yes, sir." Johnson nodded.

"Can't convict them twice," Custer mused.

Johnson said, "Sir, I'll speak to the State Police sergeant. I suspect both sides over-reacted." He glanced at Jeb and Zach. "Can I assure the sergeant you'll be more respectful of State Police in the future?" After their curt nods, Johnson continued, "I also have your assurances you're leaving town, *today?*"

Noble swiveled to bark an order. "Answer, loud and clear."

"Yes, sir," Jeb and Zach said in unison.

Noble stood, reaching a hand across Custer's desk, "I apologize for bringing this to your level, George. I appreciate your understanding. I expect

Nancy will return in a month or two. I'll ask her to write Elizabeth to arrange time for us to enjoy a private supper."

"Please do. I'm moving headquarters to Austin after this week," Custer said.

Jeb and Zach thanked Noble while they strode across the grassy plaza to their horses. "You two better behave for a while. I may not be around the next time you need help."

"Believe me," Zach said, "we'll ride out before noon."

At street side, Colonel Noble mounted his blaze-faced sorrel. "You're too late for the easy gold in California—it's all hard-rock mining now. You're cavalry, not rock hounds. I need men like you two on my Rocker-N Ranch, keeping the Comanche away. You have a job waiting when you wash the gleam of gold from your eyes." He reined left, trotting his horse along the rutted, dusty street.

"Dang," Zach said, "Why didn't the officers in the Tenth act like that gentleman?"

"They might've, but they never took the time to know their men," Jeb said. "They only barked orders."

"You still for California?" Zach asked, canting his head.

"You ever met an officer who knowed what the hell they talked about?" Jeb asked, smiling. "Especially one on the *losing* side?"

Zach laughed. "California it is."

"With all that gold," Jeb said.

Amazon, and browsing readers, rate a book by the number of reviews. I'd appreciate a review if you have the time, a few lines will do. I know it takes a few minutes of your time but consider it like a "tip" to a barista at Starbucks. It says you appreciated their work.

A tip of my hat for reading and I hope you enjoyed enough to return the tip (a review.)

amazon.com/review/create-review/B07622JJGM

If you sign-up to receive Frank's blog, Traveling the West, from the following link, Frank will send you the novella, DEATH AT CAMP DOUGLAS, which is the prequel to California Bound.

Death at Camp Douglas is the story of Jeb and Zach's experiences in the Union POW camp outside Chicago, IL. The 23,000-word story is only available to fans joining Frank's blog. The novella serves as a transition from the fight for survival at the POW camp to Jeb and Zach's next adventure, SHERMAN'S WAR ON WOMEN, planned for release in Aug 2020. Find more information at Frank's blog http://frankkelsoauthor.com

Visit the website: frankkelsoauthor.com

Join Frank's Blog, Traveling the West
frankkelsoauthor.com

Beachfront Press, LLC
25778 John M Snook Dr, Suite 2402
Orange Beach, AL 36561

Glossary

Several people commented the first book didn't provide translations for unusual words. Listed in order of use.

Oui (French) – Yes
Non (French) – No
Noir (French) – Dark or Black
Bon retour (French) – Welcome back
Me-se-este (Cheyenne) – eat
Merci (French) – Thank you
Je va a'dormir (French) – I'm going to sleep
Ca Que (French) – What
Vous parlez Français (French) – You speak French?
Voila (French) – Here (it) is
Maheo (Cheyenne) – Deity
Hombre (Spanish) – Man
La Junta del Rios (Spanish) – The junction of the rivers
Camino Real (Spanish) – Kings road
Caballeros (Spanish) – Horsemen
Vaqueros (Spanish) – Cattlemen
Señor (Spanish) – Mister
Jornada del Muerto (Spanish) – Journey of Death (Dead man's walk)
Mon ami (French) – My friend
Waugh (Mountain-man term) – Hello, what do mean, (inflection varies the meaning.)
Bonne nuit (French) – Good night

S'il vous plaît (French) – If you please

Huaraches (Spanish) – sandals or moccasins

capataz de mula (Spanish) – foreman of the mules (Mule boss)

Fonda (Spanish) – Inn, restaurant, or combination of both

Molé (Spanish) – spicy sauce (often with raw cocoa)

cherchez la femme (French) – Look for the women (the way of women)

sans joi (French) – without joy

tel joi (French) – such joy

Cache la Poudre – The hidden powder

Count coup (American Indian) – To touch the enemy in battle (A sign of bravery)

Pah (American Indian) – Water (similar sound among many People for "water.")

Via con Dios (Spanish) – Go with God

Padre (Spanish) – priest

Manitou – Deity (Bannock)

Anglais (French) – English

Chebbeniathan (Arapaho) – Deity

Hinono'eiteen (Arapaho) – word the Arapaho use to name themselves

Adieu (French) – Goodbye

Bon Jour (French) – Good evening

Arapaho is sometimes spelled with "e" on the end. I chose their traditional spelling.

BIOGRAPHY
FRANK KELSO

Frank grew up around Kansas City, Missouri, the origin of the Santa Fe Trail. He spent his teen years chasing around Liberty, Mo, Jessie James hometown, where Jesse invented Drive-Thru banking. A biomedical research scientist in his day job, Frank writes short stories and novels to keep the family traditions alive. Frank has won the Will Rogers Medallion Silver Award and was a Finalist for the Western Fictioneers Peacemaker Award. Several of his books have been #1 Best Sellers on Amazon.

If you join my blog, Traveling the West,
at https://bit.ly/ThePosseWEB
You'll receive a FREE copy of one of my books.

Printed in Great Britain
by Amazon